Praise for Tears in the Rainforest

"Zefferys weaves the tragic story of the criminal underworld of wildlife poaching and murder with the struggle of courageous wildlife agents to stop it. Along the way we are rewarded with a romance and a delectable tour of KL cuisine that left this reader wanting more!"

—NOEL ANGELL, Conservation Activist

"Marlene Zefferys's *Tears in the Rainforest* gives valuable insight into the tragic plight of exotic animal smuggling, while providing an intriguing and compelling story of the risk and profit of human involvement in the trade. One wonders if we will ever educate people enough to care more for the future of endangered wildlife than the profit their plunder brings."

—VIRGINIA BLOOM, Bloom's Winery

"This powerful story of human dynamics amidst the devastating destruction of wild animals is anchored in the author's deep experience with Malaysia."

—JARLATH HUME, Entrepreneur

"Tightly written and suspenseful! I couldn't put the book down. It was an eyeopener and a must-read for anyone who cares about the tragedy of animal smuggling."

—KATHY BENTON, Society for College and University Planning

"Tears in the Rainforest is a must-read for the world if we are to understand how we are losing our exotic animals to poaching. Zefferys's book brings tears, joy, and happiness to the reader. Could not put the book down."

—DR. JULIUS DEBRO, University of Washington

"Tears in the Rainforest is one of those books that you should read at some point in your life. It creates awareness, giving extraordinary insights into the illegal endangered wildlife trafficking, which is the third most lucrative criminal trade in the world. Brilliant!"

—SALLY TUN GHAFAR, Kuala Lumpur, Malaysia

"Timely and informative regarding the poaching of endangered animals. *Tears in the Rainforest* brings Malaysia alive with the activity, sounds and smells of Kuala Lumpur. You can actually envision yourself sitting in a café eating pepper crab."

—C. GRAVES

"I found *Tears in the Rainforest* so informative regarding smuggling and also, quite frightening about the gang behavior. My very limited knowledge of wildlife smuggling is regarding elephants. Who would have ever thought anteaters would be targets for smuggling?!"

—SUE WHIPSTOCK, Brighton, MI

"The author, with the knowledge of the multi-ethnic Malaysians, spins an intriguing story of the struggle the Malaysian Wildlife Crime Unit faces to stop the alarming increase of the illegal wildlife trade within its borders."

—SABINE HOFFMEISTER, wife of the former Malaysian Ambassador

"*Tears in the Rainforest* is an eyeopener for the outside world and a Malaysian like myself. While I was aware that such activities were possible, I did not realize the extent. The author has a deep understanding of Malaysian culture.
I couldn't put it down."

—RANI JOHNS, Senior Executive Director, PwC, Malaysia

Tears in the Rainforest
by Marlene Zefferys

© Copyright 2013 by Marlene Zefferys

ISBN 9781938467608

Published by
◤ köehlerbooks ™
an imprint of Morgan James Publishing

5 Penn Plaza, 23rd floor
c/o Morgan James Publishing
New York, NY 10001
212-574-7939
www.koehlerbooks.com

Publisher
John Köehler

Executive Editor
Joe Coccaro

Habitat for Humanity® Peninsula and Greater Williamsburg Building Partner

In an effort to support local communities, raise awareness and funds, Morgan James Publishing donates a percentage of all book sales for the life of each book to Habitat for Humanity Peninsula and Greater Williamsburg.
Get involved today, visit www.MorganJamesBuilds.com

For all my family and friends who gave their input and their support, I thank you.

My goal in writing this book is to inform the reader on the plight of exotic wild animals globally. If we work together we can stop the trafficking of wildlife and save them and their forest habitat from destruction.

TEARS
in the
RAINFOREST

Marlene Zefferys

NEW YORK

VIRGINIA

Prologue

I AM HIKING IN THE Malaysian Rainforest as I often do on weekends, having lived in Kuala Lumpur for several years. I know the forest well. I always go to the same area, about a three-hour drive from KL. I leave very early in the morning and spend the day in this rainforest teeming with life—beautiful flora and fauna, a true Garden of Eden. It is a magical place—exotic birds, giant spiders, lizards, gibbons calling in the far-off trees, swarms of insects, and a lush green carpet of tall trees and bushes.

Beautiful rare orchids grow abundantly in the jungle, each species requiring different conditions for survival. Tall, ancient, stately hardwoods form a canopy above the small plants living on the jungle floor. Giant ferns and large stands of bamboo shade other plants requiring less sunlight.

In the quiet of the afternoon heat I hear an unfamiliar sound. I slowly walk toward a buzzing, whiney noise.

I stop. A family of Malayan elephants, several tuskers, females, and three young elephants stand quietly. I remain still, barely breathing, watching them.

The pachyderms are watching too, staring at something they likely find alarming or perhaps they have never encountered. The chainsaws are cutting a large swath through the jungle, felling every tall tree in sight. Several loggers harvest the precious hardwoods and in the process cut a decimating swath of destruction. I am shocked and gasp loudly. The largest bull elephant hears me and turns toward me with tears in his eyes. He looks at me, calmly watching me. Are they tears of sorrow or moistness induced by stress, the climate, or insect bites? I don't know, but I know what I feel at this moment—sadness.

The bull snorts, turns toward the noise, then looks back to me as if to say, "Help us, help save us. They're taking our food, destroying our home."

He stares at me for a moment, then turns, taking one last look at the loggers and leads the herd away from the scene, the young elephants protected by the adults. They quietly disappear into the jungle. I can't see them as the dense jungle envelops them, hiding them, protecting them, nourishing them.

I don't know where the elephant family went, but I hope they find a safe haven. It is the saddest moment in my life, watching them slowly disappear into the jungle like orphaned drifters.

I see the future and think about the human species. Are we caretaker of this earth, or plunderers? The truth is we're both, but those driven by profits and material wealth are winning. Nowhere is this battle more apparent than in rainforests, the earth's richest ecosystems and most vulnerable.

Depletion of rainforests is taking place not only in Southeast Asia, but also in South America, Africa, and Papua New Guinea.

Some are trying to stop this devastation.

ONE
MALAYSIA

1.

FENG WAS TENSE AND EDGY. This was his first job for the secret society. He knew if he failed he would pay dearly. They don't tolerate mistakes, not even from rookies.

The night was dark—the moon, a small silver crescent in a clear, star-filled sky. His boss, Chan, was driving intently, concentrating on the road ahead. He hunched over the steering wheel, peering through his glasses at the pitch-black highway, lit only by the car's dim headlights. They came from Penang, a large island off the west coast, two hours south of the border.

Their black, compact sedan sped along the North-South expressway toward Bukit Kayu Hitam (Black Wood Hill), the main Malaysian border crossing into Thailand.

Feng's nonstop nervous chatter disrupted Chan's concentration, making him jittery. Finally, he slammed on his brakes, and the car squealed to an abrupt stop. He turned to Feng and spit out his words.

"Shut up! Zip it, kid! Stop talking! I can't drive with your noise." He angrily switched off the radio, which had blared loud

Chinese rock music that to Chan sounded like high-pitched wailing tones. Feng blinked rapidly several times as stony silence filled the car.

"Sorry, boss," he mumbled.

Chan took a deep breath, revved the engine, and drove the car back onto the highway. He increased his speed as he concentrated on the road ahead. Chan was an older Chinese man, and as a loyal member of the syndicate, always took the dangerous assignments. Stocky, with short graying hair, he wore a dirty white T-shirt with *I Love New York* scrawled across the front. His underarms were soaked. Large sweat stains covered his chest.

Feng seemed oblivious. He wiggled in his seat, tapped his fingers to some imagined rock music, and slyly glanced at Chan, who gave the youth a hard look.

Feng sat on his hands and remained still as if transported to some dream world. The young man wore a gold earring in his left ear and short spiky hair with blond tips. Chan thought this Asian hairstyle looked absurd, just like the person beneath it. Feng was pitifully thin. His sallow skin highlighted his hollow cheeks covered with red pimples and scars from a bad case of acne. Feng thought Chan looked pathetically old and boring— gray hair, creased eyes, shabby T-shirt, always angry.

They rounded a curve in the road and bright lights on either side of the highway abruptly burst into view. Large green road signs directed the traffic to reduce speed.

Chan slowed the car to a crawl. His muscular arms rested on the steering wheel revealing a large red-eyed, green dragon tattoo, winding around his right arm from his shoulder to his elbow. The dragon had its mouth open breathing fire down Chan's arm.

Chan glanced at Feng and whispered, "Don't open your damn mouth. I'll do the talking. Don't even look at the customs officers, and if you don't sit still, I'll slit your throat!"

They moved toward a short queue in the narrow lane, only wide enough for one car to move forward at a time. The brightly lit border was busy this time of night with a line-up of several lorries waiting for their cargo to be inspected.

Cars were in one lane, lorries in another, the drivers leaning against their lorries, smoking, chatting together until it was their turn to be inspected by customs.

Feng lit a cigarette, inhaled a few puffs then flicked it out the window. Their car inched toward the brown-colored metal booth with a glass window open at one side for passing documents. Chan drummed his fingers nervously against his thigh. Feng watched silently.

Azmi, a customs recruit in his early twenties, had just completed his training. New officers always pulled night duty. Only two hours remained before his shift ended at midnight, and he was looking forward to returning home.

Azmi liked his job. He felt important, questioning people, inspecting their cars and lorries.

Customs officer Mustapha was busy writing up the daily report while waiting to inspect the next vehicle. His blue uniform with short sleeves accentuated his long arms and height. He was senior to Azmi, but only by a few months.

Two army officers patrolled this border crossing. They were dressed in blue camouflage uniforms tucked into their military boots; blue berets worn jauntily at a slant, semi-automatic rifles slung over their left shoulders, pistols in holsters strapped to their right thighs. They were resting in the office, smoking and chatting.

Chan drove to a customs booth in the lane nearest the office. He opened his window as he approached. The humid hot air flowed into the car, fogging his glasses.

Azmi leaned forward and said with authority, "Passports and car registration."

He passed both through the window and then wiped his

glasses on his dirty shirt as the officer ran the documents through the computer and returned them.

"Move forward to the inspection lane."

Mustapha watched from the office as the car pulled into the lane. He grabbed his flashlight as he joined Azmi and motioned the car to pull forward into a bay.

"Turn off your engine and place your vehicle in park," Mustapha said.

He walked down the passenger side of the car toward the trunk, shining his flashlight into the car. At the same time, Azmi approached the driver, flashlight in his hand, ready to inspect the vehicle.

Feng could hear the blood pounding in his ears as his heart beat rapidly. He felt as though his heart would burst out of his skinny chest at any moment. It took all his energy to remain still. He thought about the money he would receive from this job, but he also remembered Chan's threat.

The air conditioning was off; the inside of the car quickly heated up, and Chan wiped the beads of perspiration off his forehead with his hand and then wiped his hand on his grimy pants, leaving wet stains.

Azmi shone his flashlight on the driver. "Where are you going?"

"Hat Yai, South Thailand. Be there four days," Chan said as perspiration ran off his nose. He wiped his face with the back of his hand. His glasses steamed again, and he wiped them on his soiled shirt.

Azmi shined his flashlight into the empty backseat and then on Feng, studying him for a moment, then asked Chan, "What are you taking into Thailand?"

"T-shirts for the night market."

"Open the trunk." He turned to Mustapha and signaled him. Mustapha moved to the trunk. Chan pulled the release, and the trunk popped open.

A pungent, musty smell hit him. He stepped back and took a breath of fresh air. He inspected the trunk after the smell had somewhat dissipated.

Azmi listened to him as he itemized the contents of the trunk.

"Cardboard boxes, two suitcases, and large burlap sack here. Sack smells stinky. I'll check it out."

He asked Chan again, "What's in the sack?"

"T-shirts. Some got wet so they don't smell so good." He smiled weakly.

Mustapha looked indignant. "Doesn't look to me like T-shirts." He spotted something bulging, then, *Definitely movement in the sack,* he thought.

Azmi took a step back and eyed Chan while checking on Mustapha. He kept the flashlight beam on Chan's face.

Feng tensed, but he continued to stare through the windshield, concentrating on his rapid breathing.

Mustapha peered at the burlap sack, grabbed it near the top, slowly pulling it to the edge of the trunk.

He grasped the long end of the thick cord tied around the top and tugged it with a quick jerk. The knot slowly untied. The sack opened and dropped downward.

Mustapha was frozen to the spot. His eyes widened in terror. His left hand still clutched the cord.

He stared into the cold, glittering eyes of a very agitated king cobra as it rose high in the air, flaring out its hood. He heard a bone-chilling hiss as the snake coldly stared at him. The snake continued to hiss with a sound like the throaty growl of a large dog as his tongue flicked back and forth.

He was paralyzed with fear. Then a large wet stain slowly appeared on the front of his pants.

He gradually took his eyes off the snake's face without moving his head and focused on the pattern on his neck: two black spots along each side of the yellow hood. The yellow underside of its body grew as the snake rose two feet above the sack, its head at a right angle to its body.

The cobra watched Mustapha, its body swaying slightly. He slowly released the cord. It fell on the sack. He began to lower his arm haltingly, inch by inch. The cobra struck with lightning speed, biting his arm.

In an instant he felt pain near his left wrist and fell to the ground screaming, holding his left arm with his right hand, above the snakebite.

"Help me! Help me! Please help me! Snakebite! Snake bit me! Help!" he screamed as the six-foot-long, mottled-brown king cobra slithered out of the burlap sack, over the edge of the trunk, across the inspection lanes toward the thick jungle and disappeared.

No one moved.

Azmi ran to the back of the car.

Hearing his screams, Feng and Chan quickly opened their doors, jumped out and ran. Feng followed Chan for the first few steps, not knowing where to go.

Chan yelled, "Split up, you idiot! Don't follow me!" He held his pistol in his hand. Feng watched as he ran toward the jungle then quickly ran in another direction that led toward Thailand's border.

The trunk of Chan's vehicle turned into a fountain of escaping snakes. One eight-foot python and several small black cobras slithered over the edge of the trunk and onto the road. People waiting in inspection lanes saw the snakes, screamed, jumped into their vehicles, closed their windows, and locked their doors.

Azmi took one look at Mustapha, holding his arm, then at the snakes slithering toward the dark, thick jungle.

"Oh my God!" He ran to Mustapha and put his arm around his waist.

"Walk slowly, keep your heart from racing! We're going to the Pajero."

He nodded, held his arm down, concentrating on his slow

steps. He guided Mustapha to the black Mitsubishi Pajero with the customs insignia on the doors, parked next to the office.

Azmi yelled to the army officers who ran out of the office, "I'm taking Mustapha to the clinic! Stop those two men! Go after them!"

He yanked open the rear door, helped Mustapha onto the seat, ran to the driver's seat and within seconds was speeding down the highway toward the clinic in the small border town.

The army officers saw Chan and Feng fleeing and immediately chased them. The sergeant yelled, "Halt! Drop your weapons. Hands behind your heads!"

Chan quickly turned to face the officers, raised his pistol, and fired several shots that went wide. Both officers aimed their rifles and each fired one burst. Chan was hit in the chest, jerked backward, and crumpled where he stood, blood oozing from his wound, puddling on the road.

The second bullet slammed into Feng's right shoulder, knocking him to the ground. The officer, with his side arm drawn, leaned over Chan and felt for a pulse. "He's dead, sir," he said to the sergeant.

Blood seeped from Feng's wound, pooling in a large red stain on his shirt. He whimpered as he lay on the ground. "Please ... don't shoot me! I have no gun. Please!"

The officers roughly packed his wound, then pulled him to his feet and flex-cuffed him. The officer drove him to the army base near Alor Setar, where he would be treated, then jailed. The sergeant covered Chan with a sheet, waiting for the coroner, and remained at the border.

In the Pajero, Mustapha was tightly holding his wrist, his eyes wide with terror.

"King cobra bit me!" He took short, fast breaths, sobbing between each gasp as he wailed. "I can feel pain from the venom moving up my arm. It hurts! I'm going to dieee! ... I know I'm going to die!" He lapsed into silence staring ahead, watching the road.

Azmi leaned toward the backseat and softly touched his arm, trying to comfort him while he drove. He glanced at him in his rearview mirror as he sped toward the clinic.

"Calm down so the venom doesn't travel up your arm so fast. Take a deep breath. We'll be at the clinic in a few minutes."

His only hope was the anti-venom shot. The red streak was now visible near his elbow. His voice rose to a high-pitched wail.

"I can feel the venom racing toward my heart! I am dying! Oh, Azmi ... let my family know I love them."

The Pajero screeched to a halt at the clinic entrance. Azmi jumped out, yelled at the nurse standing in the reception area, and pointed to the car. "Cobra bite! Give him a jab for a king cobra bite! Quickly! Quickly!" He ran back to the vehicle and helped Mustapha out of the car.

The nurse hit the emergency call button, then rapidly pushed the gurney to the open door. Azmi grunted as he lifted him onto the gurney and pushed him into an emergency cubicle smelling of antiseptic, bare, except for a heart monitor and an IV cart. As he watched Mustapha, he heard the nurse outside the cubicle.

"Dr. Subra, man bit by king cobra. I have the anti-venom ready."

When the doctor entered the cubicle, Azmi explained that he had to return to his post, then he ran to the Pajero and sped back to the border.

Fifteen minutes had passed since Mustapha was bitten, the effects of the venom already noticeable. His heart raced, his breathing became shallow, and he began to feel lightheaded. Perspiration appeared on his forehead like morning dew on a leaf.

Dr. Subra checked his vital signs and then quickly gave him the shot. He monitored him, stethoscope on his chest and blood pressure cuff on his arm.

The nurse watched the monitor as his heart continued to

pound. She noted his blood pressure and called out the readings. He closed his eyes. Several minutes passed, then his pulse rate dropped slightly and his blood pressure fell. The red streak stopped its advance. His rapid breathing slowly returned to normal.

The doctor breathed easier, knowing that his patient would recover. The anti-venom shot had saved him.

He still required constant care to ensure there would be no relapse. He opened his eyes, smiled weakly, gave the doctor the "thumbs-up" gesture and closed his eyes again. Dr. Subra smiled at the nurse as she wiped Mustapha's brow.

"He's a lucky man. Another ten minutes and the jab would have been useless."

The nurse nodded. "Yes, doctor. He was very lucky. We had only one vial of cobra anti-venom."

He nodded. "You had better order more tomorrow."

She nodded and noticed that Mustapha had fallen asleep and was now resting comfortably.

2.

CHRIS JOHNSON SAT IN HIS cubicle in Seattle's Customs and Border Protection building near the airport. It was a small room with two rows of cubicles back to back, each one occupied with staffers busily working on their computers.

One wall had several large windows overlooking the cargo area of the airport. The windows were covered with slatted blinds open horizontally, allowing bright sunlight to fill the room.

Startled as his phone rang, he took one last shot at the enemy, blasting away on his computer screen, scored, and only then answered the phone. He heard his boss say curtly, "Get into my office now! We need to chat."

"Right away, George."

He minimized the *Soldiers of Anarchy* game and walked down the hall to the large corner office, anxiety swimming in his stomach. He was uncomfortable around his boss, who micromanaged the staff.

Chris slumped in the chair directly in front of George Stamos's desk; his knees banged with a loud thump. He smiled weakly.

"Sorry, George."

Chris was slim, over six feet, and tried to shuffle his chair without too much noise. He was casually dressed in smart khaki pants, a light-pink dress shirt, and a natty, brightly colored tie. His boss glared at him, tapping his fingers on the desk, waiting.

"Are you finished?"

"What's up, George?"

 He ignored his question.

George smirked as he stroked the bald spot on top of his head with his left hand, a nervous habit acquired in the military. He had dark features and heavy eyebrows. His short stubby fingers held a pencil poised over a blank sheet of paper. He reached for a folder on the side of his desk. His thick, hairy arms stood out from the rolled-up sleeves of his white dress shirt and rested on the desktop on either side of the paper.

He took in George's appearance and imagined him eating a plateful of moussaka while swilling it down with Greek Retsina wine. He began to smile, but then shook his head to get rid of the image.

"Good news, Johnson. You have a new assignment. Better take some sunscreen along."

Chris smiled broadly, sat up straight, anticipating the warm sunny beaches of Florida. "I'm finally going to Miami?"

"Nope. This one is really far away. Ever heard of Malaysia?"

"Malaysia? Isn't that somewhere near Australia?"

"Thailand. Get out a map and educate yourself. You'll be there for three weeks. Here's the situation: We had a query from their Minister of Natural Resources and Environment. You'll observe their methods of inspection at their borders, take photos, and bring back a detailed report on their issues. They're a major portal for animal smuggling from Papua New Guinea, the Middle East, and Africa, as well as their own country. It's out of hand and they need assistance."

George sighed and tapped his pencil on the paper, pausing for a moment, looking directly into Chris's eyes. He continued:

"You're finally getting out of the U.S., but it's no vacation. You will be working twenty-four/seven. You've had all your training as a border officer, so you're prepared to deal with any situation that arises. You did your time at the Mexican border just like the rest of us."

"But all I've been doing for the past six months is write reports on border stats. So I just go cold into Malaysia, no briefing?"

George sighed deeply. "Look, Chris. You transferred here, away from the Mexican border. You said you were burned out with San Ysidro and, if I remember correctly, you wanted action in another field. You were hopped up about animal smuggling. You said that was your crusade and you wanted to protect wildlife. What do you have, a dog? So you're a friend of the animals now. Well here it is staring at you, and you want to be briefed about Malaysia? You're not a tourist. Go to the CIA world facts site. That's all you need to know."

Chris smirked. "Just for your information, I did have a dog and volunteered at the SPCA on weekends. And yes, that helped me to respect all animals. Besides, I've more training than just the SPCA."

George rolled his eyes. "Well this assignment will be perfect for you. You can use all your experience and training looking into the animal smuggling issue."

"OK. When do I leave?"

"Next week on Tuesday. You have five days to get your cubicle in order and pack. Your passport better be valid. Take your gun permit with you and your government ID."

He pushed a letter-size manila envelope across the desk. The sweat on his fingers left stains on the envelope. Chris gingerly picked it up between two fingers.

"Here's your ticket, expense voucher, and file. This is all the information on the assignment along with country information and stats on animals being smuggled through Malaysia to other countries. Also included is data on Vietnam and Myanmar and their problems."

"Yeah, OK." Chris frowned. "Why aren't you going? This sounds like an important assignment. It's dealing with the government more than with the smuggling."

He shuffled in his chair. He ran his hand over his bald spot again and leaned forward on his desk, looking directly into Chris's eyes with a cold stare.

"Listen to me. You asked for this assignment, kid. You're capable of collecting data. We all have to put in our time and I've done mine. So here you go, a free trip to Malaysia on the U.S. government's dime.

"My old Navy buddy is now the ambassador in Malaysia. We served together on a destroyer many years back. I've arranged a meeting for you with him. It's highly unusual for him to meet with someone of your level, but he said he would spare a few minutes. He'll fill you in on the current situation in Malaysia.

"There is one more item, however. An international animal smuggler lives in Malaysia and is one of their biggest problems, both in Malaysia and globally. The ambassador will fill you in on his activities."

George peered at him as he leaned toward him.

"You've only been here six months. You're lucky to get this assignment. Don't screw it up. Now get out of my face."

Chris picked up the packet, pushed his chair away from the desk, causing an annoying scraping sound, closed the door, and walked back to his cubicle.

He turned on his military game, threw the packet on the credenza, and picked up where he left off. He was involved in a shootout, firing rapidly at the enemy with his XM25 sniper weapon. He scored a hit on one soldier and smugly said, "Take that, George! You're wasted!"

Chris adjusted his economy class seat to the sleep position. His reading lamp illuminated the report in the darkened cabin. The flight was wearing on him and he was restless. He had already spent twelve hours on the Seattle to Tokyo flight and now he was on the seven-hour jaunt to Singapore. Sitting in the back of Delta's Boeing 777 didn't allow for much legroom. The small seats and the large man sitting next to him were tiring. He had no room to move. The armrest was draped by his seatmate's bulky arm. The heavy man snored loudly. There were no empty seats to move to. He turned on his light and flipped through most of the report, absorbing some information, making a few notes in the margins. He read the fact sheet on Malaysia and it appeared to be an interesting country: no big problems, democratic, good Internet service, and a relatively easy place to live. He thought to himself: *This is better than Miami!*

Chris stuffed the folder into the seat pocket, then ran his hand over his close-cropped light-brown hair. He covered himself with the thin blanket and closed his eyes thinking about his assignment halfway around the world from Seattle.

It was mid-January. He was content to leave damp, rainy, sunless skies, and head for the warm tropics. He reflected on Seattle, his home, and two sisters as he closed his eyes.

An attractive, slender Asian flight attendant noticed him as she walked down the aisle checking the passengers. She tapped him on the shoulder and asked if he wanted water. Chris shook his head and closed his eyes again. She lingered for a brief moment, looking at her passenger. She guessed he was in his late twenties, wondered if he was married, then continued walking down the aisle.

The plane landed at midnight at Singapore Changi Airport, and Chris caught a few hours sleep at the airport transit hotel. The next morning, he was on the first flight out to Malaysia. The flight was only one hour and on arrival he took his time walking to immigration, taking in the sights and sounds at the airport. He waited while the tourists and locals fought for space to retrieve their baggage from the carousel, then he grabbed his two bags and pushed his trolley through the nothing-to-declare lane into the arrival hall.

A tall, thin Indian man, in navy slacks and white short-sleeve shirt, held a white signboard with *Mr. Chris Johnson* in large black lettering. He greeted Chris in a Tamil-tinged English accent, introduced himself as Jega, and grabbed the luggage.

Shouldering his computer bag, Chris followed Jega through a crowd of hotel and tourist greeters. He looked haggard after the long flight and little sleep. With the fifteen-hour time change, his body was asleep. He felt like a robot that walked on cue, methodically ready for any task.

As they pushed through the revolving door to the sidewalk, a blast of hot, humid air hit him. He could feel the perspiration on his forehead as they walked to the van parked on the opposite side of the road. He stepped into the front passenger seat of the air-conditioned vehicle.

He wiped his face and thought: *A steam room would be more comfortable.*

He relaxed on the hour ride from the airport and watched the countryside pass by. Morning haze hung in the trees, shrouding his view. A beautifully tiled mosque and oil palm tree plantations floated by, a mystical appearance in the mist.

Chris wrinkled his nose. "Is this pollution or morning fog? I can smell smoke in the air."

"It's from fires, Mr. Johnson," Jega said. "The Malaysians sometimes burn their land waste at night and it smolders for several hours. Wet leaves from trees and bushes cause the acrid smoke."

"Isn't there a law against open burning here?"

"Yes, but it's difficult to control and tough to enforce. It happens in Kuala Lumpur as well, not just in the countryside."

The haze slowly subsided and the sun broke through as they drove into KL. Tall modern skyscrapers caught the warm glow of sunlight in their gold-tinted windows. The Petronas Twin Towers, the tallest twin buildings in the world, hovered over the city like an eagle with open wings protecting its young.

Traffic was heavy at this time of the day. A crush of cars and motorbikes fought for road space, slowing the traffic to a crawl, and then picked up speed as a traffic light changed to green.

Abruptly, Jega swore under his breath, "Damn motorbikes!" He leaned on the horn that emitted a loud blaring beep.

A motor scooter was weaving through the traffic and misjudged the space, bumping the right rear fender of the Mercedes sedan directly in front of the van. The rider lost control. The bike wobbled and fell over, throwing the rider directly into the path of the van. Chris saw the terror in the biker's eyes as Jega hit the brakes.

Chris lurched head first as the seat belt jerked and tightened. He put his hands out to stop himself from hitting the dashboard. The left front wheel of the van stopped inches away from the biker, his wide eyes and open mouth pleading for his life. He put his hands up to stop the impact that narrowly missed him.

"Sorry, Mr. Johnson. This happens all the time," Jega said calmly.

"Is he hurt? No one's helping him. Let me take a look. He can't be left lying there." He made a move to open the van door.

Jega put his hand on Chris's shoulder. "No need. Stay where you are. He's just shaken a bit and getting up."

The dazed rider slowly stood, wobbled, shook his head, and then dragged his bike to the side of the road. The bike was more of a scooter than a big motorcycle and easy to move.

Jega was irked. "These bikers think they own the road. This guy walked away without any injuries."

"He's not wearing a helmet. Isn't that a law here?"

"Many don't wear a helmet. Probably doesn't do much good in this mess. They buy cheap helmets that crack when dropped. The good ones are too expensive."

Traffic began to flow again. Chris tightened his seat belt and sat back warily, watching the traffic for another mishap. Jega drove down a busy street then turned into a lane and stopped at a large hotel. The hotel was nestled in a mall complex, near a major shopping center of upscale designers for everything from clothing to jewelry, restaurants to spas.

"Welcome to the Crown Hotel!" the doorman said as he saluted Chris with a clenched fist touching the left side of his chest, the Malaysian greeting used at tourist areas. He opened the door for him, and he walked up to the registration counter and registered.

A young attractive woman in a navy blue uniform escorted him to his tenth floor room. She opened the door to his room and smiled sweetly as she gave him his room key. "If there's anything you need, Mr. Johnson, anything, please call reception."

He walked through the short hallway that opened into a large bright room with a large floor-to-ceiling window. He stared at the modern city framed by the window. This was not the sleepy little village he had imagined. KL was a bustling ultramodern city. It felt strange to see it for the first time, almost like a time warp into the future with tall buildings of different architectural styles and a variety of colors. This city was very different from Seattle. After a few moments, he quickly opened his suitcase and grabbed a dark suit, blue shirt, red- and blue-striped tie, and dark dress shoes. He put his computer on the desk next to the window.

Feeling a bit lightheaded and dehydrated from the long flight and the lack of sleep, Chris grabbed a bottle of water from the minibar, quickly drank it, feeling somewhat human again. A shower rejuvenated him as he let the hot water run for several minutes, steam fogging the bathroom. He changed into his suit, and then left the hotel for his appointment at the American Embassy located nearby.

𝟑

JEGA DROPPED OFF CHRIS IN front of the embassy, a large military-gray-colored compound concealed behind a tall concrete wall. He walked to the glassed-in reception area that stood outside the main compound and spoke to the guard standing behind the bulletproof glass window.

"Mr. Johnson here. I have an appointment with Ambassador John Forbes." He presented his ID and received a numbered card for retrieval of his passport later.

He went through the security procedures and walked into the main building. He vaguely saw a Marine guard watching him from a control center behind darkened glass. A few minutes later, a pleasant older, slightly overweight lady came through a glass door.

She smiled at him and shook his hand.

"I'm Wendy Smythe, the ambassador's secretary. Welcome to Malaysia, Mr. Johnson." She led him through the door into the inner embassy, then along an atrium with large windows overlooking the inner courtyard. She punched in a code on the secure steel door then gestured him through. They took the stairs to the first floor then into the ambassador's large outer office. The long conference table in the center of the outer office was covered with Malaysia newspapers.

Her desk sat in front of the closed door. *She's the palace guard to the main man,* he thought as he watched her walk toward the door. She rapped softly once on the door then entered.

"Mr. Johnson is here," she said to the thin pale man behind an imposing dark wood desk. He looked distinguished in his dark gray suit, crisp white shirt, and blue tie that set off his piercing blue eyes and gray hair. He was in his late forties, his features sharp, face pinched.

Forbes motioned him to a straight-backed wooden chair in front of the desk, reminding him of his Jesuit school days. The chair was uncomfortable with a hard wooden seat. Guests granted an audience didn't overstay their visits.

The ambassador pulled a file from the neat stack on one corner of his desk. He opened it, took a few pages from the file, and then moved the closed file to the side. He fingered the papers as he cleared his throat, then looked up. He sat rigid in his straight-backed chair as he spoke.

"Honestly, Mr. Johnson, I don't know why you're here. We can handle the smuggling problems with our staff on hand, but..." He stared at him, his thin bloodless lips tight on his pale skin. "But when the Oval Office says jump, we ask how high."

"And I take my orders from the same Oval Office, sir." Chris smirked. His icy blue eyes flashed in anger and narrowed. This was not the friendly American welcome he had expected.

Forbes looked down at his file. "Yes, well ..."

At that moment, the secretary returned with a tray of tea and cookies and set them on a small table. Chris studied the sparsely furnished, almost sterile room that was fifteen feet long, large enough for a round table and four chairs against one windowless wall. The only pictures were a framed photo on the credenza behind Forbes's desk of his wife and three teenage children, large photos on the wall of Forbes with the U.S. president in the White House, and another of Forbes receiving his credentials from the King of Malaysia.

The ambassador waited until his secretary exited before he spoke, the tea untouched.

"Of course, we're Malaysia's number two trading partner, and we can bring in our people to assist them whenever they ask for assistance. Do you understand what I'm saying?"

"I have no plans to step on anyone's toes—not the Malaysians nor yours."

"Good," Forbes said. "Then let's get down to business."

"However, it appears your efforts haven't been enough to stop the smuggling of endangered animals from Malaysia into China and Thailand. From what I've heard, the pangolin—the region's ancient spiny anteater—and some species of snakes and lizards are rapidly vanishing.

"China is poaching tigers for medicine: bones for health and vitality, penises for aphrodisiacs, eyes to improve vision and other parts for healing a variety of diseases. Even the canine teeth are worn for protection against evil.

"Now they're developing a tiger farm in China, and they'll populate it with as many Malaysian tigers as they can smuggle in. That will be the death knell for the species. I have been following the news and the reports from organizations that are involved in protecting the environment."

The ambassador's eyes turned to ice.

"I believe you'll find that stopping the poaching and smuggling is not as easy as you might think. This country has long, poorly guarded borders, and several illegal crossings into Thailand. That's complicated by corrupt border staff, government officials, and private individuals who secret their catches in rural village houses. We can't go into all the houses in the villages—an impossible task. It's not our position to do that. We can suggest, but cannot interfere in their activities unless they specifically ask us. Obviously, they skirted us and went directly to Washington."

"Must be a reason for bypassing you," Chris said dryly.

Forbes tapped the eraser end of his pencil on the file. His voice rose slightly as his face tightened.

"The smugglers pay the villagers eight thousand dollars for a tiger. They can earn more money in one week catching exotic animals than they can in any other way in a year. We rely on paid informers to let us know if there is any activity in their villages, but we're up against a well-organized, well-funded Chinese syndicate. They sell the tigers to China and Thailand for twelve thousand dollars each. It's difficult to catch them in the act."

Forbes raised his eyebrows. "Apparently, you have something to offer that we don't have, or at least they think we are lacking in that area."

"We've had significant success with some new methods on our own U.S. borders, sir." Chris emphasized *sir*.

"Fine," Forbes said crisply. "Let's hope they work here." He stood up.

"One more thing," Chris said. "George Stamos mentioned that you would have a weapon for me."

"Oh, yes." Forbes opened a drawer and handed over a leather case. "This came in the diplomatic pouch. It wasn't easy to get permission from the police for you to carry a gun. Here's a card that you must carry, asking for assistance from the police. It's in the Malaysian language and English ... also, your gun permit.

"You must understand there's a stiff sentence in Malaysia for anyone caught carrying a weapon without a permit. That goes for the bullets as well. Both must be kept in a locked box when you don't have the weapon on you."

"I know how and when to use a weapon, Ambassador Forbes."

Chris opened the case. Forbes watched as he held the Glock .40 caliber pistol and checked it over. He placed the gun back in the leather case alongside one magazine with seventeen rounds.

The ambassador nodded curtly as he stood, signifying that the meeting was over, and opened his office door. The attack dog was standing beside her desk, waiting for her orders.

"You'll be a target once word gets out. There's too much money involved in this illegal trafficking for it to stop without a nasty fight." He gave Chris a cold smile. "Have a nice stay, Mr. Johnson. Give my regards to George."

As he was escorted out by the secretary, Chris thought: *If the American Embassy were this unfriendly, what will the Malaysians be like?*

Chris entered his hotel suite and picked up a small blue envelope that was slipped underneath his door. He walked to the side table and poured a tot of Glenlivet single malt scotch into a glass, took a sip, savoring the smoky flavor.

The envelope held an invitation to a birthday party for Tan Sri Yusof's young son at two on Sunday, one day away. No gifts please, the card said.

A handwritten note at the bottom of the card said: *Mr. Johnson, I want you to come to the party to meet a few people that you'll be working with on your assignment. It'll be good for you to get know them before our meeting on Monday.* It was signed in a scrawling script, Tan Sri Yusof, Minister of Natural Resources and Environment.

He grabbed his Malaysia report and looked up the name, not sure who he was. He found a page with pictures beside names and short bios. Tan Sri was at the top of the list and underlined by Chris's boss was a meeting scheduled for Monday in his office.

Well, it looks like my dance card is full for Sunday. He put the invitation inside the report.

Traffic was light on Sunday as Jega drove Chris to Damansara Heights, an upscale residential area of large, expensive homes in the suburbs. Jega told him that many influential people lived in this gated community: politicians, businessmen, and expatriates.

Tan Sri's expansive two-story peach-colored stucco house with red-tiled roof was built on the top of a hill with a view of the twin towers in the distance. Two armed guards stood inside the wrought-iron entrance gate. Three black Mercedes sedans sat in the driveway and a red Ferrari was parked on the side.

A large tent with ten round tables and chairs were set up on the driveway in front of the house. Several waiters wandered through the crowd serving fresh juices to the guests. At the back of the house in a floral garden and landscaped lawn, a large rectangular swimming pool was full of children playing in the water watched by several maids.

Frangipani trees grew near the pool area. The trees were in full bloom and their beautiful fragrance saturated the air. Red heliconia flowers with swordlike green leaves lined the walkway to the pool. Orchids grew in the midst of the heliconia, and four coconut palms towered over the garden.

Fifty people sat under the tent, talking and eating. Malay cuisine covered the long buffet table: curries, chicken satay with peanut sauce, noodles, rice, *laksa*—a fish-based curry noodle soup—and other flavorful dishes. Two waiters stood behind the buffet table holding rattan fans, keeping the flies away from the food as the guests filled their plates.

The birthday boy ran around the tent, laughing and playing with the other children. A large green and white birthday cake with six candles was displayed on a small table surrounded by presents—large decorated boxes hiding the offering inside. The cake was decorated like a soccer field with plastic players and goalie boxes on green icing.

As Chris took a glass of orange juice from a waiter, the small, thin birthday boy stopped in front of him, smiled and asked, "Are you from America?"

Chris knelt on one knee in front of the boy. "That's right, all the way from America. Have you been to the U.S.?"

The boy nodded. "My father took me to Disney World. I liked

it very much."

A beautiful, young Chinese woman walked over and handed a glass of juice to the boy. He took the glass and scampered away. A clown was gathering the children together in one corner of the tent for the magic show. The other children surrounded the boy, waiting in anticipation for the show to begin.

"Hello, I'm May Ling Kang. I haven't seen you before." She offered Chris her hand and smiled, her dark-brown eyes bright in the sunlight. "Are you new to KL?"

"Chris Johnson." He shook her hand lightly and gave her a warm smile. "Yes, I arrived on Friday."

Her delicate features accentuated her dark eyes that quickly scanned him.

"My parents and I live next door, and we have known the family for a long time," she said with a crisp British accent. As she pointed toward her house, her shoulder-length, silky black hair swirled.

A tall, thin man casually dressed walked up and interrupted their conversation. He looked like a man who was used to being in charge. He exuded confidence.

"Mr. Johnson, I'm Tan Sri Yusof. I want you to meet the most efficient member of my staff and my personal assistant, May Ling Kang, but I see you have already met." He smiled at her. She bowed slightly at his comment.

"Yes, she looks very capable." Chris ran his gaze over her slender figure. She gave him a brittle smile and looked away.

Tan Sri lowered his voice as they stepped a few paces away to a quiet area.

"Actually, she is more than capable. She is from the anti-smuggling unit, and her cover is to act as my personal assistant. She has a black belt in kung fu, she's a computer whiz, speaks four Chinese dialects, and is the control for several undercover agents. Many of our interceptions of the smuggled animals are due to her. No one suspects that she leads a double life, and we must keep it that way. You will be working closely with her."

"I understand thoroughly, sir. I only hope she'll work with me, but I don't foresee any problems."

The minister nodded. "I had better rejoin the family. Tomorrow, you'll meet the rest of my staff. May Ling will brief you. Enjoy the party and have some local Malaysian food. It's very tasty!"

As he turned, a Malay man approached them. Tan Sri stopped then turned back.

"Mr. Johnson, I also want you to meet Suhaimi Wahab."

As the man shook Chris's hand, the minister said, "He's from the Wildlife Crime Unit and will be your assistant while you're here. He'll also act as liaison between you, the police, and myself. I'll see you both tomorrow." He returned to his guests.

Suhaimi was of medium height, with warm dark-brown eyes. His thick black hair was cut short in military style. Chris liked him immediately.

"Mr. Johnson, I'll look forward to working with you. I have had a lot of experience with wildlife smuggling and will be able to assist you quite well."

His rather large black mustache nearly covered his mouth and moved as he spoke.

Before Chris could respond, he noticed May Ling staring at him, her face tight with anger. She cut Suhaimi off and said to Chris, "I had no idea you'd be working with me." She spit out her words. "Tan Sri failed to tell me that. In fact, he didn't tell anyone. Who brought you here? Who said we needed—"

"Is there an echo in here?" Chris interrupted and tensed as he glared at her. "Look, miss, I've heard all this from the U.S. Ambassador. It seems that neither country wants me here, but that's the way it is. Get used to it." His eyes darkened as he spit out his words.

Her eyebrows shot up; her eyes opened wide like those of a startled deer. Chris watched her clench and open her fists. He could see the veins in her hands ready to burst.

"You think you can help people who don't want you here? I don't think so. And I have no intention of helping you." Her lips tightened and her red lipstick looked like two thin blood-colored lines, slash marks on her pale skin.

Suhaimi stepped back and watched the tense interaction. He quietly blended into the large jungle plants along the walkway with his military mottled short-sleeved shirt tucked into belted khaki pants and military boots.

Chris's voice rose in anger. "That suits me just fine, but you'd better talk to your boss first. He's the guy that sent for me."

She retorted, "I'll let Tan Sri know that my time can be better spent than babysitting you. To have a foreigner brought in to help us, as if we don't know what we are doing, is definitely not true. What do you know about animal smuggling in Malaysia? You only deal with drugs from South America and Mexico and illegal immigrants. Isn't that your biggest problem? Why don't you go back to your own country and fix your problems before interfering in ours." She scowled at him and quickly turned away.

He raised his voice. Guests turned to watch. "Just a minute, lady. I've already read about the poaching problems in your country. You need a lot more assistance than you realize. Your country is a swinging door for smugglers." He gave her a cold stare, his eyes turning into steel.

She swung toward him, her hands on her hips. Her tight black silk pants and long-sleeve red silk shirt accentuated her slender figure. She said something in a low voice that sounded like *you dumb foreigner,* then stomped away, leaving the scent of her jasmine fragrance lingering in the air. He breathed in her fragrance and smiled. *Maybe this job will be more interesting than I thought.*

Suhaimi caught his eye as he watched her walk into the crowd. Chris smiled and shrugged his shoulders as he moved to the buffet table and sampled the Malaysian food, then wandered around talking to people. Some worked closely with the minister; others were good friends and neighbors. All were well known and prominent, or so it seemed to him. He suddenly felt uneasy and turned around to see May Ling staring at him, but he ignored her.

"First of all, is Tan Sri a title or his name?" Chris asked. "I want to make sure I address him correctly."

"It's his title and the British equivalent is 'Lord.' It's the second highest federal title bestowed by the King of Malaysia for honor. Only a few receive this title," Suhami said.

"Well, that helps. Are these titles left over from the British rule?"

"Basically, they are. While mostly earned based on merit, some of the lower titles have been bought from the sultans at the state level for large monetary donations. The king confers the titles based on merit at the federal level. For example, Datuk translates as Sir, and is only conferred by the king at the federal level. A lower level version of this title, Dato', is bestowed by a state sultan and is also equivalent to the British Sir."

Chris nodded, vaguely understanding the titles. "One more question while we are on the subject. What is a lorry? I have heard that term several times."

Suhaimi chuckled. "Well, you know that at one time Malaysia was a British colony. We were speaking the Queen's English for a very long time. Lorry is a British word for your American truck and semitrailer. Lorries can be small for in-city transport or, like a semitrailer, used for long-haul jobs of moving equipment and bigger things. Besides 'lorry' is a much softer word than truck. When I was in the U.S. it took me a while to get used to trucks instead of lorries."

"Now I understand. You still speak the Queen's English here and that hasn't changed with your independence."

"The Brits definitely left their mark on us."

"What do you know about Tan Sri's assistant?"

He turned to look at Chris and smiled. "May Ling? She's a beautiful and intriguing woman. Many men have tried to penetrate her outer shell but with no luck. She's very private and very self-assured—a real fire-breathing dragon lady."

Chris looked out the window, appearing to be lost in his thoughts, then answered, "She can stay that way as long as she doesn't interfere with my work."

ਮਃ

IN THE OPPRESSIVE AFTERNOON TROPICAL heat, four Orang Asli men, indigenous people of Malaysia, silently moved through the dense, humid jungle.

They wore only loincloths and carried blowpipes and machetes. Short and muscular with black shoulder-length hair, they came from their village deep in the forest. They lived off the land, eating monkeys and wild boar, skillfully killed with their blowpipes and poisonous darts.

Earlier, a Chinese man, Lee, walked into their village and asked the headman if his men would help them capture pangolins.

He told them the pangolins were wanted for zoos in Malaysia and that they would be paid well for each pangolin captured. The headman agreed. They could use the money to buy rice for the village.

One man carried empty burlap sacks. They talked softly among themselves in their native dialect as they moved single file on paths trodden by generations.

Large flowering orchids bloomed on the trees. Miniature pink and yellow orchids grew in the shaded light. As they brushed against a tree covered with white flowers, a warm fragrant smell filled the humid air.

They walked for two hours, looking and listening. A gibbon called from a high hill dense with emerald green rainforest trees. Another answered in a far-off hill. They called several times in a secret language known only to them.

Suddenly, the men stopped and stood motionless. There was a slight scratching sound up ahead. They moved toward the sound and watched a pangolin enjoying a feast from a large termite mound. The large pangolin lumbered slowly around the mound, lapping up the termites with its long sticky tongue, enjoying the food.

The ancient creature was covered with armorlike tiny gray scales from head to foot, protection against other animals. Its tail extended well past his body and long black claws were sharp for ripping into the mound. Its underbelly was soft and unprotected. When frightened, it would curl into a ball, protecting its underbelly, leaving no opening for a predator. It would remain in a ball until danger had passed.

The men moved toward the anteater. One man opened the burlap sack while another grabbed the anteater by its tail. It quickly curled into a ball, making it easy to lift the animal into the sack like a yo-yo at the end of the string. They tied the sack with a heavy cord, placed it on the ground in a shaded area then moved forward, searching for more pangolins. The pangolin remained curled into a ball inside the sack.

The men continued only a short distance before coming upon another anteater that they captured as easily as the first. They found the third one a short distance away, and put it into another burlap sack and left it on the path. This process continued until they had eight pangolins.

Backtracking, they picked up each sack as they went. They

stopped suddenly. A musky heavy odor filled their nostrils. There was no movement in the forest, no sounds except for the cry of a bird in the distance. The leader signaled quiet. He sniffed the air and suddenly the smell disappeared as fast as it had come. "Elephant," he said quietly. They continued on their way.

Each man carried two sacks. The pangolins ranged in size from four to ten kilograms. The largest one would fetch a high price in China.

The lead man stopped on the path again and looked up at a tall tree. "Pit viper." The men followed his gaze and there sleeping on a branch was a large green snake coiled tightly. They avoided walking under it in case if fell from its perch.

They walked out of the jungle onto a highway, where a lorry was parked off the road. Lee was smoking, leaning against the lorry. He was tall and thin in long shorts that covered his knees, and he wore a dirty gray T-shirt. His thick black hair hung below his ears, one small gold hoop earring in his left ear and dragon tattoo on his left arm.

He threw his cigarette butt onto the highway, ground it out with his rubber sandal, and said in their dialect, *"Have pangolin?"* The headman nodded.

"How many?"

"Eight."

Another man lifted their sacks into an open large rectangular wooden crate in the back of the lorry. Slats in the top allowed air to pass through the crate. They opened the sacks one at a time. Each pangolin was still curled into a ball.

The men gently picked them up by their tails and placed them in four crates, closed the wooden lids then nailed them in place.

They pushed the heavy crates toward the front of the lorry directly behind the cab then covered them with a large black canvas, leaving a small opening at the back for air. Around the crate, they piled other boxes labeled *Chang's Garment Factory,*

Kelantan, Malaysia. The crates were obscured from view. By the time they were finished, the sun was setting.

Lee and the men sat at the side of the road and ate fish curry and rice, chewing quietly as they waited for darkness to cover their tracks. Lee paid the Orang Asli for each pangolin and then climbed into the lorry and drove west toward the Malaysian border. The Orang Asli melted back into the forest.

Reaching the border crossing at almost closing time, he slowed to a stop at the Malaysian customs booth. Traffic was very light, as most vehicles had crossed into Thailand earlier in the evening. The customs officer was napping when he pulled up next to the booth.

The officer rubbed his eyes and asked him for the registration and passport. He handed him the documents.

"What's in the lorry?" he asked, half-awake.

"Garments from factory in Kelantan," Lee replied calmly.

The lorry moved forward to the inspection lane where two officers waited. One inspected the cab, while the other walked around the lorry shining his flashlight underneath, stopping at the back. He untied the rope holding down the gray canvas that covered the cargo. He lifted one corner of the canvas, pulling it up to shine his light inside.

Lee held his breath as the officer peered into the lorry giving it a cursory look. He saw the boxes, read the labels, then pulled the canvas back into place and tied it down. He waved Lee through to the Thai side.

A Thai officer was waiting for Lee as he crossed the border. He handed the officer his passport and lorry registration. The passport held money for the officer.

He took the documents without a word to Lee and went into the office. He returned several minutes later, handed the passport and registration back to the lorry driver, then waved him through.

He drove through the border to Hat Yai, a shopping

destination for Malaysians and a trading center for pirated
DVDs, clothing, and any goods that were manufactured in China
and Thailand. For some, it offered unsavory adventures such as
prostitution and drugs, mostly controlled by the Russian Mafia.

Lee stopped by a dreary, run-down warehouse in the
commercial district and parked the lorry next to the long two-
story building out of sight from the main road. The street was
still dark and empty of traffic as he entered the warehouse
through a side door. He walked between boxes and wooden
crates piled high and balanced, one on top of the other on each
side of a narrow walkway to the office at the rear of the dimly
lit warehouse. He was careful as he walked along the narrow
pathway. One nudge from an elbow would send the boxes and
crates crashing to the floor. He pushed the office door open and
entered.

The office was bare except for an old computer sitting on one
corner of a grimy desk covered with paper scattered between
empty food containers. In the center of the room a large
rectangular rough wood table sat with two wooden chairs on
either side. Wood boxes served as chairs on each end of the table.
One fluorescent ceiling lamp hung over the table, creating a cold
and eerie setting.

The grubby floor was rough wood planking, with paper
crumpled in one corner near a full trash bin that hadn't been
emptied for weeks. Newspapers and leftover plastic containers
filled with rancid stale food cluttered the table, fodder for the
cockroaches and rats that lived in the warehouse.

Four Thai men had just finished their dinner and napped in
chairs around the table waiting for Lee. A small, thin man in his
early thirties, eyes closed, snoring, sat on a crate at one end of
the table, using his folded arms as a pillow. He started abruptly
when Lee banged the door as he entered the room.

Yunyad was part Thai and Chinese, fluent in local languages.
He had dark hair, slicked down and parted to one side covering

a bald spot. He stretched as he rose from his crate and greeted Lee. They spoke in Cantonese.

"Any trouble at the border?" Yunyad asked.

"No. Easy trip. No one find. Customs no look."

"How many pangolin you bring?"

"Eight good ones."

"OK. You have them secure? Are they all alive?"

"Yeah, hidden in lorry. Four crates. All alive."

"OK. I pay you. Eight pangolin."

Yunyad handed the money to Lee, who counted it carefully then put it into his shirt pocket. He left the office and walked out of the building to his lorry to unload the pangolins. He removed the crates and carried them one by one into the warehouse, setting them down near the office door by a bare wall. Yunyad watched as Lee carried in the four crates and set them on the floor.

"Open the crates," Yunyad said. "I want to be certain that the animals are alive. Dead ones bring no money."

Lee opened the crates and Yunyad inspected each animal and nodded. "Give them water and food. They still have a long journey."

He did as he was told then returned to his lorry and drove off to a cheap hotel to sleep.

In the morning he would sell the garments to the local shops and then return to Malaysia to repeat the routine. Considering the price he paid the Orang Asli for the pangolin, he was pleased with his profit. He was already planning his next trip.

5

CHRIS SENT E-MAIL MESSAGES OFF to his family, giving them his contact information. He let his sister know what had transpired so far. Next, he wrote an e-mail to his boss outlining his efforts to date in detail.

I met Ambassador Forbes, and I'm not impressed with him. Is he a career ambassador or a political appointee? He was defensive and cold. Basically, the embassy doesn't want me stepping on their turf.

His words: I am only here because the U.S. gov't wanted someone with my qualifications to assist the Malaysian gov't, not some untrained official from the embassy. He felt that his embassy staff could handle any problems. Obviously, he thought it was a snub. What does that tell you?

I've met the agent assigned to me. She is very self-assured and thinks she knows everything about smuggling. It will take time to bring her around to be of any use to me. Unfortunately, with the three weeks time limit on my trip, it may be difficult to get the information you require and I plan on staying longer if

I need to. I'll keep you posted on my progress.

He prepared for his afternoon appointment in Putrajaya, the capital city for the government of Malaysia. He was feeling tired, jet lag catching up with him. He sat on the sofa and closed his eyes for a minute, but woke an hour later to the sound of the telephone ringing. He reached over to answer it.

"Jega here, Mr. Johnson, I am waiting at the lobby. We are a bit late for your appointment. We must leave soon."

"Thank you, Jega. I'll be down right away." He splashed water on his face, grabbed his suit jacket and left. In the car, he received a text message from his supervisor on his phone.

The ambassador is a career appointee and retiring at the end of his term in Malaysia. Don't expect too much help from him.

Pressure your agent to come around to your way of thinking as soon as you can. You are there for three weeks, not to analyze people. Get the information required and get back here.

He shut off his phone, dropped it into his briefcase and thought wryly, *George is an idiot.*

They walked into a large square six-story brick edifice that housed the ministers' offices, rode the elevator to the second floor, and walked through glass doors into the Interior Minister's well-appointed waiting room.

Six large rectangular teak panels carved into elaborate scenes of Malaysian flowers, hornbills, and other animals graced the walls of the outer office. The secretary sat near the private office door at a large teakwood desk. Lower staff members had small desks off to one side. The minions were banished to an isolated corner.

The Malay secretary smiled politely. "May I help you?"

"I'm Mr. Johnson from the U.S. I have an appointment with Tan Sri."

She scanned her daily appointment list and ticked off his name. She was wearing the typical Malay outfit with a blue batik decorated headscarf that covered her hair and shoulders. Not one wisp of hair was visible. The scarf was pinned tightly beneath her chin with a tiny rhinestone brooch. She reminded him of a full moon shining in a dark sky.

He looked around the office and saw that the women were all dressed similarly in brightly colored batik dresses with a long top that stopped just below the knees and an underskirt that covered their ankles. The only body parts visible were their hands and feet. Matching headscarves were pinned tightly underneath their chins.

"Yes, Mr. Johnson, you're right on time." She smiled pleasantly. "Please be seated while I inform the minister." She picked up the intercom phone and spoke quietly in Malay.

A few minutes later the private door opened. The minister stood in the doorway.

"Mr. Johnson, please come in."

He walked into the office. The minister warmly shook his hand and nodded to Suhaimi, who was sitting at a table in the inner office.

"Good afternoon, Mr. Johnson." The minister's thick black mustache dominated his thin, handsome face and moved when he spoke. He wore a pink shirt with matching tie and foulard and a beautifully tailored dark-olive suit. Chris noticed the large ruby- and white-gold ring on the pinky finger of his left hand.

The minister gestured with his hand toward the round teakwood table. "Please be seated."

The minister walked over to his desk, removed his suit jacket and placed it over the back of his black leather desk chair, then joined them at the table.

He leaned back in a swivel chair, placed his hands together, fingertips touching, and looked at Chris, then at Suhaimi and smiled briefly.

Chris looked around the office at the hand carved teakwood panels with scenes from Malaysia, jungle birds, and flowers. The spacious office was impressive with large multicolored Persian carpets covering the hardwood floor. Large picture windows overlooked the beautiful pink-tiled mosque.

"I have the office with the best view," he quipped.

"Quite spectacular, sir."

"Well, Mr. Johnson, we'll do all we can to make your visit successful. I see in the report that you are assigned here for three weeks. Certainly not enough time to make any changes."

He watched Chris for a moment, studying him. "By the way, most people address me by my title, Tan Sri, and I'm fine with that. Actually, it's easy because you don't have to remember names."

Chris relaxed, already feeling more comfortable with this Malaysian minister than he had with the American ambassador.

"Thank you, Tan Sri. I'm looking forward to seeing more of your beautiful country. Of course, I'm here to give you some new ideas on preventing smuggling. We found some methods that work well in some areas of the U.S. and we'd like to offer you our experiences, successes and of course, failures. I can certainly extend my stay if there is value in my doing so."

"Our Malaysian tigers are our biggest concern. They'll be extinct in the next twenty years if nothing is done to stop their demise. Unfortunately, poachers are the biggest problem with the tigers. They are hard to find and they hide what they have killed."

"And I've been told it's almost impossible to bring tigers back from an endangered level. I was briefed on the state of the animals here before I left the U.S."

"Actually, it's worse than most people realize," Suhaimi said. "They see the tigers in the zoos and think all is well. Unfortunately, the stats go unnoticed here."

Tan Sri handed him a one-page paper decorated with Chinese symbols. "Here's a menu from a local restaurant that we closed down several months ago, Mr. Johnson. This dinner was intended for a Chinese New Year's party for eight very wealthy businessmen and visiting Chinese officials. We had it translated into English for you."

Chris studied the menu. "Tiger penis soup with herbal broth, two hundred dollars per serving?"

"Times eight people is sixteen hundred dollars for one dish," Tan Sri said.

He continued reading: "Sun Bear claw baked in jungle fern, two hundred dollars. Python steak at eighty dollars per serving. One ounce of king cobra blood, mixed with Chinese wine, thirty dollars."

"That's mostly wine with a small amount of blood," Suhaimi said. "They make more money by cheating their customers."

"Wealthy people will pay any amount for a chance to try something exotic," Tan Sri said. "It makes them feel special in some way."

Chris shook his head in amazement. "Pangolin in red curry sauce, one hundred and seventy-five dollars per serving. Skinned monitor lizard with onion, garlic, and herbs, fifty dollars per serving. I wouldn't pay one dollar to eat any of these. Give me an old-fashioned beefsteak any day."

Suhaimi grinned. "Are you sure you wouldn't like some steamed clouded leopard intestines served with black bean sauce, seventy-five dollars per serving?"

"Imagine all the animals that lose their lives for one dinner," Chris said quietly. He tossed the menu onto the table in disgust. "What a waste."

Suhaimi turned serious. "That dinner cost over six thousand dollars, a pittance for wealthy Chinese who want to impress their guests. It makes me angry that they have no feelings for the animals." He banged his fist on the table.

Tan Sri walked over to his desk and took several newspapers out of a drawer. He placed them across the table. He pointed to the front-page photo of anti-smuggling unit officers holding up five seized tiger skins mounted on red cloth.

"Look at this. Each skin is worth fifty thousand. These tigers lost their lives so that their skins could hang on some collector's wall."

Chris read the article and frowned. "So how do we stop the demand for these animals?"

"Traditional Chinese medicine is not easy to change. It's imbedded into the culture, almost part of their DNA. Remember, the Chinese eat anything that has its back to the sun. That doesn't exclude too many exotic animals.

"Education is difficult as they believe that animals and plants give them health and vitality. Men are especially interested in powerful animals as aphrodisiacs. They've used parts from predator birds and animals for centuries."

Suhaimi sighed. "I went to the market in Guangzhou, China, and saw firsthand the appalling conditions that the animals live in waiting to be bought. Not a sight for the fainthearted. Thailand, Vietnam, and Cambodia all sell exotic animals."

Chris shrugged. "I sincerely hope that I can help you, but it will take an all-out effort by everyone concerned. Slowly, slowly catch the monkey."

Tan Sri raised his eyebrows. "That's a very old Chinese proverb, but it's true. I'm dedicated to preventing this type of activity and have created many enemies in doing so. I am convinced that education in the schools is the only way to stop the trafficking. But how do you stop a forty billion dollar business?"

He looked at Chris, suddenly stopped, and gave him a sheepish smile.

"Sorry, Mr. Johnson, I was giving you my political talk. I wish dedication were all that it would take, but greed is the driver in this smuggling activity. It'll take a joint effort from both our countries to put a dent in the smugglers' supply chain." He sipped his tea, lost in thought.

"Tan Sri, I'm here to tell you that the U.S. government will give Malaysia whatever resources they require. Our country is suffering from the same disease—we are at the top of the list for trafficking animals. We feel strongly about this issue too. If we can put a dent in the smuggling here, it'll slow the trade in the States."

He arranged the newspapers into a stack and handed them to Chris. "I appreciate that, Mr. Johnson. I'd be remiss if I didn't tell you there are many people who will not be happy with your presence here. They feel the U.S. has overstepped its bounds. Be patient with them, please."

Chris decided not to mention the ambassador's concerns. "Thanks for the heads-up."

Tan Sri looked at his watch. "I want you to meet the heads of departments involved in your project. They should be gathering in the conference room right now."

They walked down the hall and into a large room. Eight people were standing, chatting, waiting for the meeting to begin. Tan Sri moved to one end of the long oval conference table and gestured them to sit on either side of him. The others sat on black leather chairs around the table. His secretary placed a small stack of bound folders in front of him and then sat nearby ready to record the minutes.

As soon as they were seated Tan Sri introduced the staff. Chris caught some of their names and titles, most too long to take in at a first meeting. He made a point of remembering the name of the deputy director of Wildlife and National Parks—Abdullah Razak. He listened to the titles of other departments: customs, anti-smuggling unit, police. Suhaimi could fill him in on the names and positions later.

Tan Sri invited the group to sample the sweet Malay cakes and tea in the center of the table and spoke as they were passed. Everyone took one or two pieces except for Abdullah Razak, who filled his plate. It appeared that no meeting was complete without refreshments. Perhaps that was the only way to entice people to attend meetings.

Chris glanced around the room and saw an ornate gold-framed portrait of the king and a matching portrait of the queen, side by side on one of the oiled teak walls next to the portrait of the prime minister. A thick gold-colored carpet deadened the sound, and media equipment, including a laptop on the table, faced the large screen on the wall.

He noted that everything in the room was first class, no scrimping here. Quite different than the bare meeting rooms in the U.S. More civilized, he thought.

The minister picked up the small bound stack of reports and passed them around. "This report details smuggling activities of our endangered animals and suggestions on preventing this illegal activity. Read the report later and e-mail me any ideas you may have."

Tan Sri gestured toward him. "Mr. Johnson was sent from U.S. Customs and Border Protection to offer us his assistance. While he and his department may not have all the answers, they have some advanced techniques that we can use in tracking animals. We can learn from the Americans and they can learn from us. Please give him all the help he needs."

They all turned to look at Chris, smiled and nodded.

"Thank you, Tan Sri. I'll need support and input from everyone here to do my job." He glanced around the table as he spoke.

The minister gestured to the overweight Malay deputy director. "Abdullah, I expect you to work closely with Mr. Johnson."

Abdullah nodded his agreement without looking up and continued to devour a small cake.

Tan Sri cleared his throat. "Abdullah, pass Mr. Johnson your contact information." His tone sharpened.

Abdullah stood, brushed the cake crumbs off his portly belly, waddled over to Chris, and placed his business card on the table.

Without a word he returned back to his seat and took another piece of cake.

Tan Sri surveyed the group. "The prime minister will be kept informed on a weekly basis. Do not send anyone in your place with your report. It will not be accepted. I want this understood by everyone here. Are there any questions?"

Abdullah slowly stood and wiped his mustache. "Tan Sri, why do we need an American to interfere in our affairs? They should spend more time looking after their country rather than interfering with us. We can handle our own internal affairs."

He looked at the group, ignoring Chris. The others waited in silence, frozen in their chairs, staring at Abdullah. From what Chris had been told, outbursts like this were uncharacteristic for Malaysians. He glanced at Tan Sri, who stiffened with the outburst.

Abdullah seemed to puff up a bit and spoke louder. "We can handle our border problems better than you can, Mr. Johnson. Look at the mess at your borders." He slapped one hand with his fist.

"I'll not work for anyone … anyone who interferes in my ability to do *my* job!"

Abdullah looked at the minister. Again no response.

"Go home and fix your problems first," Abdullah continued, finally fixing his gaze on Chris, "and perhaps then we will listen to what you have to say." He was red in the face, out of breath.

The minister glanced at the staff. "Does anyone else want to add anything?" he said in an even tone. "If so, now is the time to do it."

The department heads looked at each other, nervously waiting for someone to speak. Finally, a thin Malay woman wearing a pink headscarf and a traditional long pink floral-patterned baju kurung, rose at the far end of the table, and said quietly as she looked at all the participants individually, "I am the assistant to the deputy director and I agree with Abdullah

Razak." She looked around the table again and then sat down as uneasy silence filled the room.

Chris waited a moment, gathering his thoughts. After a long moment of silence, he said, "I couldn't agree more with what you have said, Abdullah. However, my government sends me to any country as a resource to solve a common problem. No one works for me; I am here to work for you. You direct me."

Abdullah was sipping his tea with loud slurping noises. A woman sitting next to him was annoyed. "Abdullah, stop the noise. You are ill mannered and make us look like country bumpkins." She looked at Chris and smiled politely.

Abdullah put the teacup down and gave the woman an angry stare. Chris placed his hands palms down on the table and leaned forward.

"Mr. Razak, I'm not here to challenge your policies or your control over your department, only to offer suggestions and learn from you. I don't want to waste your time or mine.

"For your information, I headed the wildlife smuggling unit in the U.S. and worked at ports of entry in California, Texas, and JFK airport. They are among the busiest entry points in the U.S. Thirty-four million people enter the U.S. from Mexico into California each year, far busier than any border here. I'll teach you what I've learned, and then I'll leave. Simple as that."

Abdullah wiped his face with a napkin.

Tan Sri's dark eyes flashed with anger as he peered at Abdullah. "Are you finished or do you have anything more to add?"

Abdullah rose again and cleared his throat. "I think I speak for everyone here. We will work with you, Mr. Johnson, but that doesn't mean we have to accept your suggestions." He sucked air into his mouth, making a clicking sound. He looked at the minister for approval but found none forthcoming, then sat down.

Chris shrugged his shoulders. "I can only make suggestions

and you must decide whether they have value or not."

Tan Sri stood. "Good. I think the air has been cleared. I hope there'll be no more doubt about Mr. Johnson's role here. If anyone has any other objections, see me at my office."

The meeting quickly broke up and most of the people filed out. Abdullah walked over to Chris and limply shook his hand. "We'll wait and see."

Chris looked at him and said nothing. Abdullah reminded him of a bantam rooster strutting around the barnyard to mark his territory and impress the hens.

After Abdullah left the room, Tan Sri said quietly, "You don't want him to be your enemy."

Chris nodded. "Point well taken."

As the minister turned away, Chris muttered under his breath, "That went well."

ҧ

AS THEY LEFT THE MINISTER'S building and walked into the bright warm sunlight, Chris could feel the humidity and began to sweat. He wiped his forehead. "How do you take this heat? It's hot, humid, and draining."

"You'll get used to it. A good method is to eat some spicy food," Suhaimi said. "How about I take you to my favorite Indian restaurant for good spicy chicken curry?"

"Sure. I like Indian food. In fact, there's one authentic restaurant in Seattle where I eat. It's the best one I've found, although it's probably suited for American palates. It'll be interesting to try real Indian food."

"We'll give it a try then. This place has tasty food. You like it spicy?"

"The hotter the better. Let's go."

The driver went toward Petaling Jaya, a large suburb with several factories, businesses and houses. They parked on a small side street and walked up a short hill to a strip mall with several restaurants, Chinese, Indian, and Malay, all open air with tables on the sidewalk.

Suhaimi stopped at a small indoor-outdoor restaurant. He turned to Chris. "This is it. It may not look like much from the outside, but believe it or not, it has the best Indian food in the city. Everyone comes for the food, not for the restaurant's appearance."

He was hesitant. "Are you sure it's safe to eat here? It doesn't look very clean."

"Yes, it's fine. You can drink the water here too. You don't have to worry."

He nodded and laughed. "OK, let's do it!"

They settled onto wooden stools at the only small empty table on the sidewalk. The air-conditioned indoor restaurant was full with the lunch crowd. They watched an Indian chef place long skewers of half-chickens into a round opening at the top of a hot, pumpkin-shaped tandoori oven.

Diners' conversations, noise from the street, and the sizzle of food cooking created a chaotic atmosphere. The heat from the oven was so intense that the cook wore a towel around his neck to protect himself from the heat.

Naan bread dough was sprayed with water and placed along the inside of the oven, using a round white-cloth-covered tapper. The cook pulled cooked flatbread from the oven on long black metal skewers. Sweat dripped off his nose as he worked.

He yelled in Tamil, a South Indian language, to the waiters when their orders were ready. They carried heavy trays of hot spicy food in stainless steel bowls to the diners. Chris could smell the warm spicy curry as the trays passed by. The aroma made him hungry. The harried waiters ran back and forth, serving the tables and clearing the empty plates.

Suhaimi ordered chicken curry and naan bread served on a banana leaf and then continued on about his time in the States, oblivious to the sounds and sights around them.

When the food arrived, they ate with their fingers, both

noisily expressing their enjoyment.

"You speak English very well," Chris said, "but with an American accent. What's the story behind that?"

"I was on a government scholarship at the University of Indiana, back in the seventies. After my degree I worked at Yellowstone National Park for a year as a ranger, then returned to Malaysia and worked at wildlife and national parks here, watching for poachers. I became a jungle guard, just like a lifeguard." He laughed. "Except I didn't wear a swimsuit."

"The mosquitoes must have been disappointed."

"Yeah, I would have been a tasty meal."

Chris tore off a piece of naan, dipped it into the curry and ate it, then sipped his tea. He ate the tandoori chicken and smacked his lips, savoring each mouthful. "This is fantastic! I have never had Indian food this good anywhere in Seattle."

Suhaimi grinned. "I knew you would like it. It's eating in the tropical heat, fresh spices, and hot curry that make the difference."

"So what took you to the U.S.? Don't most Malaysians end up in Britain?"

"The Malaysian government sent many students to the U.S. in the early '60s, '70s, and '80s, mostly in the hard sciences. They needed engineers to develop the country. Back then there was little animal poaching. It has increased dramatically in the past six years. Beside the animal poaching, we also have a problem with timber smuggling, but forest management takes a backseat."

"I heard that hardwood trees are being taken out of the rainforest at an alarming rate."

"Yeah, going to China and Japan for wood flooring, chopsticks, and toothpicks, not only here, but from all over Southeast Asia. I recently discovered that a lot of the logs end up in South India. Malaysia won't have any forests left if this continues uncontrolled."

"So you didn't become an engineer?"

He shook his head. "I studied zoology. I was lucky to be able to study what I liked. I got the scholarship because of my father."

He suddenly stopped, looking embarrassed. "In America, I also learned to talk a lot!" He wiped his hands on a napkin and took another sip of tea.

"Where are you from, Chris? You haven't said a word about your background."

"Not much to say, really. Grew up in Seattle, went to the University of Washington for my science degree and master's in public affairs then became involved with customs and border protection. I like the work. It's exciting. Not much else to tell you, rest is pretty boring."

He laughed at himself. "I have two sisters and my parents live in Seattle."

"Married?"

Chris hesitated and then lowered his eyes. "No." Finally, he said, "This job takes all my time. You?"

"Still single and living at home with my mother. My father was an army officer and murdered on patrol in the north by smugglers. That's why I'm involved with the Wildlife Department. I don't want that to happen to anyone else.

"They killed the smugglers in that firefight, but the army lost two good men. I look after my mother now. She receives an army pension, but it doesn't amount to much. She had a girl all picked out for me when I was younger, but she wasn't my type."

At that moment, five Chinese men walked past their table into the restaurant, two on each side of an older man. He looked muscular and clean-shaven and wore a colorful short-sleeve shirt open at the neck with black trousers.

Suhaimi looked over at the men and said quietly, "See those guys walking over to a room in the corner?"

Chris looked and nodded. "What about them?"

"The man in the middle of the group, the heavy guy? The one

wearing the black trousers and the silk shirt?"

He turned to look. "Yeah."

"He's the head honcho, the Tai Ko, in KL. His name is Kwang Li. The other men are in charge of different areas in the city and report to him. That's who you're up against."

As Kwang Li entered the restaurant, he looked around aware of his surroundings. His alert eyes landed on Chris and Suhaimi for a moment, registered their presence, then he walked into the restaurant, musclebound entourage in tow. Tattoos of snarling tigers and fire-breathing dragons adorned their upper arms. Their hair was pulled back into a ponytail—a typical style for gangs. Chris could see a bulge in the back of their jackets. It was barely noticeable.

"Bodyguards," Suhaimi whispered.

"They're armed. I can see the bulge."

"Yup, they're always ready for anything. They've been well trained."

Chris noticed two tall muscular Chinese men leaning against the outside wall near the open walkway to the restaurant.

Suhaimi followed his gaze. "More bodyguards."

The owner greeted the Triads leader and his men, escorted them to a private room off to the side of the main dining area, and closed the door. The small room held a round table with eight chairs.

With a grunt, Kwang Li lowered himself onto a chair and gestured for the other men to sit down. Eight settings of small white plates, silverware, chopsticks, and small dishes containing peanuts and sliced green pickled peppers were arranged on the table. A sideboard held several bottles of Scotch whiskey, ice and mix.

Outside the private room, another table was set for the six bodyguards. The waiters immediately served the gang. The men ate in silence, shoveling in the food with their hands, wiping them on paper napkins.

Pint-sized glasses and two large pitchers of beer sat in the middle of each table. The Triads leaders finished their meal, dipped their food-covered hands into bowls of limewater and then sat smoking and drinking. Talk was minimal. They barely looked at Kwang Li's grim face.

After the waiters had cleared the tables and left, he hit the table with his fist and barked at his second in command across the table. His eyes darkened with anger.

"Kiow, who tipped off the police?"

He replied matter-of-factly, "The anti-smuggling unit was involved, boss. They never bothered to check our lorries before. They get paid a nice tribute to let them pass through without inspection. An informer told us the border patrol was watching for a lorry carrying Intel chips stolen from the Penang factory. They stopped our lorry and found animals instead of the chips. It was a mistake."

Kiow was his first lieutenant, his "go-to" man. He was well known in Triads circles as trustworthy and loyal. Younger than Kwang Li, he was an unassuming man, quiet spoken, neatly dressed. His black hair was short, and he wore a thin gold bangle on his right wrist.

He adjusted his glasses and spoke directly to him in hushed tones. "It's becoming more difficult to cross the border to Thailand. Even cars are being inspected carefully. The government is aware of all the activity and the people want more arrests."

His face flushed. "What happened to our connection at the border? Isn't he working for us?"

"He was transferred to another border. We will have to entice someone else to work for us with money or threats to their family. This will take time."

He gulped his beer and put the empty glass down on the table. He looked around the table at his men, challenging them. "We're losing money if we wait. China has a big stomach. So ...

how to move the animals to China, without getting caught? If we can't provide the product, China will find someone who can."

They offered a few ideas, but he only looked at them in disgust and threw his napkin on the table. "You're all too lazy, too comfortable, thinking this will go on. You must be on top of your units and keep the men working to improve our methods. That's the only way the Chinese dragon will stay quiet. If the flow of products stop, so do we!"

He looked around the table at all the men, scowling at them. "Get out of here! I don't want to see you until you get the job done."

The men left in a hurry. One of them knocked over a chair as he rushed from the table. Kiow motioned to him, pulled him to one side, and quietly spoke to him.

"There's something else, boss. I got a tip from my informer in the government. An American came into town to advise the Malaysians on their border problems and capture methods. He may be a problem if he gets too involved. I don't like it. He has already met with Tan Sri Yusof. My contact in the government informed me of his presence, and I sent an enforcer to take his photo at his hotel."

"Tan Sri doesn't work for us," Kwang Li said matter-of-factly.

"No, and he can't be bought off. We may have to use different tactics on him. There are other people in his organization that would help him to change his mind if he becomes stubborn."

"Let's wait and see what this American does first." His eyes hardened. "Does he have a wife and family?"

Kiow smiled slightly. "I'll check it out, boss."

"Get me all his information. I want it now."

He left in his black Mercedes and two bodyguards followed behind in another black Mercedes. Chris and Suhaimi watched them leave and finished their meal.

Chris remarked, "That guy looks tough. I noticed the thick gold chain he's wearing. Do they all dress like that?"

"Well, they're no different than any of the gangs in the U.S. Big bullies and enforcers, money handlers and always involved in crimes against humanity. They dress the part."

Suhaimi nodded. "Yeah! They all take training from the same book. The only difference is that each country has its distinct group that picks on certain people in society. Their trademark is a dragon tattoo and usually a gold earring and a bracelet or neck chain. Some are more showy than others with their ornaments."

They paid their bill and left. Suhaimi dropped him at the hotel. When he stepped out of the car he saw a black Mercedes on the opposite side of the road, engine running. He noticed the driver looking out the window at him then saw a glint of light reflecting off something the driver was holding. He saw the flash when the driver took his picture. He walked over to the Mercedes. The driver revved the engine and took off.

Suhaimi jumped out of the car. "What happened? Who was in the car?"

"The driver took my photo. I guess they know who I am now."

"Not only you, but me as well. They may think I was just your driver. I hope so, for my sake and yours as well." He spoke in a serious tone. "I have to maintain some cover or my job is in jeopardy."

"Not much we can do about it now. Just have to be careful, that's all. Time for the sunglasses and hats."

7.

MAY LING TEXTED HER BEST friend: *Sue, I'm on my way over to your condo for a cup of tea and a chat. See you soon.* The two women lived in the same condo complex, so May Ling parked her car at home and then climbed a few flights of stairs to her friend's. Sue was smiling as she greeted May Ling. They hugged each other and walked to the sofa in the main room of the small condo. "What's up, May Ling? You sounded excited on the phone."

Sue made green tea and poured them both a small cup.

"Well, I went to the minister's party for his son this afternoon. I was just standing around looking for someone to talk to when a handsome, young American man walked in. The American was soooo good looking! Chris Johnson is his name, and he has beautiful blue eyes and pale skin."

May Ling waved her hand in front of her face as if to cool down. Sue giggled and covered her mouth with her hand.

"I introduced myself, and we started to chat. He was easy to talk to, and we were just getting into a good conversation when the minister walked over to introduce us. I found out the real reason he's there."

"Is he a spy for the U.S? An American James Bond? Does he drink martinis?"

"You've been watching too many movies. He's here to assist the government with wildlife identification, and I'll be working with him—very closely."

"Just how close?" Sue eyed her carefully.

"Never mind that. I was furious with the minister because he didn't tell me ahead of time that the American would be here. In fact, he told no one. He kept it a secret.

"I got angry. The American and I got into a spat with both of us jabbing at each other. I stomped off in anger and left. But ..." she gesticulated with her index finger, "he can't expect to come into Malaysia to solve our problems. We can look after our own country. I'll make it so difficult for him, he'll leave."

"Why would you want to do that? I thought you liked him."

May Ling was still agitated and ignored Sue's comment. "I'll see how this plays out, but first I want to know more about him." She paused and became serious. "I'll take him out to dinner and see how he acts. Sue, you must not mention this to anyone."

"Our talks are always between us and no one else. Keep me up to date, OK?"

They went on to other gossip.

Tan Sri's secretary called Chris on Monday to set a late afternoon appointment. Suhaimi picked him up and drove him to the minister's office.

The minister greeted them as they walked into his office. "Mr. Johnson, thank you for coming on such short notice. Please sit down, gentlemen."

"I enjoyed the party yesterday. You were very kind to invite me."

"I'm glad you could make it." Then, the minister's tone turned serious. "Let's get right to the point. I understand you and May Ling had a disagreement at the birthday party."

Suhaimi grinned. "I think a fireworks display would be more accurate." Tan Sri glared at him and the smile slid off his face.

Chris cleared his throat. "She was offended that she wasn't informed of my status. And she's not happy about having to, uhh, babysit me. I was testy with her as well. In fact, we were both at fault. We ended up sniping at each other."

"It was partially my doing," the minister said. "I told no one but the other ministers about your mission. I felt that if too many people knew, it would have been dangerous for you. KL is a small town and gossip travels faster than the Internet. As it is, the syndicate knows you're here."

"If I am working with her, I think she should have been high on the 'need-to-know' list."

"Yes, well, unfortunately I neglected to do that. I spoke to her this morning, and she's ready to cooperate with you. Please do so and let's move forward on this project."

"All right. I'm realistic that I can work with her, as long as she doesn't get in my way."

"Thank you, Mr. Johnson. She'll call you today and explain what we have planned."

"By the way, when I got out of the car at the hotel Monday, a man in a black Mercedes was waiting for me outside the hotel and snapped my photo. Before I could get to him, he drove away. Do you have any idea who that might be?"

"I'm sure it was one of the gang members. They knew where you were staying and wanted a picture. You must take extra precautions now that they know who you are. The Triads are well informed and their syndicate is like a spider's web, encompassing all of Southeast Asia and China. Indonesia is losing their animals at a rapid rate."

Chris nodded. "I'll be on red alert from now on and keep my

weapon close at hand."

On the drive back to KL, Chris said, "The minister is a good manager. He takes immediate action and doesn't let people stew, does he?"

"No. That's why he's well liked and his staff will go out of their way for him. You won't have any trouble with the dragon lady now."

"Let's wait and see. She has a very high opinion of herself, and she will try to prove that she can do her job better than anyone else."

The red phone light was blinking when Chris walked into his suite. He listened to May Ling's crisp message as he sat on the sofa.

"Mr. Johnson, I'll pick you up at six tonight and explain the operation. Dress casual."

OK, so the dragon lady is going to be all business, cool and formal, about as friendly as a dog guarding a bone. It should make for a great evening.

He quickly changed and freshened up before he met the dragon lady. He entered the lobby and stared at the only woman seated in a large red leather chair. They glanced at each other, two strangers waiting in the lobby.

He looked at his watch—six. A few minutes later the woman walked toward him and Chris gave her a closer look. "May Ling? Is that you? Oh my God, I would have passed by you without a second glance!"

"That's good. I won't be recognized by anyone." Her light-brown, long-haired wig, heavy eye makeup, long artificial eyelashes, and bright red lipstick were outrageous. People passing through the lobby stopped and stared before continuing on their way. Chris looked into her brown-striped cat's eyes and said, "Contact lenses? That color?"

As she nodded, her dangling flashy earrings shook and sparkled. Her tight black miniskirt barely covered her backside and it matched her low-cut black shirt.

He continued to stare at her. "If I didn't recognize you no one else will either."

She tossed her hair in a haughty manner, with a flick of her head.

"I always wear a disguise when I'm working." She gave him a sexy stance with her hands on her hips, her oversize handbag over her left shoulder. As she moved, the smell of jasmine caught his attention. It reminded him of exotic places and unforeseen excitement. He followed her scent as he walked beside her to the car.

"What's happening?" he asked as they got into the car.

"My sources have told me there's a new restaurant specializing in exotic animals that opened last week outside of the city and frozen animal meat was delivered to this restaurant earlier in the week.

"Entrance is by password—pangolin. There's also a rumor that a top man involved in animal smuggling will be there tonight with fellow Triads. The restaurant owner is also a Triad."

As they drove through the outskirts of the city Chris asked. "So, what do we do?"

"Let me give you a brief rundown, Mr. Johnson."

He interrupted: "We're working together now. Let's drop the formality. Call me Chris."

"I'd rather call you Mr. Johnson," she said coolly.

He shrugged his shoulders. "Makes little difference to me, just as long as you do your job and let me do what I came to do."

She ignored his comment. "At the restaurant, another undercover officer or UC will be inside. The police videoed the restaurant yesterday to get the layout so they know what to expect before they go in."

"OK. That's usually what we do in the U.S. on these busts."

She tensed. "Let me finish. And please, don't compare us to the U.S."

"I was just telling you that we work in similar ways, and I'm not unfamiliar with the routine," he said curtly. "It's standard procedure."

She smirked. "Well, this is how we work here, Mr. Johnson, not like your Keystone Cops in the U.S."

"You've been watching too many movies, lady." His jaw tightened.

He turned away from her, and they both sat in stony silence as they stopped at the tollbooth. The driver paid the toll, and they continued along the highway.

The monsoon storm began as a light sprinkle, soon followed by heavy droplets pelting the car, drumming on the roof in a military rhythm. Vertical lightning flashed nearby, with loud thunder.

The rain increased in intensity, becoming solid sheets of water. The driver slowed the car to a crawl. Visibility was less than two feet, and the wipers couldn't clear the windshield fast enough. Water flooded the road in minutes. Chris could barely make out the lights from the businesses set back from the highway, and the windows in the car began to fog over as the air conditioning blew ice-cold air into the car.

Traffic inched forward slowly, plowing through axel-high water, leaving rooster tails of spray behind them. Finally, after several minutes, a side road came into view. As they turned onto the poorly paved road it slowly became a deep-rutted dirt track.

The driver skidded on the water that filled the ruts as he traveled along the road. The black sky and heavy rain changed day into night. The driver turned the headlights on high beam, allowing him to see a short distance ahead.

Suddenly, the rain subsided as quickly as it started and the heavy downpour slowly became a light drizzle. Lightning continued to flash in the distance as the storm moved toward the city. Darkness lifted as the clouds moved quickly and water disappeared, draining into the soil, leaving a wet and slippery path.

A yellow glow appeared in the distance and several minutes later, a small restaurant lit by strings of ethereal yellow lights. The parking area at the side of the building was crowded with cars.

The well-lit restaurant contrasted with the dense, black, foreboding jungle a few feet away, and the cicada's loud hum from the jungle mingled with the clattering noises from the kitchen.

The air was fresh after the rain, heavy with moisture and cool, a change from the intense heat of the day. The driver stopped the car in front of the restaurant.

May Ling spoke rapidly. "Here's the scenario: The backup police team is on its way and will be in place after we enter the restaurant. You're a wealthy tourist and I'm your date. When the meal is served, we eat the food. If it's exotic animal meat, I light a cigarette as a signal to another agent eating in the restaurant. They'll wait for the signal from the agent and then enter the restaurant. Don't interfere with the ops. I know what's going down so you just be an observer and that's all."

"OK. I'll just follow your lead. By the way, are we eating a real dinner?"

She gave an "are-you-stupid" look. "Yes, of course. That's part of the act. What did you think, we would just sit there?"

"I just wanted to know, that's all." He followed her into the restaurant like a puppy behind its master.

The restaurant was small with several old dark wood tables and dirty white plastic chairs. A makeshift bar sat in one corner near the kitchen door. The wall behind the bar held several bottles of whiskey and scotch, nothing elaborate. A few short glasses sat on the table with an ice bucket beside them. The wood floor and walls were grimy and greasy.

Several ceiling fans whirred slowly, circulating the humid air. An electric bug killer in one corner zapped each time a mosquito flew into the coils. Its blue fluorescent lights gave an eerie glow to the room.

Twenty men sat eating, drinking, and smoking in the crowded restaurant. There were no women.

The Chinese owner met them at the door. May Ling spoke to him in Cantonese, and Chris recognized the word *pangolin*. The owner glanced at him, nodded, and then returned to the kitchen.

"There's no menu here," she whispered. "You eat what the cook has prepared and that depends on what is available that day."

They made their way toward the back of the room to an empty food-stained table still covered with crumbs, chewed bones, and wet drink stains from the last customers.

Chris looked at the table with revulsion. "These tables are filthy! This is disgusting. I've eaten in some dirty places in Seattle that are clean compared to this."

She glared at him as she called the waiter to wipe off the dirty table. He quickly pushed the leftovers onto the floor with a grimy cloth and then brought steaming bowls of soup, spilling some broth on the table.

"Don't the waiters ever change their clothes? It looks like they have the menu on their shirt," Chris said. The waiter's shorts were wrinkled and spotted with food stains. He walked away in his rubber sandals making a slip-slop sound with each step.

"I hope food poisoning is not on the menu." As he spoke, a tiny green-colored lizard fell from the ceiling and splashed into his soup. Chris jumped up, knocking over his chair. "What was that ...?"

The lizard crawled out of the bowl, onto the table, and didn't move, stunned by the hot soup. Finally, he disappeared over the edge, dragging some greens on his hind feet. The waiter came running over. "What is wrong? What happened?"

"A lizard fell into his soup." May Ling pointed to the ceiling. "Bring him a fresh bowl." The waiter looked at Chris, grabbed his soup bowl, and took it to the kitchen. He brought him a fresh bowl and placed it in front of him, splashing the soup onto the table. Chris made a move to stand to wipe droplets of soup that splashed on his pants.

"Sit down," May Ling said quietly. "Don't make a scene!" She gave him a dirty look. "You can leave at any time."

He sipped the hot soup, then looked at her, eyebrows raised.

"Herbal chicken soup with greens and some special spices. I ordered it specifically so you could be seen actually eating something."

"It's delicious, but like nothing I've ever eaten before."

The waiter arrived with a sizzling black-iron platter on a wood board and placed it in the center of the table. He set down another plate of stir-fried vegetables and two small bowls of rice. May Ling spoke to the waiter. He replied and left.

"The waiter said this is real pangolin meat. Put some vegetables on your plate. You can eat those and a bit of the meat."

He picked up a tiny piece of the meat with his chopsticks and mixed it in with the vegetables then pushed it to the side of the plate.

"It makes me sick to see the meat. I can't stomach it. Those poor animals."

May Ling ignored him as she placed her chopsticks on her plate and then took a sip of tea. She pulled a packet of cigarettes out of her handbag, lit one stick with her lighter, took a few puffs, and then stubbed it out.

A Chinese man in his mid-twenties sat alone at a table near the far wall. He had finished eating and was sipping his tea. When he saw May Ling's signal, he called for the bill. She glanced at him and watched as he put his money on the table and left the restaurant.

Chris watched her movements quietly. After her outburst in the car, he didn't want to interfere with her plan.

While Chris and May Ling continued to pick at the vegetables, the agent went to his car and opened the hood as though he had engine trouble. Another police officer hiding nearby watched through night lenses. He hid under the open hood and used his walkie-talkie to call the police that were parked near the entrance to the side road off the highway.

He said quietly, "Stand by. Stand by. All quiet ... it's a go." He put the walkie-talkie away, lowered the hood, and drove away from the restaurant.

A police van drove up to the restaurant with a unit of men sitting in the back of the van wearing yellow vests over their uniforms. Two unmarked cars followed.

The van parked near the side of the restaurant. Four men moved to the back exit, ten headed to the front; some watched the parking lot while the others waited, ready to enter.

The chief investigating officer received a signal on his walkie-talkie that they were in place and gave a signal for the unit to enter the restaurant. They spread out along the walls, their weapons visible as they secured the area. All the while they watched the diners. No one moved. The cooks were caught trying to escape out the back door.

Three officers entered the restaurant. The chief investigating officer was in charge of the operation. He shouted to the customers, "Police! Hands on the tables in full view! No talking."

Customers were startled. They looked around the room at the police on either side of the room, then at other diners. Some attempted to stand but the investigating officer repeated the warning: "Remain seated!"

All was quiet. The customers watched the police as two Indian officers, one holding a drawing of a known criminal, walked by the tables comparing the photo of a man with the diners' faces.

At a table near the kitchen they found their man, a Triad lieutenant and known animal smuggler, sitting with the restaurant owner. The Triad lieutenant was Chinese, thin, and tall with slicked back greasy hair, smoking a cigarette. He was wearing jeans and a white short-sleeve shirt. After taking a long drag on the cigarette, he flipped it onto the floor and stubbed it out with his foot. He glanced at the owner then stood quietly as they flex-cuffed him.

The restaurant owner nodded to the lieutenant. The owner was a heavyset man and his black shirt and stained black pants hung on his body in an effort to cover the flab. He stubbed his cigarette out on the floor, took a long gulp of beer, and slowly set the glass on the table. He turned to look at the police officer, sneered at him, and then slowly stood.

The officer flex-cuffed the owner and shoved them both toward the front entrance. "You can talk to your lawyer at the jail," he said gruffly.

Two other Malay officers escorted the restaurant owner and the Triad lieutenant to the patrol car. They drove to Bukit Aman, the main jail in the city where they would be booked on charges of animal smuggling and serving illegal wild meat at the restaurant.

Chris had his passport and visa ready as the Indian officer walked down the tables. When he came to Chris he stopped and asked for his identification. He looked at his passport. "American?" Chris nodded.

The officer looked at May Ling and asked for her ID. He looked at her, then at Chris. "She your girlfriend? How much does she charge?"

Chris glared at him silently. The officer laughed as he continued to walk past the tables looking at each customer as he did so.

The chief investigating officer spoke to the diners, "You haven't been charged this time for eating in this restaurant. You're free to go."

The diners jumped up, knocking over chairs in their rush to leave the restaurant. The restaurant was soon empty except for the police and the waiters.

The wildlife officer stormed into the kitchen. He saw cages with three large pangolin alive, waiting to be butchered. They grabbed the cages and dragged them outside, putting them alongside other cages with turtles, lizards, and snakes.

The police wagon backed up to the kitchen, and the men loaded the live animals onto the back of the van. When they had all the animals and meat they found in the freezer loaded into the van, they quickly departed for the animal shelter to give the animals food and water.

Chris and May Ling left with the other diners.

"What happens now? I want to help with the animals. Can I go into the kitchen or is that off-limits to me?"

"Sorry, you can't go there. A wildlife officer is there to take any evidence of exotic meat being served. You can't do anything. It's up to the Wildlife Department to photograph the animals, alive and dead."

Chris took a deep breath and waited. "I won't interfere. I know how to handle evidence."

She ignored him. "The restaurant will be shut down for several days and a fine levied against the owner. As for the Triad lieutenant and the owner, they will be booked and then released on bail." They watched the lorry carrying the animals leave the site.

They were silent on the drive back to the city. Chris finally broke the silence as they stopped next to a police car at a highway tollbooth.

"Well, that went smoothly! Congratulations! At least a few animals are safe. That's what's really important. We were there most of the night. It took that long to clean up the operation."

"Most of the time our ops are like that. Our officers are well trained. I am going to the police station and this officer will drop you at your hotel." She got into the waiting police car without another glance at him. She lowered her window and said distantly, "I'll be in touch."

As she drove off, he muttered under his breath, "She may not be pleasant but at least she's professional. A real fire-breathing dragon."

⁂

Chris retrieved the morning paper from the outside doorknob, then called room service and ordered a simple breakfast.

He opened the paper to the front page and saw the article complete with a photo of the exotic meat laid out on a plastic sheet. Several cages of live animals were displayed alongside the meat. Deputy Director Abdullah Razak and a wildlife officer stood at the side with police officers all holding bags of frozen evidence.

Later in the morning Chris and Suhaimi drove to Putrajaya for the meeting with Tan Sri and his staff. They were all sitting in the meeting room when Chris and Suhaimi walked in and sat down at the end of the table.

The minister handed each member copies of the latest smuggling incident reports. Tan Sri congratulated Abdullah on the raid. He puffed up as he thanked the minister, and gave Chris a smug look. Chris ignored his behavior and offered Abdullah his congratulations. Tan Sri discussed the raid and briefed everyone on new items of interest.

As the meeting was about to end, Chris stood and said, "The operation last night was successful. We saved several animals from the cooking pots in the restaurant. Your police did an excellent job throughout the operation. I congratulate your team, Tan Sri."

He sat down and Tan Sri spoke. "Thank you for your kudos, Mr. Johnson. I and my staff appreciate your input on their ability to do their job well, and I am pleased that the ops went off without a hitch. The meeting is now adjourned. Thank you all for coming."

Later in the morning, May Ling called Chris. Her voice sounded pleasant as she greeted him. "How about a real dinner tonight to make up for the bust last night? My treat and it will be great food you can enjoy."

"Why the sudden change of heart? You were like vinegar last night and now you are all roses and honey."

"Well, I was concentrating on the ops. I think I owe you an apology for my briskness and thought it would be good to get to know you better rather than not understanding your foreign ways. I know you don't have the experience necessary for this ops and I will try to assist you. After all, you're leaving in two weeks."

"Wait a minute! Did Tan Sri put you up to this? *Be nice to the foreigner because he'll be leaving shortly.* How do you know what my experiences are? You think your police force is the only one that does these type of operations? Get real, lady. You just want to be a one-woman show, that's all." His face flushed with anger.

She slowly enunciated each word: "Mr. Johnson, this is my country and you are a foreigner in it. Don't push me. You will get your chance to assist soon enough." She continued, "I'm trying to help you here. You have to turn in a report to your supervisor, and I will help you do that so you don't look like a new recruit."

"I thought so. You had your hands slapped, didn't you? You were told to back off."

Silence, then she said in a softer tone, "Mr. Johnson, I said I'll to take you to dinner and show you the town. Do you want to meet me or not?"

"Yes, I'll meet you in the hotel lobby. And by the way, hamburgers and French fries are not my favorite food. I like the Malaysian cuisine."

He put down the receiver and wondered about her change in attitude. *She runs hot and cold, and I never know which way the tap is turned.*

May Ling met Sue Hwee and Jessica Ting at a Chinese restaurant for lunch. They chatted as they ate their noodle soup and drank their tea.

Sue asked, "So, how's it going with the American? Is he easier to work with now that you have had a few days with him?"

May Ling sighed. "No, he's unrelenting and stupid. He doesn't know the Asian ways and makes a lot of mistakes in talking to people and eating. He holds his chopsticks near the bottom like a peasant. All he talks about are the animals and how they should be protected. He's obsessed with it. It's annoying."

"Aw, come on, May, don't be so hard on him," Jessica said. "He's just not used to our ways, and you're treating him miserably. Lighten up, and perhaps you'll find he's a nice guy."

"I know he's doing his best and working very hard, but I could do the job better myself and we really don't need him out here."

Jessica pointed a finger at her. "You've said that before." She waved her finger as she talked. "You're jealous that he's here. You're upset that the minister didn't ask you to do the job. Did it ever occur to you that he might know something that you don't, or are you just trying to cover up your feelings for him?"

May Ling picked up some noodles with her chopsticks and ate them slowly. She said firmly, looking at her soup, "I have no feelings for him."

Her friends smiled, and they nodded their heads.

"I've had enough of this conversation. I have to get back to work." She stood and said to her friends, "Don't try to make something out of this. I'm meeting him this evening, and it's work related only. Besides, Tan Sri wants me to babysit him."

They nodded knowingly as she turned to walk to her car.

CHRIS STEPPED INTO THE MERCEDES and sat beside May Ling. She turned to him and smiled as he closed the door. The driver pulled away from the hotel and headed toward the main street and edged into the traffic.

"Thanks for meeting me tonight. I wanted to show you some of the city. You've been here less than a week, and I'd hate to have you return to the U.S. without seeing some of KL."

Her voice softened. "I thought it would be good if we had a chance to enjoy an evening together. I'm not all business and like to have a good time too."

Chris was civil. "You turned me off at that operation last night with your cold attitude, so I wasn't sure I'd meet you tonight. But after some thought ... here I am. Besides, who said I was leaving next week?"

"I can understand your feelings, but I was working last night, not out for a social affair. I didn't have time to teach you how we work here. You of all people should understand that. When you're working there is no time for politeness. Anyway, lets drop it, OK? Let's start over by seeing some of the city's attractions. That doesn't sound too threatening, does it? I thought you were here for only two weeks and then going home."

She gave him a brittle smile that disappeared quickly.

"I'm not sure I'll be leaving next week," Chris said. "Disappointed?" He waited and she was silent. He continued, "Perhaps I should keep a report on our evening out tonight and turn it into the minister tomorrow so you can be graded on your personality skills?"

Her tone softened. "We'll keep it simple, just between you and me and not let the minister know, OK? Ready to just be a tourist? No, I'm not disappointed."

"Well, it's nice to have a tour guide as pretty as you." She ignored him.

Oh well ... she's still a dragon lady. Best to keep it simple.

He sat back and looked out the window as she leaned forward and told the driver where she wanted to go.

As they drove through the Golden Triangle area, she gave him a short history of the city. She directed the driver to Bukit Nanas (Pineapple Hill) in the center of the city. They parked near the brightly lit tall observation tower. Famous city towers from around the globe had been etched into the two sidewalks leading up to the tower.

Chris saw the tower from Seattle. "Hey! Look at this! It's the Space Needle!"

"I thought you'd enjoy it. Do I get points for bringing you here, Mr. Johnson?"

At that moment his mobile phone rang. He looked at the sender—"unknown"—and decided not to answer it. It rang a few times then stopped.

"I don't recognize the caller. No number came up. Must have been a wrong number."

They were walking back to the car when it stubbornly rang again. He answered it.

"Johnson here. Who is this?" He looked at her, pointed to his phone and walked a short distance away and sat down on a nearby bench. She could still hear him.

"Why are you calling? What? You spent all the money in Vegas and now you want more?" His voice became still louder. "I don't care if you're broke. I'm not your lovesick boy who wants you back. Can't you find another diamond to pawn? ... You're sorry? Too late, sister, sorry doesn't repair the damage. Go find someone else to scam."

He walked back to May Ling, his face red with anger. He turned off his phone. "I won't be bothered by that caller again. Sorry about that."

She gave him an embarrassed look. "I wasn't really listening. I was on my own mobile."

She held it in her hand. He gave her a look that said, *smart girl.*

It was already dark when they stopped at a busy back street off the main road in the center of KL. She sent the driver back to the hotel to wait for her.

The narrow street was filled with local and foreign restaurants: French, German, Dutch, Cuban, Italian, Indian, and others. Tourists and locals were eating and drinking, talking and enjoying themselves at crowded food stalls along the roadside and in air-conditioned restaurants. Each restaurant had its own outside eating area separated from its neighbors by small palm trees in planting boxes.

The street lights, loud music, food hawkers in stalls alongside the road calling out to the tourists about their food varieties— all of this mingled with the aromas of the curries, exotic spices, grilled fish, stir-fried chicken, and mutton that filled the air. Cars and motorbikes drove slowly, avoiding the people walking along the congested street.

Chris could smell the different foods being cooked as they walked by each stall. May Ling pointed at the different cooking styles and foods. "This stall is cooking oysters with scrambled eggs, a very tasty Chinese dish. They only prepare it in the late evening."

He watched as the Chinese cook stirred two scoops of oysters into the eggs cooking in a large wok, using a large wooden paddle. The cook looked at Chris and smiled. He placed a small bit on a paper napkin for him to taste.

"This is delicious. I haven't had anything like this before." The Chinese cook beamed, and they continued walking along the road.

The last restaurant on the street was a small Chinese seafood place, famous for its great food and cheap prices.

It was crowded with noisy locals and tourists talking in several languages, the clatter of the plates, waiters clearing tables and resetting them for new diners, then carrying hot food and ice-cold beer served on large trays.

Twenty wood tables with round marble tops filled the small room. Four café chairs of old dark wood were placed around each table. The walls held several Chinese brush paintings of scenes from China, each painting in a gold frame. An old white marble tiled floor, yellowed with age, marked the entryway.

The restaurant had a 1920s look to it. It was clean and well lit by several heavy-metal black-iron Chinese lanterns hanging from the ceiling offering dimmed lighting.

May Ling grabbed Chris's arm and pulled him into the restaurant. A short, thin Chinese man with slicked back, black hair watched them enter and walked over to greet them. He smiled and spoke to May Ling in Cantonese. She turned to Chris. "This is Jimmy Lee, owner and very good friend."

Jimmy Lee looked at him, gave a slight bow, and then led them to the only empty table near the kitchen door, and left. Immediately, a waiter poured tea into small china teacups, then handed them a menu.

May Ling smiled sweetly and said, "Mr. Johnson, you'll be

able to eat the food here. There is nothing endangered, just the best seafood in town. Also, they don't serve hamburgers and French fries."

"That's a change. I can enjoy it and not worry about what's coming to the table."

He glanced around the crowded restaurant and the diners as she ordered the dinner. They appeared to be enjoying the food, laughing, and talking as they ate. The waiter brought steaming hot and sour crab soup in small bowls, followed by spicy chili crab, and a green leafy vegetable sautéed with garlic. Steamed fish was served on a special platter with parsley and onions sprinkled over the fish and served with small bowls of rice. Ice-cold Tiger Beer in frosted glasses and fresh tropical fruits completed the meal.

"You said the owner is a very good friend? How do you know him?" Chris asked as May Ling placed some steamed fish on his plate then spooned the special sauce over the fish.

"I have known Jimmy for many years. We grew up together on the same street. His family was very poor and had too many mouths to feed—six children. His father was a cobbler and many times they were short of money. They raised a few chickens and my mother bought eggs from them every week. She gave them a little extra money now and then. My mother helped Jimmy as he grew up, with his education and clothing. He has never forgotten his humble beginnings and watches over us. He will do anything for my parents."

"That's quite a story. Your parents must be very caring people. I hope I can meet them sometime." He drank his beer and ordered another.

"Of course, it would be a pleasure to take you to meet them. They are quite elderly now, but would like that."

"What did your father do? Was he in business?"

"He was a tailor and had a small shop in our house. He supported the family, and we were comfortable, better off than

Jimmy's family."

"Do you have any brothers and sisters?"

She looked at him for a moment. Her eyes became cold and the warmth in her smile disappeared. She stared off into the distance.

"I had a younger brother ... I think it's time to leave. It's getting late, and I have a busy day tomorrow."

Sorrow clouded her face. Chris tried to hold her hand, but she pulled away and stood.

"It's time to go," she said.

As they walked toward the exit, he noticed Jimmy Lee standing by the kitchen door, talking on his cell. His lidded eyes watched as they walked to the street.

They strolled down the side of the street as cars passed by. Motorbikes slowly weaved between the cars and the people walking along the roadside. A motorbike with two riders came up behind them, attempting to pass.

Both men wore helmets with dark visors covering their faces, and they wore heavy jackets. Chris turned to look at them as May Ling began to move off the road to make a path for the bike. As it edged by them, the pillion rider grabbed her shoulder bag.

She screamed. Quickly she grabbed her bag, but the rider pushed her backward. As May Ling stumbled, he tore the bag off her arm. Chris immediately jumped toward the bike and yelled at the biker, "Hey! What're you doing? Stop right now!"

The rider turned to look at them and stopped for a brief moment. May Ling quickly grabbed the bag's strap and yanked the bag from the pillion rider's hand. He let go. She lost her balance and fell onto the street. She rolled with the fall, still holding onto her shoulder bag. "Help me!"

The bag fell open, and the contents scattered on the road. She screamed again as she hit the cement with a thud, her head barely missing the curb.

Chris shoved the biker, and the bike tipped to one side as

the driver lost his balance. The biker tried to stabilize the bike, one foot on the ground for balance, as it continued to wobble. He regained control and quickly turned the bike around then increased his speed.

As the bike sped toward him, Chris sidestepped. As the bike passed him he caught a flash of light on a long steel blade.

The biker turned the bike around again, facing him, and the pillion rider raised his machete. The biker revved the engine as he sped toward Chris.

The rider swiped the blade toward his shoulder. Chris sidestepped out of the way, then quickly turned and grabbed the collar of the pillion rider's jacket. With a quick yank, he pulled him violently to the ground; his helmet rolled across the road with a clatter.

The machete flew out of his hand striking the ground with a loud clang. The biker revved his engine, raising the front wheel in the air and took off without stopping.

The rider jumped up and shoved Chris, who stepped back and quickly smashed him in the face. He threw a punch as Chris pivoted to one side and grabbed his outstretched arm and twisted it behind his back, kicking his feet out from under him, forcing him facedown on the rubbish-strewn pavement.

He screamed in pain, bleeding from his broken nose. Chris twisted the man's arm toward his shoulder and put his foot on the man's back, holding him on the ground.

"Let me go! Let me go! I'm sorry. I'm sorry. I don't want to go to jail."

"Not on your life, you jerk! You'll pay for what you did!"

May Ling quickly stood then rushed forward to help.

Chris raised his eyebrows. "Are you OK?"

"Yeah! He just took me by surprise." She finger-combed her disheveled hair back into place.

"Someone call the police!" he yelled to the crowd that had gathered.

Several minutes later a tall, thin Malay policeman ran to the scene and quickly flexi-cuffed the pillion rider's hands behind his back and pulled him to his feet.

The officer ignored his cries as he took down Chris's description of the attack.

"You'll receive a call from the station asking you for more details. Thank you for capturing this man." He shook Chris's hand. "We have been watching this area for some time and haven't been able to catch these thieves."

The paddy wagon arrived. The rider was secured in the back and the paddy wagon drove away.

The people watching began to move out of the way, and the noise in the street returned to a normal level.

Chris put his arm around May Ling, comforting her. "Do you hurt anywhere?"

She composed herself and quietly said, "I'm OK. No, I don't think I have any broken bones, just some scrapes."

She brushed her clothes, picking off pieces of rubbish that had stuck to her skirt and she picked up the contents of her handbag.

"I wasn't alert. I was enjoying myself and forgot about being cautious."

He brushed some dirt off her shoulder and hugged her, but she remained stiff.

"I'm OK!" she said brusquely.

She moved away from him, but her ankle twisted and she stumbled. He caught her. She looked at her shoe. One of the heels had broken off in the scuffle.

"Well, there go my Jimmy Choo shoes! I'll just limp on the other one." She smiled weakly as she held her broken shoe.

He hugged her again. "You can always replace your shoes."

Chris reached down to pick up the broken heel. As he did he noticed a crumpled paper with a photo on it. He picked it up and smoothed it out.

"Hey, look at this. This fell out of the guy's pocket when we were scuffling."

He held out the photo for her to see. "What? Where did he get this? This is a picture of you by your hotel. When was this taken?"

"It was taken Monday. We came back from lunch at an Indian restaurant and some man in a Mercedes took my picture and drove off."

"So this attack tonight was not random! Someone was looking for you and meant to do some serious damage."

"Yeah! I think I know who it was. A gang member was at the restaurant and checked us over. They must have found out who I was real fast. Someone followed us to the restaurant. Now I have to be doubly careful."

Chris looked around but saw no one watching them.

"I don't think they knew who I was," she said. "The purse snatching was a ploy. The machete was real and meant for you."

Chris stopped a taxi, and they headed back to the hotel. Once inside his room, he cleaned the scrapes on May Ling's legs and arms with soap and water. He gently wiped up the dried blood with his handkerchief and bandaged the worst scrapes. He opened a bottle of brandy from the minibar, poured two shot glasses, and handed her one as he sat beside her on the sofa.

"Drink this."

She looked at him then drank it in one gulp.

"You certainly know how to entertain a tourist. What other surprises do you have for me?"

As she set the glass on the low table in front of the sofa, she gave him an odd look.

He laughed. "That's American humor. I'm trying to make you smile."

She shrugged her shoulders. "It's late. I'd better leave and take care of my scrapes."

She put her hand on his arm and looked at him.

"Thanks for saving me from the purse thief, Chris. Purse snatchers work the area all the time. The police patrol the area, but it's difficult to catch them. I think this guy was trying to make some extra cash on the side as well as take you out."

She pushed the down button on the elevator. The door opened, she turned, smiled at him and left. He stared at the closed elevator door. She had stopped calling him Mr. Johnson.

Suddenly, he didn't want to leave. He decided then and there that he would stay and help the government. Or was it that he wanted to see more of her?

He went to bed, all the while thinking of her, but he wasn't prepared for another rollercoaster ride so soon after his last one.

Best to keep it business only.

9

SUHAIMI DROPPED CHRIS AT THE American Embassy for his meeting with Riley Logan, Homeland Security. They exchanged greetings as they went into Riley's small second-floor office, standard issue for lower-level staff.

Riley walked behind his desk and sat. Chris dipped into one of the two modern blue and chrome chairs facing the desk. He glanced at the large Boston poster on the wall behind Riley.

"If I took a guess, I think you've an Irish background?"

Riley laughed. "You think? Freckles and red hair? People wrongly assume that I am new to Homeland Security. I've had lots of experience in my field, more than many experienced officers." He emphasized his words with a strong Boston accent.

"I received a memo from the ambassador outlining your project and his expectations. Smuggling of any sort is always on our radar screen."

"Thanks, Riley. I appreciate any help you can give me. What can you tell me about the wildlife smuggling activities in Malaysia?"

"Many articles have been in the local papers on smuggling here and in other Asian countries. Penang, an island on the West Coast, is a large part of the picture. It's a hub for the smugglers because it's a free-trade zone for international electronics companies. Containers are given cursory inspections when they leave the port. Customs are lax in their inspections of vehicles. Animal smuggling isn't high on their list."

"I'm going to the Kangar border this Thursday to watch their vehicle inspections," Chris said. "I've not been happy with what I've seen so far and want to take another look. I want to see if the inspections are any better at this crossing. It's in the state of Perlis and is off the main expressway."

Riley nodded. "I'll come with you. You can always use a guide."

Just then the ambassador walked into the office. He stopped, surprised to see Chris Johnson, and gave him a curt nod.

"I thought we had covered all the issues when I met you earlier. Why are you here?" He tensed as he moved toward Riley's desk.

"I required some information from Riley. I didn't think it was necessary to clear my visits through you. Has there been a breach in your security?"

"Our security is tight. It's your presence here that's not wanted."

"Wait a minute. I've a right to have a meeting with any of your staff that can assist me. What's your problem?" Chris glared at the ambassador.

"I don't want you here. I thought I made that clear. I run a tight ship and don't appreciate you interacting with my staff." He crossed his arms as he glowered at Chris.

"Yes, sir." Chris mockingly saluted. "I won't require anymore information from your staff at the moment. If I need further assistance I'll have my supervisor contact you for clearance."

Riley's door slammed behind Chris as he left.

Chris got into the car but said nothing. Suhaimi looked at him, frowning.

"What happened? You look, like, distressed."

His cell rang. It was Riley.

"Sorry about his attitude. He's not liked here but we have to tolerate him until he leaves. Don't let him bait you. I'll see you as planned."

"Thanks, Riley. The guy's way out of line." He told Suhaimi about the altercation.

"This guy sounds like a tyrant. When does he leave?"

"Not soon enough. I hope they send him to some god-forsaken outpost where he can't do any damage." He calmed down and gave Suhaimi the schedule.

"I'll meet you at the airport. Better bring your weapon. I'll have mine, and we can carry them with us in a locked box aboard the plane. I'll take care of the paperwork tomorrow."

As they walked out of the airport in Kangar, a car pulled up. "Mr. Logan?" the driver asked through the open window. Riley nodded and the three men sped toward the border crossing, parked at the side of the small building and walked into the office.

A customs officer wearing a blue uniform was standing at the long counter reading the newspaper. He looked at Chris and Riley as they entered. "Can I help you?"

"We'd like to speak with the officer in charge please," Riley said.

The officer called out: "Osman, someone wants to talk with you."

After a few minutes, Osman sauntered out of his office. He was short, heavy, with bulgy eyes. His bushy black mustache looked stiff, as though it had been dipped in candle wax.

He looked them over and curtly said, "What do you want?"

"I'm Riley Logan, U.S. Embassy. This is Mr. Johnson from U.S. Customs and Border Patrol." Both men showed him their IDs.

Osman gave them a cursory look, peered at Suhaimi standing in the background, and said in a bored manner, "Who are you?

"I'm Suhaimi Wahab, Wildlife Unit."

Osman stared at him for a moment, ignored him, and spoke to Riley.

"I wasn't informed that you would be visiting the border tonight. Why are you here? This is a busy border crossing and we have no time for visitors." He cleared his throat and continued to stare at the men.

Suhaimi looked out the window at the few cars waiting to cross into Thailand.

 "The embassy sent a letter to your department informing them that we would be here. Did you receive notification?" Riley pressed.

Osman was edgy. "I received nothing—no written approval for your visit. What is it you want to see? Just look out the window and you'll see it all. Singapore doesn't miss much and lets us know if there is a problem." He gestured toward the window.

"Why don't you drive your car through inspection and test out our methods? Then you don't need approval to watch us. You can see how busy we are here."

Riley produced a letter from his satchel and showed it to Osman, who simply glanced at it.

"Officer Osman, we are here to watch your methods of vehicular inspection, not participate in them. We're investigating wildlife smuggling across Malaysian borders, not here to disrupt your routine." His mustache twitched slightly.

"I'm here to make suggestions that may improve your inspection methods," Chris said abruptly. "I want to help you find the animals and rescue them."

Osman shuffled his feet and looked at the letter.

"Well, as long as you're here and this letter was sent to my department, I'll explain our procedures." He continued to shuffle papers.

"How do you handle your inspections?" Chris pressed.

Osman paused then said, "Well, if we are suspicious about a load, we pull a crate or box and open it. That's how we found the civet cats last week." He puffed up as he spoke.

"I'd like to see your inspection routine firsthand," Riley said.

Osman nodded. "Then you'll have to go outside and watch the officer inspect the lorry that's in the lane." He made no effort to move.

Chris waited. "Officer Osman, are you coming with us?"

"You don't need me. Just watch the officer in the inspection lane. You can watch him."

Chris and Riley walked the inspection lane while Suhaimi watched from the office, keeping an eye on Osman.

The inspecting officer walked around a large lorry covered with a black canvas tarp, opening the doors to the cab, looking under the seat, lifting the canvas on the back of the lorry, peering inside at the cargo with his flashlight. Then he called over another officer and together they moved a few boxes, opened one, gave a cursory inspection to the rest and waved the lorry through.

"Not good enough," Chris whispered to Riley. "They're lax."

"Short of taking every crate out of the lorry, there is not much more they can do and most of the time they don't even accomplish that."

He nodded. "I agree. But they could be more aggressive about their search of the lorries or at least look busy. They are lazy and probably on the take. His attitude said it all. We may not see any animal smuggling tonight, but we sure know who should be removed from this border."

When they returned to the office, Osman gave them a cold stare.

Chris was curt. "Thank you for your cooperation. We would

like to do it again if we have your permission."

"Yes, yes, you can come here, but please inform me before you do so." He watched them through the window as they drove away.

He turned to the other officer. "Call the lorry driver and give him the all-clear signal to cross over." He returned to his office to sleep.

Chris read the morning paper in his hotel room in KL. The front page had a spread on the main port in Klang on the West Coast. A customs inspector recently discovered a container with fifteen tons of elephant tusks shipped from Kenya through Malaysia on their way to China. The tusks were valued at an estimated one point three million dollars.

The container was labeled as *recycled craft plastic.* Some tusks would be ground up and the ivory used in traditional medicine, and the majority of the tusks would be carved and sold on the open market for more than three million dollars.

A month earlier another container was discovered at the Penang Port of six hundred and forty-four ivory tusks bound for China from the United Arab Emirates. They were in a container labeled *plywood.* Their estimated value was over one million.

Chris reread the article and commented to himself in anger, "That's over six hundred elephants destroyed for their ivory so someone in China can drink some potion and think they feel better?" He felt nauseated, angry, and disgusted.

He calmed down enough to read his e-mails. He had a message from George.

Your reports offer little new material—only the usual garbage. If you can't get to the teeth of the matter, then get back here ASAP!

He read the e-mail and slammed his fist into the desk and kicked it, then hollered, "The idiot is a bureaucrat and can't understand that it takes time! What a jerk!" He furiously wrote back a caustic e-mail, punching in each key, finally satisfied.

He went to the Traffic.org site to read more about the elephant tusks and got the full story on the discoveries at Malaysian ports.

Later that afternoon, he called May Ling. "Are you free for dinner this evening?"

"Yes, I am. Where would you like to go?"

"Someplace not too far from the hotel. That'll make it easy. Let's have an early dinner."

She was waiting for him as he emerged from the elevator. Her stiletto heels clicked on the marble floor as they walked out the door. Her short skirt crept up her thighs as she got into the Mercedes. It did not go unnoticed by him.

"We are going to a popular old restaurant near here. The food is local with some tasty twists. I think you'll like it. This restaurant has been in the area for many years and is well known to the locals and expats. They serve only real food, nothing illegal."

"It sounds like a real gem. I need some downtime. I feel very frustrated with our results."

"We both do ... not just you." She stared out the window in silence.

The restaurant was in an old British bungalow, situated on a large piece of property. The inside was brightly colored with many Malaysian antique furniture pieces and wall decorations in several small rooms. They chose to sit in the small glassed-in atrium with a view of the towers. No one else was seated there, and it became their private retreat. The scent of the flowering plants in the atrium was relaxing.

May Ling was beautiful, and the full moon bright and romantic.

As they sipped wine, they watched the twin towers coruscating like multifaceted diamonds, brightly shining in the darkness. After a few moments, May Ling broke the silence.

"This is a great spot for a quiet dinner, so peaceful. How was your trip to the border?"

Chris was relaxed and smiled back. "It went well but uneventful, but it's nice to be back in the big city. I'm a city boy at heart."

"But did you learn anything?"

"Yes. Not all customs officers are on the ball. That border crossing is very busy with not much control over inspections. They need more personnel on duty to assist. They should have dedicated people, not just people that sit on their thumbs doing nothing."

"That's typical of all Malaysian borders. Don't get so angry. That's the way it is. Some of them are just uncaring. It's just a job that doesn't even pay that well. It's not an unusual problem globally. Our borders are short-staffed and the border traffic is increasing daily. Inspectors burn out fast. Anyway, enough about work. Let's order."

May Ling signaled the waiter and ordered the house specialties. The food was a fusion of Malay and Western, creating interesting combinations and flavors. As their food was brought to the table, the aroma of curry and spices filled the air.

Their signature appetizer of little top hats was filled with vegetables and served with a spicy, sweet chili sauce. They spooned the sauce over the top hats and ate quietly, each thinking their own thoughts. Chris broke the silence.

"You mentioned earlier that you have a brother? What happened to him?"

She looked at him and said sadly, "I had a brother, but no longer." She didn't add anymore and changed the subject.

"What about you? Tell me a little about your life in America."

"Nothing much to tell and very boring. I had a girlfriend but broke it off when I came out here."

"Why? You didn't want any long distance attachments?"

"It's a long story, and I am not in the mood to talk about it right now." He took a sip of his wine, stared out the window, and finally looked at her.

"What happened to your brother?"

"It'll take a few more glasses of wine for me to talk about him. It's too fresh in my mind right now ... please ... no more questions."

"Well, here we sit and neither you nor I want to talk about our personal lives, so let's go." He paid the bill and stood up.

He watched her as she fidgeted, tapped her fingers on the table and looked out the window.

"What's the problem? Do you want something else?"

She sighed. Her shoulders sagged. "Sit down and I'll tell you about my brother. I guess it's time I got it off my shoulders."

"OK." He sat down and waited.

"This is very difficult for me. He was murdered two years ago." She looked away as tears welled up in her eyes. She took a large gulp of her wine and twirled the wine stem several times.

"We were very close. He was my best friend."

Chris reached across the table and held her hands in his. He was silent for a few moments then said, "What happened?"

She looked at him with a vacant stare. The expression on her face changed and her voice became monotone.

"Ben was younger than me and in university, a bright star in engineering in the best school in Malaysia, well-liked by everyone." She took another sip of her wine.

"He and his friends were out at a bar where he met an attractive Thai girl one night. She was working the tables and smiled at him several times. Ben felt something for her and returned to the bar every weekend to see her. He always stayed until the bar closed. There were always two men who escorted her and several other girls when they left the bar.

"One evening before the bar closed, she whispered that she loved him, but was working off her debt to the Triads and couldn't leave the bar. He found out that she was brought into Malaysia from Thailand by the Triads and had to pay back the cost of her expenses.

"She was told she would work as a secretary and make good money, but it was a scam. She was brought in with fifteen other girls to work in prostitution and make money for the gang. They were literally kept prisoners in locked rooms."

May Ling paused a moment, sipped her wine thoughtfully, and continued. "The girls lived together in one apartment and worked for years, never getting their debt paid off. If they tried to escape, they were killed. Some of the bar girls lived in secret rooms off the bars, hidden by false walls. The rooms contained several beds and nothing else.

"When they remodeled one hotel in the Ampang area, they found one large room hidden behind the bar. It contained several cots."

Chris listened quietly. May Ling stopped and looked at him, waiting for him to say something.

Finally, Chris said, "I don't understand how this can happen without someone reporting these dens to the police. Isn't there anyway that someone, anyone, can help these girls?"

"No one will talk because of the money they make from the girls. These guys pay off everyone. That's how they operate, either by bribes or murder ... Let me finish my story.

"My brother said he would talk to the gang lieutenant and pay off her debt. They went to meet him at a condo in the suburbs. The lieutenant said the girl belonged to him and would work for him until she was too old to work for anyone else. He laughed then told Ben to get out.

"My brother was insistent. He threatened the lieutenant that he would go to the police. That's when the trouble started. The lieutenant ordered the bodyguards to beat him. The girl pleaded to let him go, but the bodyguards held her and beat her with a rubber hose. She fell on the floor screaming, trying to cover her head.

"Ben fought with them, but he was no match for those goons. They beat him until he was unconscious and bleeding, kicked him several times in his head, and then dragged him to the balcony.

"The girl tried to stop them, but was knocked unconscious too. They pushed him over the balcony railing and he fell ten stories to his death." May Ling was sobbing.

Chris handed her his handkerchief. "Dear God, that's terrible. Did you go to the police?"

She wiped away the tears.

"The bodyguards brutally raped the girl. She was found strangled, lying in the gutter on a dark dead-end street. Ironic isn't it?

"The autopsy report listed Ben's death as an accident, confirming that he slipped and fell over the balcony. This is the easiest way to kill someone here and it happens all the time."

Tears flowed down her cheeks. Chris moved to the empty chair next to her and put his arm around her shoulders.

"What a terrible outcome. The gangs are ruthless and kill anyone who gets in their way. It happens in the States too."

She put her head on his shoulder, and he hugged her.

"I vowed to kill the leader to honor my brother, and I'll get him."

"Do you know who it is?"

"Yes, I do. He won't get away with it."

Her face flushed and her hands tightened into fists.

They sat quietly while she regained her composure, then she wiped her face with the napkin and took a sip of wine.

"No one knows what happened, and I want to keep it that way."

He nodded. "How did you find out about the murder?"

"The bodyguards are stupid, good for nothing else but following orders. They were at a bar drinking and bragged about it. A friend overheard them talking and told me the story. I have no proof and can't go to the police."

He moved back to his chair and they finished their wine in

silence. He put his arm around her as they walked back to the hotel.

As they neared the hotel, he stopped and asked her, "May Ling, I am curious. You have such a beautiful name. Is there any meaning to your name?"

"Yes. May means beautiful and Ling, petite."

He hugged her gently. "Well, the name fits you perfectly. You're beautiful."

She looked at him and smiled. "Thank you for the compliment. What about your name? Is it a family name?"

"I was named after my grandfather, Christopher. He had an Irish background."

"Well, I think it suits you too." She gave him a warm smile.

"Thank you for your compliment." He bowed slightly.

Her car was waiting in front of the hotel. She opened the door, turned, and smiled.

"I really do feel better telling you about my brother. It makes it easier to bear when you can tell someone you trust. But it changes nothing." The smile slid off her face and her eyes darkened. "That gang leader will die."

She got into the backseat of her car and opened the window. He leaned into the open window. "Your brother was a hero for trying to save that girl. Revenge may not be that sweet. Try not to let it take control of your life."

"It already has."

She closed the window, and the driver drove away.

10

FIVE IBAN MEN WORE ONLY loincloths. Their legs and arms were strewn with tattoos and their heads were covered in jungle-decorated cloth hats. They carried blowpipes, poisonous darts, and burlap sacks. Their forefathers were headhunters, but they no longer practiced the art of shrinking human skulls, although some still shrank monkey heads for tourists.

It was twilight and darkness slowly fell over the jungle. The large monitor lizard was hungry, looking for food, flicking its tongue back and forth, catching movement of prey nearby—small mammals and birds.

The men were walking silently, keenly aware of the sounds around them. They were the true forest people and had developed special survival instincts, but they had come on difficult times. The forest was changing: logging destroyed animal habitats, forest fires cleared areas for planting crops, and timber companies logged the hardwoods. Trapping animals gave Iban and jungle dwellers money to buy rice, sugar, and other staples.

They saw a large monitor lizard just ahead of them, off the

trail near a large termite hill. They split up to surround the five-foot-long reptile. It would fetch a good price. The animal weighed at least sixty-six pounds.

One man jumped out in front of the lizard and another grabbed his tail before he could disappear. They carried it to a wooden crate, gently placed it inside, and nailed the lid shut. They continued to capture both pangolins and lizards.

They had collected five sacks. In the morning, a lorry would come by their village, pick up the bounty, and pay the men the equivalent of eight dollars per animal.

The lorry arrived at Sarikei, a small town on the Rajang River that emptied into the South China Sea, a smuggler's paradise. There was no customs here, only a lonely jetty. A rusty tramp freighter sat high in the water, waiting for its precious cargo. Then it sailed on the next tide for China.

Sometimes, smugglers killed the animals and labeled the meat as beef from Sarawak, frozen in containers, difficult to identify. The animal parts were packed carefully and stored in refrigerated compartments in holds of ships and then shipped to China.

Smugglers are crafty. They leave from hidden coves, paint new names on ships and change the registry to countries involved in illicit activities.

One of the most notorious ports is in Guangzhou, China, a city on the Pearl River. The city has a population of six million people and a metropolitan area of nine million—the third most populous metropolitan area on the mainland.

Zhang Chen was slurping pork noodle soup when Wang Ju walked into the small Chinese restaurant located in a suburb of Guangzhou. The restaurant was on a narrow street where the old buildings were tightly jammed, one next to the other, crowded with people and bicycles trying to navigate the narrow street.

Bicycle carts carried goods, vegetables, and people through the small streets where driving a car was almost impossible. The streets were filled with noise, sellers yelling about the quality of their goods, horns honking, dogs barking, bicycles wending their way through the traffic with their bells incessantly ringing.

The smell of roasted pork wafted from the old restaurant that held only eight square wood tables with four plastic chairs at each table. The green walls were faded and dirty.

Old-fashioned lights hung from the ceiling, and a few potted plants graced the front by the door. Once inside the restaurant, the street noise subsided. Bodyguards stood outside the door, barring anyone from entering. The waiter brought tea, sugary buns, and roast pork..

Wang Ju looked thin, almost bony with almond-shaped dark-brown eyes, pale skin, and a small mustache. His fingers were stained yellow from obsessive smoking. He wore a cheap black suit, white shirt and black tie, standard for government officials. He was nervous and did not like Zhang Chen; moreover, he did not trust him.

Zhang Chen nodded curtly and picked up his teacup, his large meaty hand engulfing the small delicate cup. He sipped thoughtfully and put it down delicately. He killed many who betrayed him or would not cooperate.

His appearance suggested a normal working-class Chinese man. His clothes were cheap and hung on his body. His long shorts covered his knees, a stained short-sleeve shirt open at the neck and the standard plastic sandals that the lower class wore. As he picked up his teacup, the dragon tattoo flexed on his arm and the fire moved as though it were real. The tattoo identified him. He only belonged to one society.

Wang Ju asked, "How many shipments have you received this week? How many have been delivered to special restaurants?"

He pulled out a small notebook, wet his index finger on his tongue, then delicately turned the pages one after another, finally stopping at the last page and read from a list.

"So far this month, shipments have arrived from Thailand

and Borneo. Total number of pangolins is eighteen hundred, lizards two thousand, turtles four hundred and seventy-five, and other animals four thousand. We were able to get a Malaysian tiger, big male. Penis will sell for large amount yuan. Other body parts will sell for good price. Made big money this month."

"The total?"

He checked his book again. "Two million U.S. dollars."

"That includes protection money from the restaurants?"

"Yes." He closed his book and put it back into his shirt pocket.

"We have one problem that has slowed the shipments. U.S. government inspector is watching the Malaysia borders."

His eyes narrowed to slits as he hissed. "Kill him. Throw him to the tigers. Let them eat him."

Wang Ju laughed nervously. "If he causes any trouble, we'll take care of him."

"Send him back to the U.S., then no problem. Malaysia big trouble when someone killed there, secret police too good. Must be very careful. You take care of this problem quickly or else. There is no room for failure."

He stared at Wang Ju, his eyes becoming slits on his face.

Wang Ju's hands shook slightly as he picked up his cup. He knew Malaysia well. The Triads there were strong, the Indian gangs were always in the news, but the government kept control.

"Big shipment coming by sea from Sarawak. Will arrive next week. It will make up for confiscated shipments."

He smiled. "That means good money. Restaurants can raise their prices, and we make more. Watch that shipment closely so we don't lose any animals."

"Not to worry. Everything under control." He took a sip of tea, the tremor gone.

They continued to talk for a few minutes more, and then Zhang Chen left with his bodyguards. He was an important Triads leader—a longtime member and very powerful.

Wang Ju sat drinking his tea thinking about the shipment.

He finished the buns and pork, wiped his mouth and picked his teeth. He burped, stood, adjusted his pants, and left. The unhappy restaurant owner standing near the kitchen watched him leave.

The haze was thick, and he put on his mask as he rode his bicycle back to the office. As he pedaled and thought about the conversation, he noticed a black Mercedes with dark windows following him. He pedaled faster but the car immediately pulled alongside almost touching his bike. The window came down and the man inside pulled out his weapon, pointed it at Wang Ju for a few seconds, then closed the window, and sped away.

Wang Ju shook with fear. He quickly pulled off the road, stood while he wiped his face, looked around and then continued to his office. His hands shook as he locked his bicycle with the other bicycles in front of the building. He had difficulty climbing the three flights in the dimly lit stairwell to his floor.

The door opened onto a long rectangular room of men and women sitting in rows working on computers. The room was austere with a few fluorescent lights on the high ceiling and drab, yellowed walls. A gray tiled floor was almost invisible, covered with old wooden desks and chairs.

Pictures of party officials and the President of China hung on one wall. Small windows on another wall overlooked the city. The men and women looked as drab as the walls in their black uniforms.

He walked into his small windowless office and shut the door. The nameplate beside his door read, *Tan Wang Ju, Head of Division*. He was often out of the office on business so no one paid much attention to him.

A quiet, self-effacing man who managed to do his job without complaining. No one knew about his other business. He kept his mouth shut.

He put his head down on his desk and cried. When he gained control over his emotions, he opened a secret compartment in the bottom drawer of his desk and pulled out a small black notebook, turned to the last page, dated it, and wrote the minutes of the morning's meeting.

He replaced it in the drawer and locked it. He wiped his eyes with a tissue then reopened his door and ordered tea from the tea lady as she pushed her cart by his door.

The crew was armed—semi-automatic weapons and ammunition loaded into a secure locker. The captain locked the door and held the key. The ship's engines coughed and began their melodic drumming. Bowlines were untied, stern lines next. The ship pulled away from the dock and slipped into the darkness, running lights off.

In the bridge, electronic equipment monitored the ship's movement and the captain gave orders to the engine room. Green lights from several computer screens emitted an eerie glow. The ship set sail for Guangzhou, China, where the animals would be off-loaded. There was little food or water for the animals.

This was a special shipment. A large party for a wealthy Chinese government official was planned. They wanted the animals alive for the best taste.

Meanwhile, a lorry with animals hidden in the back was on its way to Hat Yai on the North-South Highway to the Thai border. The lorry crossed the Malaysian border into Thailand before it closed at midnight, paying tribute to the officers on both sides, a paltry amount enough to satisfy them. The lorry continued to Hat Yai where the animals would be off-loaded into a warehouse, ready for the next stage of their journey into China.

Chris sat at the desk in the hotel room working on his

computer. His report was due, and he felt the pressure from his boss to return home. He had to develop a broader plan to stop the animal trade and also demonstrate to his hard-nosed boss his need to stay longer. Not an easy task.

There was a slight improvement in the number of lorries caught with animals but still a long way to go. He would make one more run to the border then meet with the Minister of Natural Resources and Environment and finalize his proposal.

He was working on his recommendations when he received an e-mail from George. His boss was his usual curt self, nothing in his e-mail warm or encouraging.

Chris, I want you at the meeting next Friday to present on your findings in Malaysia. Other border staff will be at the meeting. No excuses. George

Chris wrote back: *I'm working on the report but it's not completed. I need another two weeks to finish my study. I can't lose the momentum by leaving. Postpone the meeting or I'll send you a brief of what I am doing.* He reread the message, was satisfied and sent it off.

He envisioned George tearing his hair out over this last sentence and smiled.

His phone rang. "Suhaimi here. I have some great news!" He spoke rapid-fire. "I had a call from the Marine Police Commander in Pahang on the east coast of Malaysia. Last night, they caught several gang members loading a ship with animals.

"Slow down, Suhaimi. What's the location?"

"A jetty near Kuantan, Pahang, a large town on the South China Sea. The ship was bound for Guangzhou. The police had a tip from an informer and captured the crew and the workers loading the vessel."

"That's terrific! Finally, some results."

"Well, let's hope so. However, the Triads are ruthless when it comes to money. I am less enthusiastic than you."

"You're right, but I can't help feeling euphoric over the

rescue. I have a thought. Perhaps this would be a good time to go to the East Coast. We could check out the jetty and the ship, and it would give weight to my report. What do you think?"

Suhaimi shouted, "Yes! Let's do it. This is the season when the sea turtles come into Malaysia to lay their eggs. You haven't seen that, and it's not too far from where we will be going. It's about two hours farther north."

"I like that a lot. Let's head out tomorrow. It'll be great to get out of KL for a while and see something totally different."

"OK. I'll make the arrangements."

Chris returned to his report, revising it as he added more details.

Suhaimi called an hour later. "OK, it's all set. We leave on the eight a.m. flight to Kuantan. Go to the jetty and then drive to Rantau Abang, Terengganu. This is where green turtles nest. I talked to the ranger there, and he said there have been turtle sightings this week. We may be lucky and see one. They actually saw a leatherback last week. That's becoming a rare sight."

"Great. See you at the airport tomorrow."

The long wooden jetty was located in an unpopulated area on a deserted strip of sandy beach. It stretched two hundred feet out into the South China Sea. The rusty ship was still tied alongside midway down the jetty, floating high in the water. Two police officers were sitting in chairs on the jetty, stopping anyone from boarding the ship. Suhaimi spoke to them in Malay, flashing his ID. He pointed at Chris. They looked at him, nodded, and continued to talk. Suhaimi turned to Chris. "We have permission to board the ship but not to disturb anything."

"Fair enough."

They walked up the gangplank and looked around the unpainted worn deck. The hold was open, exposing the dirty, empty hold. They stood in the bow looking toward the open water.

Suhaimi related the incident. "An informer called the police.

He saw several lorries pulling up to the jetty and unloading crates. It was dark, and he suspected something illegal was happening.

"The informer's house is over there." Suhaimi pointed to the last house in a small row of tiny Malay-style wood houses on stilts.

Fisherman had their trawlers moored inside a man-made small rock breakwater, safe from the strong winds and tides.

Suhaimi continued: "Our informant was looking out his window and saw the activity. Several police from the Pahang anti-smuggling unit arrived within ten minutes and surrounded the trucks and the men. The police had assault weapons and were prepared to shoot. The men loading the ship didn't put up a fight and were taken to the jail in Kuantan. The unit was surprised when they opened the crates and found animals, not drugs as they had originally suspected. They rescued three hundred animals. The informer has already been paid. They receive a sum of money for reporting any illegal activities."

"Well, that's a good deal for everyone," Chris said. "They earn money, and we get the animals back. I like that approach."

Chris looked around the ship. "There's no sign of any life here, not even a rat. We aren't going to learn much from this ship. Actually, I'm glad we came as it gives me a different aspect of the smuggling operations. "

Suhaimi nodded. "Yah. Now you can understand how difficult it is to protect the animals from the criminal element."

They drove north to Rantau Abang and found a small hotel to stay the night. It was a typical rural hotel with one bare lightbulb in the middle of the murky green painted room and a ceiling fan to cool the air.

"This'll be a long night," Suhaimi said. "The turtles come ashore after midnight and before dawn return to sea. We have to wait it out. We may not see anything tonight, but that's the way it is. The turtles aren't on our schedule."

They ate dinner in a small Malay outdoor restaurant near

the hotel and waited until ten, then walked to the beach. The tide was incoming and small surf gently lapped the beach as though waiting for the turtles. They sat quietly on a log near the underbrush several yards from the water, watching for any movement from the sea. The night was clear and millions of stars coruscated in the sky. The white crests of the waves contrasted the black water.

"I didn't realize the East Coast was so rural," Chris said. "I take it that fishing is the main industry."

Suhaimi started to answer him but Chris interrupted, looking down the beach at the surf.

"Is that movement at the edge of the water? Can you see where I'm looking?"

"I see something. Let's walk toward it."

As they approached they saw the flippers of a large turtle pumping back and forth in the sand slowly dragging itself up the sand to the underbrush. She looked like a rowboat with oars in the sand trying to move ahead. It was a struggle and took all her effort.

Chris watched, amazed. "It's huge. It's almost three feet across the shell. It takes a lot of energy to move itself up the sand."

It left a long trench in the sand, with flipper marks on each side. Suhaimi shined a flashlight on the turtle.

"It's actually dark green-brown and has white markings on its shell, but the shell is smooth. The flippers and head have white makings in patterns. Look at the size of the flippers!" The turtle paid no attention to them, focused on getting to the underbrush.

As they continued to watch, six Malay men in sarongs joined them. Each wore a T-shirt and small black hat called a *songkok*. They were from a nearby fishing village.

Suhaimi whispered, "These men are the local fishermen. They are here to collect the eggs. Don't say anything, just watch, OK?"

Chris nodded.

Everyone stood quietly as the turtle began to dig a large hole with its flippers, resting several times from the exertion. Tears flowed from the turtle's eyes. It appeared that the turtle was crying, but it was only dryness in her eyes from coming ashore.

When the hole was deep enough the turtle placed its back end over the hole. Suhaimi shined the flashlight on the hole, and they all watched as the turtle laid one round soft-shelled egg after another. The eggs dropped silently into the hole and piled up, staying intact as the dexterous shell prevented the eggs from cracking. The turtle would stop after several minutes, resting before it continued to lay more eggs. The process continued for an hour. Everyone watched in silence.

Suhaimi quietly said, "There must be at least fifty eggs in the hole. It's finished laying and is resting before it makes the journey back to the sea."

"I've never seen anything like this," Chris said. "It's totally awesome!"

Suddenly, one Malay man reached into the hole and began to pick up the eggs. Two men grabbed one egg each, broke a hole in the top with a finger and sucked the liquid into their mouths. Chris tensed in anger, aghast at what he saw.

"Hey, what do you think you're doing? Put those eggs back into the hole!" He stood up as he yelled at the men.

One of the men looked at him and laughed. He spoke in Malay, gesticulating rudely.

Suhaimi translated: "They think it's their right to take the eggs. Drinking the liquid gives men virility."

Chris yelled angrily, "Virility? Put the damn eggs back now!"

The men looked at Suhaimi as he translated Chris's anger. Suhaimi was agitated as he pointed to the hole and stared at the men.

The men stood, keeping the eggs in a basket, then turned away as if to leave. Chris jumped up and grabbed the basket.

"These eggs are going back into the hole so the turtle can cover them. You can use chicken eggs for virility." His face turned red as he continued to shout.

One of the men grabbed at the basket, but Chris shoved him away. He fell into the underbrush. Another man pulled out a machete and brandished it at him. He was still holding the eggs and stood his ground.

"I'm ready for you. Come on, let's see if you can carry out your threat." He put his fist in front of his chest, feigning punches.

"There is no way you're getting these eggs."

Suhaimi stood beside Chris, ready for an attack.

"The foreigner will not give up the eggs. If you want trouble we are prepared. So, come on!"

The leader was angry and spit out his words.

"Those eggs belong to us. The turtle laid them, and we can eat them. There will be more turtles to lay eggs. So give them back. We sell them at the market and make money for food. You can't deny us that." He held his hands out, palms upward in a pleading gesture.

"Yes, but if you leave no eggs, there will be no more turtles," Suhaimi said. "You must learn to make sacrifices for the good of the country and the preservation of our animals."

Then Suhaimi whispered, "I am hoping that they all don't rush us at once."

"They don't look that strong. We are heavier than they are and taller."

One of the Malay men rushed toward Chris, trying to grab the eggs. He shoved Chris. He stumbled backward over the turtle but managed to right himself still holding the basket. He looked at the turtle that was covering the empty hole and sat down beside it, gently placing the eggs back in the hole.

Suhaimi stood on the other side of the hole, his fists ready. The man with the machete jumped forward. Suhaimi deflected the blade with his foot then chopped the man on the side of his neck with his hand. The machete fell onto the sand and the man fell on top of it. Suhaimi quickly reached down and slid the machete from under the man's body and picked it up. The men moved toward him. Chris jumped up and stood beside him as he brandished the machete.

Chris shouted as he held up both fists. "Come on!"

The men looked at them and backed away.

Chris emphasized his words. "You will not get these eggs! They stay in the nest. Go home and eat something else."

A small man spat at him. Chris jumped forward and grabbed him by his T-shirt, lifting him in the air and said in a cold, hard voice, "Don't you ever do that again!"

He threw the man onto the underbrush.

"I'm with the Wildlife Crime Unit and special forces," Suhaimi interjected to them in Malay. "If you want to take me on, we're ready." He beckoned them with his fists, and Chris started to move toward the men. The men backed off, then turned and left. One man turned and brandished his fist at them.

Chris was breathing hard as he watched the turtle finish covering the nest. It slowly made its way down the sand and disappeared into the surf. They brushed the sand clean, leaving no trace of the turtle's path to the water. They smoothed the sand over the hole and gently covered it with some underbrush to hide the nest. They sat for a while near the nest waiting for the men to return, but no one did.

"Well, I hope we saved those eggs and the men don't come back tomorrow," Chris said. "They will probably wait until we leave."

"We'll just have to spend some time here tonight, but let's move away from the spot and sit where we can watch the nest without the men seeing us."

"Good idea. I don't mind. Call your ranger friend in the morning and let him know about the turtle eggs."

"I had planned to do that. He will protect them from the

locals. By the way, you can buy turtle eggs in the local market, ten eggs for RM 25, about eight U.S. dollars. Not much for a year's work by the turtle."

Before they left the next morning for Kuala Lumpur, Suhaimi showed the ranger where the nest was, and he began to remove the eggs to the turtle sanctuary for protection.

11.

CHRIS'S CELL RANG NOT LONG after the turtle egg rescue. It was May Ling, and she sounded excited.

"We found a syndicate warehouse full of animals and birds. Some of the birds are very rare. One pair is worth one million on the black market. It's the biggest haul we've had. They even had leopard cats that are difficult to find in the jungle. The warehouse has been turned over to the Wildlife Department for care and feeding of the animals and birds until they decide where they should go. That's all I can tell you."

He exclaimed, "Wow! That's terrific! Who collected the animals?"

"We don't know yet. An informer gave us a tip on the warehouse, and it was raided last night. I guess it's good enough that we found the animals and were able to rescue them. We'll eventually find the culprit or poachers. Some of the birds were dead and a few animals were in poor condition, but most were OK. I was also informed of a large shipment crossing through the Thai border tonight just before midnight." She ended the call.

Chris immediately called the director of the anti-smuggling unit.

"Idris, I just had news that a warehouse full of exotic wildlife was found. Have you heard anything on this raid?"

"Yes, I was involved in the raid. It's a blessing that they were found. But who told you?"

Chris was silent, then said, "I received a call from an informer."

"Who is your informer?" Idris replied.

"Sorry, Idris, but I can't give you that information. I have to protect my sources."

"You seem to be well connected lately. Be careful. You're playing a dangerous game."

"Thanks for the tip. I'll watch my back."

Idris stared at his phone, then called the Wildlife Department.

"Good morning, Director. I've just had news of your warehouse raid by a surprising source. There's a leak in your department, and you'd better find it."

"Yes, I know. The raid has already been leaked to the morning newspaper, and there's a story in tomorrow's edition. I couldn't squelch the story so I'm sure you'll be receiving many calls."

"So much for our secrecy. There are eyes everywhere. Next time keep the info on any raids to only a select few."

"Yes, I know, but with the size of this raid it's difficult to control everyone. I know there's a mole in our operation but I'm not sure who it is. We will find them and shut them down. If word gets out to the smugglers then they will move the animals to another location. This farm has been in operation a long time under someone's protection, and we will get to the bottom of it and find out who it is. I suspect it is someone with a lot of power in Malaysia."

Chris looked at his watch. It was almost four o'clock and he had time to check his e-mails. They were meeting Idris at the airport for a flight to Johor Bahru, a border town with Singapore. They were going to watch the Malaysian border staff's method of operation. He sent a report on his East Coast trip to his supervisor and messages to his family.

He dressed in black pants and shirt with a dark jacket and packed his weapon in his hand carry bag. Chris got into the car and looked at Suhaimi.

"Hey, man, we look like gang members from LA." Suhaimi laughed. "Yeah, we sure think alike, dude. Black is the ops color of the day."

As they drove out to the airport, Chris related the news on the warehouse raid and then asked, "Who is Anson Wong? My boss told me to ask the ambassador, but he didn't give me any chance to do that."

Suhaimi glanced at Chris. "He's a notorious international animal smuggler living in Penang. He spent time in prison in the U.S., seven years I think. It was not enough to stop him from continuing to smuggle animals. He came back to Penang and has been transporting animals through Malaysia to other global buyers and doing it with impunity." Suhaimi was tense. "I have a great dislike for this slime."

Chris nodded. "There's more to this business than just transporting animals across Malaysian borders. I didn't realize how sophisticated smuggling of animals has become. I feel like a tire that's gone flat. I can't move fast enough to keep up. It's overwhelming, the number of people involved and the endangered species we're losing. We've just scratched the surface of this problem. That's what my supervisor, George, doesn't understand. He's a bureaucrat, just a pencil-pusher and is only interested in the final report, not what could be done while I'm in Malaysia. I've decided I'm staying for as long as it takes to get the job done. Then I'll go back."

"Be careful, Chris. You're impetuous, still young and you could ruin your career. With the smuggling business bringing in forty billion dollars, it's tough to stop it altogether."

Chris sighed and looked out the window. Both men were quiet as they reached the airport.

Idris was waiting for them at the check-in counter and had the weapons cleared. They arrived in Johor Bahru at the border crossing next to Singapore.

Idris cautioned them: "I don't want to arouse the suspicions of the customs officers, so I'll tell them that you're here to watch the process at the border, just a courtesy visit. They've seen you here before, so they won't suspect anything. I know you've watched the vehicle inspection before, but I'll inform them that you're helping us with the procedures and that you must view the activities again. That should take care of any suspicions they might have. If we stay with them in the office, they won't be able to call the lorry driver to alert him."

"OK, I'll play the dumb inspector act."

❧

The air conditioning was blowing cold air on the thin customs officer standing behind the office counter. He was reading a newspaper and looked up as they walked in. He immediately put the paper away and stood at attention. The dark-skinned Malay officer saluted Idris.

He nodded to the officer and said to Chris, "Officer Zorab has worked at this border crossing for two years. There is heavy traffic on both sides. Singaporeans like to travel to Johor Bahru because the prices for goods are cheaper than Singapore. Singapore's dollar is much stronger than ours. Officer Jamal is in the inspection lane. They will go through their inspections, and you are free to ask any questions."

He spoke to Zorab. "This is Mr. Johnson from the U.S. Border Patrol. He is here to learn how we inspect the traffic for people smuggling animals across our border. Please give him all the assistance he requires."

Zorab shook his hand and said to Idris, "Yes, sir."

"Mr. Johnson, follow me. Officer Jamal will do the inspection. He is ready to inspect the lorry in the lane now."

Chris watched as Zorab took the lorry driver's car registration and passport, scanned them, and motioned the lorry forward to the inspection lane. The lorry was entering Malaysia. The contents of the lorry were off-loaded at the Singapore Port bound for Penang.

Jamal looked in the cab and then walked to the back of the lorry. Zorab waited at the back of the lorry. Idris remained in the office with Suhaimi, who casually leaned against the window watching the outside activity.

Jamal read the manifest, untied the canvas, and shined a flashlight into the back of the lorry. Zorab moved a few feet away to cover both the cab and the back of the lorry. He pulled down the canvas, tied it up, and motioned the driver to go. The lorry held cardboard boxes filled with food products bound for Bangkok—nothing unusual.

Chris watched this routine several times and then the border quieted down about eleven-thirty; another half-hour to go and the border would be closed. Zorab finished his inspection, and they returned to the office.

Chris was prepared for something to happen, but he was calm and relaxed. *Perhaps, it is too early yet,* Chris thought as he watched the officers.

About eleven forty-five, Zorab looked at the wall clock and then out the window.

"The traffic is light tonight. Not too much activity for you. Perhaps a weekend would give you a better idea of our inspection procedures, Mr. Johnson."

Zorab tapped his foot nervously on the wooden floor, then lit a cigarette and threw the match on the floor. He smoked the cigarette briefly then stubbed it out in the full ashtray on the desk.

Chris yawned and stretched. "I think you're right. We should wrap it up. I'll wait a few more minutes before doing so."

He could hear the long sigh of relief from Zorab. His black mustache twitched as he fidgeted and shuffled a few papers, then glanced at his watch. "My wife has dinner waiting for me." He smiled weakly.

Out of the dark, a twelve-wheeler rolled into the side lane and waited. A heavy, muscular Chinese man sat in the cab and watched the officer approach. He could see the muscles in his right arm flex as he held his paperwork out the window of the cab. The officer took the papers, walked to the booth and scanned them, flipped through the passport and passed it through the computer. He returned the documents to the driver in less than a minute. Next, he read the driver's manifest—craft plastics from Indonesia bound for Penang.

Chris watched the action on a security camera that focused on the officer in the booth, stood, stretched, and said, "I want to watch the procedure once more."

Zorab followed him as he walked toward the lorry. Jamal motioned the lorry forward to the inspection point then shined his flashlight onto the Chinese man's face, quickly moving it around the cab.

Chris joined him at the back and watched as he undid the canvas, lifted it, and shined his flashlight into the back of the lorry. Jamal watched the driver.

Zorab made a cursory inspection of the boxes that were labeled *Jakarta, Indonesia, Craft Plastics Manufacturing.* The wooden crates were stacked five high in four rows making it difficult to move in the lorry. He scrutinized the boxes then asked him for his flashlight and a crowbar. He took it and shined it further into the back of the lorry. He saw nothing but more crates.

Chris turned to Zorab. "I'd like to climb into the lorry and see what else is in there."

Zorab looked toward the office then replied, "Yes, Mr. Johnson, you can climb into the lorry, but there's really nothing to see."

Idris watched the action from inside the office, and Suhaimi slowly walked over to the inspection lane all the while watching the driver sitting in the cab.

They lifted one heavy wooden crate and set it down on the ground. Chris opened the nailed crate with a crowbar. He stopped, silent for a moment, then exclaimed, "My God, look what is in here!" He lifted a short ivory tusk out of the box and held it up to the light.

"Elephant tusks, not craft plastic! The box is full of the tusks. Bring down another box."

Suhaimi had his weapon ready, safety off, partially hidden from the driver by a steel pole.

Idris grabbed the manifest from Jamal and read it. "Forty boxes of craft plastic! That means there are forty crates of elephant tusks and no craft plastic! The manifest says the boxes go to the Penang Port for shipment to Shanghai. The crates came through Dubai from Nairobi. They were to be transshipped through Malaysia, the open door."

At that moment the driver's door burst open. He fired at Suhaimi with his weapon. Suhaimi rolled out of the way of the gunfire and ran behind a sedan parked in the next lane. Chris jumped down, grabbed his weapon, and peered around the side of the lorry.

The cab driver riddled the side of the car with bullet holes. Suhaimi opened the car door and dragged the frightened driver out and pushed him down on the pavement.

Suhaimi ran to the rear of the car, crouched, and then peered around the fender at the shooter. He was hiding behind the lorry's door and looking wildly around, pointing his weapon at everyone. He caught sight of Suhaimi and fired. Suhaimi ducked down as the bullet skimmed over the trunk, missing him. He moved to take a shot at the shooter. As he did, another bullet grazed his shoulder. Suhaimi recoiled and shot back, hitting the lorry's door.

Chris jumped out and pointed his weapon at the driver, who was firing at the sedan. He yelled, "Stop. Put your weapon down on the ground, hands over your head!"

The driver quickly turned toward Chris and fired. Chris flattened against the side of the lorry, crouched, then quickly aimed at the driver and returned the fire. One bullet went through the driver's upper arm and passed through his chest, then out his body. He looked at his chest and collapsed where he stood. Blood gushed from the chest wound, and the red stain quickly grew on the pavement.

Suhaimi rushed over, weapon pointed at the driver. He leaned over and felt for a pulse but found none. He shook his head and stepped over the dead driver to the cab. He looked inside and found a young Chinese man cowering on the floor between the seat and the dashboard.

Suhaimi shouted to Chris, "Get over here!"

Chris joined him and looked into the cab. Together they pulled the unwilling teenager out of the cab and onto the ground, pushing him facedown. Suhaimi grabbed his arms and flex-cuffed him then stood him up.

"Who are you and why were you in the cab?"

The young man was crying. "I was the second driver. He never told me what was in the back. He hired me in Singapore and said he would pay my way back to Singapore once we reached Penang."

Suhaimi dragged him into the office for further interrogation by Idris.

Jamal drove the truck to the side of the building, out of the inspection lane.

Police arrived and stood guard while they waited for the

Wildlife Crime Unit to get to the border.

Blood seeped from Suhaimi's wound as he and Chris waited in the border crossing office.

Chris looked at his shoulder, grabbed a cloth off the desk and pressed it to the wound.

"You were very lucky. It's only a flesh wound."

The police were already investigating the shooting and the identification of the dead driver. One officer was interrogating the teenager in the office.

Suhaimi said, "The driver was Singaporean Chinese, according to his passport. He had the usual gang markings, no surprise there. They'll unload the lorry at a warehouse and count the tusks and anything else that's in the back. This is the second load of tusks that was on its way to China. We were lucky with this one."

Idris shut down the border to traffic, closing it until the next morning. He informed Singapore, and they closed their border to Malaysia. Within fifteen minutes, a paddy wagon appeared at the border. The teenager was taken to a holding cell in Johor Bahru, where the police would interrogate him before transporting him to the jail in Kuala Lumpur.

"I wonder if Anson Wong was involved with this shipment," Chris said quietly. "It's obvious that it was passing through Penang to be reshipped to China. His client won't get the order."

"Yeah, he'll probably be a little miffed." Suhaimi chuckled.

They both left for a hotel in the city. Idris stayed behind to work with the police.

Chris received a text message from his boss as he entered his room.

Don't waste my time with your daily reports. Save your information for the final report and present it when you return shortly. There will be no more extensions of your stay in Malaysia. If you stay without my permission you will do it at your own expense. George.

Chris smirked as he shut off his mobile.

We'll see about that.

⚜

Over the next two weeks, Chris and Suhaimi traveled from one border crossing to another, watching the inspection procedures and making notes. At the end of each shift they met with the staff pointing out how they could improve their inspections of the different types of lorries and cars.

It did not go unnoticed by Chris that each time they arrived at a border crossing, it was obvious that they had been expected. Someone was tipping off the animal smugglers.

12

Wang Ju sat at his small wood desk composing a business letter when the red phone on his desk rang.

Zhang Chen was terse. "The Malaysian lorry driver was arrested and the ivory confiscated. A shipment coming by sea was also stopped, and several members loading the ship were arrested. I will not tolerate this interference."

"Yes, I heard about the arrests," Wang Ju sheepishly replied while squirming in his chair. "The customs and police are becoming overzealous in their inspections. I heard that the American is visiting every border. We have alerted our contacts at the borders. It's the American who is causing the problems."

"Do something to stop their inspections!" Zhang Chen shouted. "Our men were arrested and jailed. Our last good customs officer was arrested when the shipment was confiscated."

He continued to vent his anger. "Stop the American from interfering! What are you going to do, Wang Ju? What are you going to do? We talked about finding someone close to the minister. I think it's time. It had better be quick or else."

This was not an idle threat. Sweat beaded on Wang Ju's forehead. He held the phone away from his ear and tuned him out, thinking only of the consequences, but he could still hear him shouting.

They lost over two million dollars from the confiscated shipment. Not only that, there would be no exotic food for the Party Minister on his birthday celebration. He would have to think fast in order to placate Zhang Chen and also have the food for the birthday.

He put the receiver back to his ear and when there was silence, he calmly said, "This was unexpected. There must have been an informer who talked to the customs officer. We will find out who it is and have them eliminated. I'll call you back. Give me some time to work this out. I'll get the information and call you immediately."

"Make it fast ... or there will be trouble for you!" The phone went dead. Wang Ju dabbed his forehead with a tissue.

His hands shook as he pulled open the secret drawer in his desk that contained all the files on the shipments from Southeast Asia. He shuffled through the top papers looking at the shipment dates of the lorries and the vessels from Malaysia, Borneo, and Indonesia.

He found what he was looking for. He pulled a paper out of the stack, read it, and smiled as he called Zhang Chen.

He answered the phone on the first ring. "What did you find?"

"There's a shipment leaving Borneo in a few days that should arrive in time for the minister's party in two weeks. I'll fax the ship and get their exact date of arrival."

"That's more like it. You know this dinner is important and we must make sure there is exotic meat on the menu, otherwise—"

Wang Ju interrupted, "Yes, I understand. I'll monitor the ship and put pressure on the captain to get here as quickly as he can. He must be cautious on the sea and care for the cargo. I'll pay him a small bonus for an earlier arrival date."

"The minister will be very unhappy if he doesn't have his birthday celebration with the food he ordered. He must not lose face or there'll be big problems for us. You'll call me daily on the ship's movements?"

"I'll call you every day and let you know the ship's position."

All was going to be OK. Wang Ju would still get his commission from the sale of the animals.

A few days later Wang Ju updated Zhang Chen.

"Shipment will leave Borneo tonight. It'll make up for the smaller shipments that have been lost. Ship will be in open water outside country boundaries and can't be stopped. I am in contact with the ship daily following its movements. Everything is under control. Inspectors at port are waiting for the ship to arrive."

"There better not be any problems," He warned.

Wang Ju rubbed his hands together in satisfaction as he thought about this payoff. Nothing could stop the shipment now that the ship was leaving on the tide.

Ten o'clock in the evening and the rusty ship was waiting to be loaded. It was tied to an old jetty in a hidden bay on the South China Sea. The ship's lights shined on the jetty witnessing the frenetic activity. Lorries were backing onto the jetty; the Chinese crew oversaw locals unloading animal cages from the lorries. The first mate was yelling at the locals, "Don't drop the cages on the jetty. You won't get paid if there are wounded or dead animals."

The men looked at the first mate and nodded, continuing to unload cages. The ship was just a one-hundred-and-fifty-foot long rust bucket, a tramp steamer, leaking oil from its bilge into the river.

Several pangolin were crammed into one cage; the frightened animals rolled into balls. Monitor lizards received the same treatment. Several were put into a small crate and crawled over one another trying to escape. Snakes were held in mesh sacks tied tightly and ready to be put into barrels. Over one hundred crates were tied down on the deck, covered with a canvas; another two hundred crates were in the hold. The ship was ready to sail as soon as food, water, and a crew of ten were on board.

⁂

Suhaimi called Chris with an update from their sting operation. "The army put the confiscated animals from that ship into cages, tagged them, and will return them to the rainforest when they recover. I have the breakdown on the animals counted."

"That was a large haul. How many did they find?"

"One hundred pangolins, two hundred monitor lizards, fifty star turtles from India, fifty kilos of python skins, twenty live snakes, ten palm civet cats, and about three hundred various other animals. Several were dead, others dehydrated, and some close to death, but with water and food, they will recover."

"Good. The more animals we can save, the more we cripple smuggling."

"I'd like to know who discovered the shipment. That was quite a feat, but they are in danger."

Suhaimi was right about that. The informer would be killed if discovered.

⁂

Wang Ju kept close tabs on the animal-laden ship steaming

toward its drop point. It arrived as scheduled at the Guangzhou Port and was ready to pass through customs. He called the port and talked to the customs inspector, Leong, a party member whose job it was to ensure that any ship on Wang Ju's list was legal and the cargo could enter the country.

Leong was in Wang Ju's back pocket and would answer to the Triads if the cargo were confiscated. He was nervous when he received the bill of lading from the ship stating that the cargo was miscellaneous Borneo handicrafts.

His small sparse office held only a desk and one small chair. He was reading the fax while tapping his fingers on the desk. Finally, he stood, put on his cap, and walked out the door to the ship tied up at the jetty. It was a bright day as he walked up the gangplank to the dirty vessel. His hand shielded his eyes and he could see that it was rusty, in need of paint and cleaning. The captain greeted him in Cantonese as he walked onto the deck.

He read the bill of lading, which stated that the cargo contained teakwood carvings, wood bowls, sarongs, clothing, and food products. He lifted the canvas, gave a cursory inspection, then walked over to the hold full of boxes, all labeled according to the bill of lading from which he could see standing at the side of the hold. He stamped the bill of lading, gave it to the captain, and walked off the ship.

He returned to his office, hung his gray cap on a wall hook, sat at his desk, and ordered tea. He knew that if the real contents were found he would be arrested and imprisoned. He was afraid of Wang Ju and felt he had no choice but to do the syndicate's bidding. Plus, he knew the animals were for a minister's dinner.

He watched out his window as the crates were being unloaded from the deck onto a lorry. The driver tied down the load, climbed into the cab, and drove away. Leong let out a long sigh. He picked up his phone and called Wang Ju.

"All is in order. The lorry just left the port."

"You will be rewarded for your efficiency. The minister

thanks you as well, and you'll receive my gratitude shortly."

Wang Ju immediately called Zhang Chen to advise him that the precious cargo was on its way.

He was pleased. "You will receive a bonus, Wang Ju, for your efficiency."

"Thank you." Wang Ju breathed a sigh of relief as he put down the receiver. He was in his good graces once again.

He left his office, locked the door, and walked out of the building. He decided to leave early to celebrate the shipment's arrival. He unlocked his bicycle, put on his mask, and pedaled home. He thought about his wife and how loving she was. He knew what he wanted when he arrived home.

Sex was on his mind as he pedaled faster. Traffic was heavier than usual but he was able to weave through the cars and bicycles. He could feel the hardness between his legs and wanted to get home quickly before his children arrived from school.

❧

The lorry left the port and drove to the large restaurant that was hosting the birthday dinner for the minister. It pulled around the back of the restaurant and began unloading the crates into the kitchen. Six chefs were ready for the animals as the crates were unloaded into the wet kitchen, where they would start the preparation for the meal. The head chef paid the lorry driver and locked the back door.

Immediately after the door closed, they started to open the crates, one at a time. The animals were docile and weak. Each chef pulled out an animal. Some had died on the voyage but there were still enough to satisfy the minister and his guests. They acted swiftly in ending the animals' misery. None were left alive by the end of the morning. The pangolins, lizards, turtles, and snakes were now part of the auspicious birthday feast.

The chefs prepared snake blood with Chinese wine for the

toast and turtle soup. Exotic dishes from the other animals would be prepared tomorrow on the day of the dinner. Two hundred people were expected to join the celebration.

The head chef read the menu pinned on the wall. Long life noodles in pork broth was the last course, an auspicious dish for the birthday. Other dishes offered health, power, and prosperity for the minister and his guests.

Twenty-five fish from the coral reefs in Indonesia and Malaysia were already at the restaurant, swimming in the tanks of seawater. Indonesian fishermen used small bombs to stun the reef fish. They floated to the surface and could be easily scooped up and placed in seawater tanks on board the boats to keep them alive. The blasting destroyed the reefs.

The restaurant was closed to allow the staff to decorate the dining room and complete the food preparation. It would be an elegant dinner with some of the top party officials attending. Everything had to be perfect for his dinner—no mistakes. The Triads were always in the back of their minds if something went wrong.

The dining staff set up twenty tables with ten seats at each table. Red tablecloths and chairs covered in white with gold ribbons were set at each table. The VIPs and the minister and his wife would sit at the head table. The ten-course dinner included a large cake created by the pastry chef to celebrate the birthday.

Gold-rimmed porcelain plates, soup bowls, and spoons to match adorned the tables, along with red-colored chopsticks and teacups; crystal glasses for a fine imported single malt Scotch were placed in the center of each table for the toast to the minister. Everything was set. The chefs finally relaxed.

The next evening, the guests arrived wearing elegant evening clothes—tuxedos and long sequined gowns—and diamonds and green jade graced the women's necks. Flashy diamond earrings and rings, large and gaudy, were displayed on several fingers.

Guests milled about drinking wine and eating appetizers

passed by waiters as they made their way through the crowd of guests. Finally, the minister and his wife arrived with a fanfare of drums and loud music.

The restaurant owner greeted the VIPs, bowing low before them, escorting them to their table, bowing along the way. Following them were friends and other party officials.

The lights dimmed to darkness when everyone was seated. The small Chinese band struck up a march, and the waiters marched into the room carrying plates of appetizers with a large candle in the middle of each tray. When the appetizer was placed on the head table, the lights were turned on. Everyone clapped at the performance.

Waiters carried a large plate with four cold appetizers and placed it in the center of each table, then served each guest with the appetizers on a small plate. The appetizers represented the four corners of the earth and included fried baby octopus, fish balls in bean curd wrappers, abalone, and crab dumplings.

Shark fin soup was served, and no one turned it away.

Steamed garoupa fish followed, along with several dishes of the smuggled exotic meat, stir-fried mushrooms and broccoli, fried rice, then longevity noodles. Dessert was snow fungus in herbal soup.

The grand finale was the large cake lit with fifty candles wheeled in on a cart and placed in front of the minister. People stood and toasted the minister.

13

WANG JU ANSWERED HIS PHONE on the first ring. Zhang Chen was brief. "Meet me in thirty minutes."

He quietly put down the receiver, grabbed his jacket, then closed his door, locked it, and walked out of the office. His hands trembled as he unlocked his bicycle, then rode off through the heavy traffic to the restaurant.

The pollution was exceptionally bad, and he covered his mouth with his handkerchief tied behind his head. Twenty minutes later, he arrived at the restaurant and parked his bicycle against the wall, locked it and walked into the restaurant past the two bodyguards leaning motionless against the wall. He took out the handkerchief, wiped his face, and then folded it neatly, placing it in his pocket.

Zhang Chen was sitting at a table in the back of the restaurant and motioned him to the seat facing him. Wang Ju felt as though it were a policeman interrogating him at a Chinese prison.

His "hot seat" was uncomfortable. He watched Zhang Chen pour tea. He picked up his teacup, took a sip ... waiting. Zhang

Chen glared at Wang Ju, then ... "What're you doing about the problem in Malaysia? The shipments have slowed; the goods aren't making it to the restaurants. You have a big problem, Wang Ju." Deathly silence filled the room. Wang Ju cowered in his seat, staring vacantly at him.

Suddenly, he shouted and hit the table with his fist. "How're you taking care of this problem? We are losing money! Do you understand me? How many times must I tell you before you do something? Do you value your life?"

He slammed his fist onto the table again then reached over and grabbed Wang Ju by his suit lapels and shook him several times. He fell off his chair onto the floor, got up quickly, and sat back in the chair, quivering. He looked down at his teacup as if the cup would save him.

"The Dragon Master is on my back to keep the shipments coming. If I lose, you lose." His face turned red as he yelled, "Do something to stop the American! Do it now. Kill him!"

Wang Ju paled. His hands trembled.

He pointed his finger at Wang Ju and warned him, "All right, I'll give you one week. If the problem has not been fixed, we will use other methods to fix it." He gestured menacingly with his finger sliding across his neck.

He looked at Wang Ju, sneered slightly and said, "How's your wife and daughter?"

Wang Ju stuttered, trembling with fear. "I'll have good results for you by next week. Give me a little more time. Please, boss."

"One week. After that ..." He pointed his index finger at his head and mouthed *boom,* then blew on the end of his finger and put his hand down.

Wang Ju stood, knees weak, and wobbled out of the restaurant, past the bodyguards toward his bicycle. His hands shook trying to unlock it as tears flooded his eyes.

He rode back to the office, forgetting to wear his mask. He

was almost hit by another bicycle but swerved onto the side of the road. He stopped, took a large breath and sat for a minute, then peddled back to the office and locked his bicycle by the side of the building. He wiped his face as he slowly walked up the stairs to his office. He sat at his desk, put his head in his hands and cried. After several minutes, he opened his secret drawer and began to work out a plan.

14

CHRIS MET SUHAIMI FOR BREAKFAST and they drove to Putrajaya for their ten o'clock meeting.

"This session with Tan Sri is important. I received an e-mail this morning from my department in Seattle. They have allocated some money to support the project here, and we will outline the details to him."

"That's good news. He'll be pleased with the cooperation between the two countries."

"He should be. It's a big step. I also left a call for the dragon lady to attend the meeting but haven't heard back from her. She's usually prompt in answering any messages."

"Perhaps she's busy this morning. Who knows?"

Chris mentioned a new, positive e-mail from his boss.

"Your e-mail from your supervisor is more moderate to your returning home? He seems to have accepted the fact that you are staying until your job is done."

Chris groaned. "Well, he is more open to my staying to complete this phase. I am OK for another two weeks. He is now seeing the benefit for himself of my results. It put him in a better light with his boss and justifies my stay here."

Tan Sri greeted them as they walked into his office. "Good to see you both again. Thank you for coming."

They walked into the conference room, where the rest of the committee members were already seated sipping their tea and eating cake.

Tan Sri put his hand on several reports that were on the table in front of him and continued. "Our progress is good and we have saved several hundred animals from death. The animals were tagged and relocated back into the forest reserves."

The deputy director of the Wildlife Department said, "Tan Sri, how can they be protected in the forests when it's the Orang Asli, the Iban, and Penan who are collecting the animals? They are the ones that need the protection from the smugglers. They see the animals as a way of making a small amount of money to buy food for their people. You have to stop the smuggling there, not at the border where it's too late for the animals. Too many shipments of animals are getting through the borders without being stopped. You must catch the major smuggler in Malaysia and that will definitely slow the trafficking."

Tan Sri raised his eyebrows. "Who is the major smuggler?"

"The one that lives in Penang."

"I don't know whom you are talking about," Tan Sri said. "The only man I know in Penang has permits from the Wildlife Department. The assistant to the deputy director issued them herself."

Chris changed the subject. "Who will take responsibility for developing the education program for the tribes?"

The education director raised her hand. "I will take responsibility."

"Thank you all for your help," Tan Sri said. "I expect a first draft by the next meeting."

He turned to Chris. "Now, Mr. Johnson, what is this proposal you wish to present?"

Chris stood. "Dogs can be trained to sniff out certain animals. I recommend two dogs at every border crossing. The U.S. K-9 Corps trains dogs for specific jobs. I've been in touch with them, and the government has approved two dogs and will also train Malaysians on how to handle the dogs. They'll accept four Malaysians to come to the U.S. for the necessary training. The dogs could work one border crossing a week and then move on to another. In the meantime, when the handlers return they will train other Malaysians, and more dogs would be brought in until there would be two dogs at every border crossing. This would surely help cut down on the smuggling."

"An excellent plan, Mr. Johnson. We already have experienced dog handlers in the armed services. Our police and fire department use dogs to detect drugs and explosives and also for search and rescue.

"Two dogs were on loan from Ireland recently. They helped us find pirated CD shops and worked with us for several months. The dogs uncovered one outlet with over one hundred thousand CDs hidden in a secret room in a shop wall. They also found several other hidden sites that the criminals were using to store their CDs.

"I agree that dogs who can sniff out animals would be very helpful. We can build a separate shelter at each border crossing for the dogs and their handlers. Yes, I like your idea, Mr. Johnson."

"Like humans, dogs will need rest time, especially in the tropical heat," Chris added. "That's why a pair of dogs is necessary for every crossing."

"I'll ask the departments to recommend four men and advise you when they are ready to leave for the U.S.," Tan Sri said. "Please give me the proposal in writing as soon as possible. This will be another nail in the smuggler's coffin, as you Americans say."

Abdullah Razak approached Chris. "I think it's a good plan.

But let's wait and see how long this will take. Usually, anything coming from America gets bogged down in your government and may take years to implement." He smirked at Chris as he left.

"Could I have a word with you?" Tan Sri stood next to Chris.

"Of course, Tan Sri," Chris replied. They left the room and stood in the hallway.

"Chief Inspector reported that they picked up a gang member in Penang with a badly damaged face, broken nose, and jaw. The doctor's receptionist reported the gangster to the police. They arrested him and the doctor.

"This doctor has a reputation of treating Triad members with no questions asked. Both men are under police remand for seven days. The man says he was in a fight in a karaoke bar. He's not talking, at least for the moment, and he has no previous record so the police can't really hold him unless they charge him with a crime. The karaoke bar in question said there was no fight on the night that he was there."

"Hmm. Sounds as though the Triads are starting to lose control of the smuggling and are using force on their members here," Chris said. "Our surveillance must be working."

"Just be careful," said Tan Sri.

Suhaimi nodded. "We will be on red alert."

Tan Sri started to walk away. He stopped and said to Chris, "More and more people are becoming aware of why you're here."

"Perhaps it's good timing that this meeting came up in Seattle. It takes me out of the country for a while."

Chris and Suhaimi stopped for coffee on the way back to KL. Chris took a sip of the coffee and said, "What do you think of the education plan? Do you think it'll work in stopping the smuggling?"

"It will to a certain degree, but only if it's implemented quickly. The tendency is to develop the plan, let it sit while the people involved continue to change it and it gets bogged down in the development. No one can settle on the final plan. It'll be up to the minister to move it from development into implementation as soon as possible. But I think he means business."

Chris called May Ling, but heard her voice mail. He looked at Suhaimi. "Looks like our dragon lady is out of reach at the moment. It's strange."

Suhaimi offered, "Let's stop at her flat on the way back and see if she's there."

"Good idea." They drove to her flat and asked the gate guard if he had seen her. He said, "Not for two days. She hasn't been around. I thought she was away."

"She lives on the fourth floor. Let's try her door," Chris said.

They took the stairs two at a time and walked down the hall to the end door. Her gate was unlocked. Chris opened it and knocked on her door, waited, but there was no answer. Suhaimi banged on her door. Nothing ... silence. He looked at Chris and then he stepped back several paces and slammed the door with a flying kick against the side of the lock. The wood near the lock splintered and the door flew open.

An eerie silence hung over her flat. The main room was neat and tidy. Suhaimi looked in the bedroom and found it undisturbed. Chris walked into the bathroom and saw a lipstick, comb, and two towels crumpled on the floor near the shower.

The shower curtain was on the floor and the shampoo and cosmetic bottles on the small counter were knocked over and the liquid spread out on the floor. Broken skin care bottles lay on the floor oozing their liquid onto the crumpled floor mat.

"There's been a struggle in the bathroom," Chris said. "Whoever it was overpowered her. No wonder we didn't hear from her." He ran his hand through his hair as he looked at the damage. "We have to find her before something happens. I don't want anything to happen to her."

As they left the building they explained the break-in to the guard. He said he would patch the door and watch the flat.

Chris mulled over what they had found in the flat. "Someone found out about her and grabbed her. I'm worried that they may kill her so we have to move quickly."

They sat in the car as Suhaimi used his cell phone. "Good evening, Tan Sri. I think something happened to May Ling. We haven't heard from her in two days. The guard hasn't seen her either. We broke into her flat and found signs of a struggle. I fear she's been kidnapped."

"I haven't seen her or had any contact with her since last week, but I don't hear from her every day," Tan Sri replied. "Let me make a few calls and see if anyone has seen her, and I'll call you immediately if I hear anything. I hope what you just said is not true. I don't want anything to happen to her."

The phone rang after ten minutes. "Tan Sri here. No one has seen her or talked to her here. I have my secretary calling around, but it's very strange. She usually connects every few days to give me a report. My secretary has some numbers for May Ling. I'll pass you to her, and she can assist you with any information you may need."

Suhaimi took down the phone numbers for her parents and her girlfriend, thanked the secretary and dialed her parents' home.

After several rings, May Ling's elderly mother answered.

"This is Suhaimi Wahab speaking, a friend of May Ling's. I am trying to reach her but she doesn't answer her cell. Have you talked to her in the past few days?"

She paused. "No. Why are you asking? Is something wrong?"

"We haven't heard from her and wondered if she was out of town."

"If she calls here, I'll give her the message. Usually, she calls every day but she hasn't called in a few days. It's very unusual not to hear from her. I'll have May Ling call you as soon as she contacts us. I'm sure she has been busy."

They returned to the hotel. Chris plopped down on the sofa next to the window and stared at the towers. A few minutes later he went to his computer and e-mailed George.

I won't be coming to the meeting. We have a situation here that requires my immediate attention. Will let you know in a few days if it's resolved.

Suhaimi began calling other friends. "Hi, Sue, Suhaimi here. Have you seen May Ling this week?"

"No, I haven't seen her. She called Monday and said she would meet Jessica Ting and me for coffee around eleven today. We went to the coffee shop but she never showed. We found it odd, but thought she may have been called by the minister for an assignment. I called her cell phone but got her voice mail. She has done this in the past, and we hear from her a few days later."

"Something funny is going on. I'll call you when I have information."

"Please call me immediately. I am concerned about her. Please, let me know if I can help in any way at all."

Suhaimi called Tan Sri. "Do you have any news for us?"

"Yes, I called the chief inspector, Hassan. He said we must wait twenty-four hours before the police can help out."

Chris grabbed the cell and yelled, "Twenty-four hours! She may be dead by then. I'll start my own investigation. Never mind sitting on our thumbs waiting for the sky to fall. She is missing, and no one has seen or heard from her. Don't you have any ideas?"

"At this point I don't," Tan Sri replied. "No one has seen her or knows her whereabouts. Do you know where to start?"

Chris felt helpless. He handed the phone back to Suhaimi. He sat on the sofa, quietly thinking. A few minutes later, he jumped up with his idea. "Where do we start?" He thought for a minute. "Wait, I have an idea. Her good friend Jimmy Lee may have a lead."

They left the hotel and drove to Jimmy Lee's restaurant.

The driver stopped the car on the congested street, and they got out in front of the restaurant. Jimmy Lee was standing at the open door greeting a customer. He saw Chris coming toward him. "You're May Ling's friend. You were here a few weeks ago."

"That's right, Jimmy. Only now May Ling is missing, and I want to know where she is. Any ideas?"

Jimmy Lee looked startled. "What do you mean?"

"She's disappeared, and no one knows where she is. Come on fella, tell me what you know."

Chris stood directly in front of Jimmy Lee, who backed up against the door and couldn't move. He could feel Chris's breath on his face.

He sneered. "I don't know anything. I don't keep track of her activities. She's probably out with some other guy having a good time."

Chris grabbed his shirt and pulled him closer, tightening his grip on his shirt.

"You know who kidnapped her and where she is. I want an answer now!"

The restaurant became quiet. Customers stopped eating and watched the altercation.

Lee broke his hold. "Get out of here! I don't know anything. Go find yourself another woman. There are plenty on the street! May Ling isn't your toy."

Chris grabbed him and shoved him against the wall. Suhaimi stepped in and grabbed Chris.

"Hey, Chris, calm down. This guy doesn't know anything."

Chris stepped back, and Suhaimi pulled him out of the restaurant. He turned to look at Lee and saw a slight smile on his face.

"I'll get you if any harm comes to May Ling," Chris threatened him as they got into the car. Lee watched them leave and then made a call on his cell phone.

Zhang Chen called Wang Ju on his cell. He was having dinner with his family and looked at the caller ID. He immediately rose from the table, went to the bedroom, closed the door, and then spoke to him quietly.

"Yes, no one is listening. What happened?"

"The Malaysian has been taken care of. It was no problem. They are guarded by our friends and will remain there until we decide what to do. This person is very close to the Minister of Natural Resources and Environment, so the kidnapping will have some meaning. We will let him worry for a while before we contact him with the terms."

"Good. Now the shipments can continue without any problems?"

"Yes, all under control. There is a shipment crossing the border tonight and will arrive in Bangkok tomorrow, then to China by ship. Part of the shipment will remain in Thailand for their restaurants, but the major portion will be shipped to Guangzhou. The paperwork is in order for the shipment out of Bangkok. You'll receive a fax on the vessel and the arrival date."

"Good. I'll make the preparations at the port."

He put the receiver down, sat on the bed, and thought about what Zhang Chen had said. The prisoner was hidden somewhere in Malaysia. What happened next was up to the Triad leader. Wang Ju went back to the table to finish his dinner. They continued to eat in silence.

❧

Suhaimi and Chris drove to Kwang Li's hangout at the Evergreen Bar. It was situated off Petaling Street in the Chinese trading district, the oldest part of KL. The driver parked the car with the motor running. Chris waited in the backseat.

Suhaimi put on his black watch cap and then walked through

a stained wood door into the dingy, dark wood room. Several round wooden tables and chairs were scattered throughout the small room with a long bar against one wall. Liquor bottles behind the bar stood in a row on a mirrored counter. The bartender was frail and hunched over. He looked as old as the bar.

Kwang Li was sitting at a table drinking Scotch with his girlfriend. They were alone in the room. He looked up as Suhaimi approached the table, grabbed a chair, and immediately placed it next to Kwang Li's chair. He glanced at him in surprise and tried to get up.

Suhaimi put his hand on Kwang Li's shoulder, holding him down. "You know who I am?"

He stared at him. "I've seen you before. What do you want?"

He turned to his girlfriend and said roughly, "Get lost." She glared at him as she slowly strutted from the room. Her hips swayed in the tight, short black skirt and sandals with four-inch stiletto heels. She pushed the kitchen door open then slammed it shut.

"All right, talk."

"My friend has disappeared. I want to know where and why."

"I don't know who you're talking about, and I don't really give a shit." He took a gulp of Scotch and put the empty glass on the table.

"Someone kidnapped my good friend." Suhaimi quickly grabbed his throat and squeezed it. He struggled, but Suhaimi tightened the stranglehold on his throat, and he remained motionless.

"Where did they take my friend?"

Kwang Li gurgled. "I told you, I don't know nothing. You're wasting your time, man."

He tightened his grip and calmly said, "My friend is very important to me. I want you to understand that."

He grimaced in pain and squeezed out his words: "Listen, asshole. I told you, I don't know nothin'. You must be looking for some other guy, but it's not me."

"You sure, man? I can make it a lot harder for you. I can crush your larynx in a second." He squeezed his throat again.

Suddenly, he yelled in a strangled voice, "Tong!" As he did, Suhaimi pulled him off the chair, released his grip, then moved behind him and quickly put his left arm around his neck and tightened his grip. With his other hand he reached for his weapon hidden in his back holster and shoved it into Kwang Li's right temple. He screamed in pain.

The kitchen door burst open. Two tall, muscular Chinese men ran into the room, weapons drawn, and moved toward Suhaimi.

"Stop right there or I'll kill him!"

He walked backward to the bar door holding Kwang Li as a shield. At that moment, Chris pushed the door open and saw the situation. He drew his weapon and held it on the bodyguards. "Don't move!"

He glanced at Suhaimi. "Need help?"

"Yeah, be nice."

As they moved out the door, the bodyguards inched toward them. Suhaimi gave Kwang Li a shove that propelled him onto the floor.

Chris and Suhaimi ran out the door onto the street. The bodyguards fired at them. Chris returned the fire, hitting one guard in the head. He fell forward, blocking the entrance.

They disappeared down a narrow lane that opened into an ancient wet market between the buildings. They ran through the narrow dark market filled with food tables on either side of the narrow wood floor. Several large rats scampered out of their way, climbing the ancient walls, disappearing quickly into openings in the walls.

In the meantime, two other Triads joined the chase and followed them into the market. As they ran toward Petaling Street, they tipped over the fresh fish table, spilling fish onto the walkway, and then pushed over the fresh pork table as they went by.

The Chinese sellers yelled and shook their fists. The man selling fresh pork tried to grab the meat but was knocked over by the Triads as they slipped their way through the fish and fell into the pork pieces.

They ran from the market onto Petaling Street then ran down to the end of the crowded narrow street, dodging the tourists and traders hawking their products. The car was waiting at the end of the street with its back door open. They jumped in and quickly sped off.

"How did the car end up down here?" Suhaimi asked, breathing rapidly.

"You took too long in the bar, so I assumed you were in trouble. I told the driver to meet us here while I went to see what was going down."

"Smart move. Thanks for the help."

"Better than me sitting in the hotel."

"I got nothing out of him. I don't think he knew who did the kidnapping. He wouldn't admit to anything anyhow."

"So what do we do now?" Chris asked, frustrated. He looked out the window as they sped away from the area and said desperately, "May Ling, where are you?"

15

MAY LING'S EYES SLOWLY FLUTTERED open. She felt groggy, nauseated, and her head throbbed. She tried to move. Her arms and legs felt as though they were embedded in cement. She took in the room. Slowly, the headache eased. She became more aware of her surroundings.

A Chinese man was standing near an open door. He watched her. His eyes bored into hers. Suddenly, she felt naked. She remained still, trying to remember what happened, all the while staring at him.

Her mind became a film on rewind. She saw herself standing in her bathroom then heard a noise coming from her front door. She watched as two musclebound goons blocked the bathroom doorway. One man moved into the bathroom and overpowered her. The men put a damp cloth over her nose and mouth and that was the last thing she remembered.

She tried to think. *How many days have I been here? Have I been drugged the entire time? Who kidnapped me and why?*

Her hands were tied behind her, and her feet were roped

together at the ankles and the rope tied to an iron cot. She could not turn or sit up and lay on her back. She could smell the dirty mattress beneath her, making her gag. She swallowed, choking back the vomit rising in her throat. Her arms tightly tied forced her pink short-sleeve T-shirt to stretch tightly across her breasts. The tight black skirt fell just above her knees, exposing her thighs. Every time she moved, her skirt crept higher.

The Chinese man watched her as she squirmed trying to move her arms and legs. He watched her skirt slowly creep up her thighs. He smiled in anticipation. He stared at her tight shirt. She could feel his eyes on her body, waiting.

The cot mattress was grimy and stained. A rusty iron headboard and broken footboard held the bed together. The bed was in the middle of one wall facing the door in a large bedroom. The walls were unpainted with only the unfinished concrete on the walls, chipped in some places. One floor lamp near the door dimly lit the room.

The room was dusty with stale air. One small fan blew warm air on the guard. May Ling felt hot and sticky; perspiration rolled down her face. Her mouth felt like cardboard—dry, a bad taste, as if she swallowed dirt. She needed water.

As she looked around she realized she was in an unfinished row house. The developer ran out of money to finish it and the other row houses in the development, and walked away from the project during a downturn in the economy. No one came into the abandoned site except stray dogs, drug dealers, and gangs.

The guard sat on a grimy white plastic chair near the door. He leered at her. He knew what he wanted to do, but had to wait for orders from his boss, a Triad lieutenant. His boss would kill him if he touched her. He taunted her, telling her what he would do to her.

The guard belonged to the secret society and had joined them when he was sixteen, leaving school to work as a low-level enforcer, a bully, and a killer. Now in his early twenties, he was perfect for this job, loyal to the gang—no fear and no conscience.

He was of medium height, heavy, but muscular with thick black hair, blond tips on the ends. Chinese dragons were tattooed on both his upper arms. She could see his tattooed legs under his long, dirty shorts.

May Ling watched him, memorizing his features for identification later … she hoped. He was good-looking with a round face and pale skin. He spoke only Cantonese.

She had to escape somehow, but nothing came to mind. She closed her eyes, tired of seeing him watch her. The dusty, stale smell in the room choked her, the tropical heat stifling.

She coughed quietly, pleaded with him. "Water, I need water, please can I have some water?"

The guard laughed. "Sorry, no water. You won't need any." He had a bottle of water and took a long sip. She felt thirstier and swallowed.

She closed her eyes. She didn't want to see him leering at her. She waited a few minutes, then said to him, "I have to go to the bathroom. Please, let me do that."

He laughed at her. "It's not time yet. You will have to wait or piss on the bed."

"Can I at least have some water? I am so thirsty."

He grinned. His gold hoop earring and thick gold chain caught the light coming from one dirty window.

She tried again. "Please, let me go to the toilet. I am in pain, and I can't wait any longer. Please—"

"I'm tired of your whining. I'll let you up but only if you obey me. Don't try anything funny. If you do, you will die."

"I won't. Please, I need to go, now!"

The guard slowly rose from his chair and watched her squirm. He put his hand on her thigh and grinned as she tried to move away from his hand. He untied her legs, moved his hand up the inside of her thighs, laughed, then pulled her to a sitting position.

"Untie my arms. I can't go to the toilet this way."

He thought a minute and then he untied her arms. "Just watch it. Any false moves, and you will be tied down again."

"I won't do anything." She turned to walk out the door toward the bathroom.

He stopped her and grabbed her shoulder roughly. "Not there. Here! Use this." He kicked the metal paint bucket that he used as a footstool.

She looked at it, then at him, pleading. "No, please, I can't relieve myself in front of you." Tears rolled down her cheeks.

"Don't cry. It won't help you, and you won't piss at all." He laughed. "Just turn your back and do it. That way you won't see me watching you!"

He kicked the bucket toward her. She looked at him then took the bucket by the handle, turned away, then quickly turned back, swinging the bucket with all her strength, catching him at the right side of his head and across his face, tearing skin from his nose and cutting his cheek. His face started to bleed, and he screamed in pain. He clutched his head.

"Damn you, you bitch!"

She kicked him in the head, heard him scream, pivoted, and gave him a final kick in his groin, knocking him backward as he doubled over in pain, trying to catch his breath.

She quickly ran out of the room, down the long hall, and out the open doorway of the house. Glancing up and down the row, deciding which way she should run, she headed toward the nearest corner and turned right. She ran fast, past the houses to the end of the row, and turned right toward the next row, then continued running past the rows toward the end of the development, not stopping to look behind.

She stopped, gasping for breath as she listened for footsteps but heard none. She continued to run past five rows of houses, one after the other, then past another five rows, breathing rapidly, panting, heart racing.

The guard struggled to his feet, doubled over in pain, still holding his head, bleeding from the scrapes. He staggered to the door, holding a bloodstained handkerchief to his face. He looked left then right, but she was nowhere around.

He panicked and ran to the left, stopping to look in each house as he made his way down the row.

May Ling ran past the last row of link houses, crossed a dirt field littered with concrete and garbage from the development, and continued into the dense jungle. She hid behind a palm tree, waiting and watching to see if he was following her. She didn't see him and took time to catch her breath.

The dense jungle surrounded her. She was hesitant to leave the jungle, but cautious about going deeper into it. If she got lost, no one would find her. She shivered. It would be dark soon.

She ran straight into it, pushing the vines and the thick branches aside, away from the link houses and with luck, toward an area where she could get help.

Just as the guard was running down the street, a black Mercedes drove along the dirt road toward the house. The guard stopped, then turned and ran back to the house. The lieutenant got out of the car in front of the house and watched, sensing there was trouble. The guard came to a stop in front of the lieutenant, out of breath and puffing.

"What happened? Where is the girl?"

"She escaped and I was searching for her. Give me a few minutes and I'll bring her back! She has not gone far."

The lieutenant shouted in anger. He scowled and spat out his words, "You stupid fool! How could you let her escape? You had a simple job to do and you failed. You're no longer of use to us."

"Please, boss, let me explain. I'm sorry," the guard said, weeping. The lieutenant nodded to his bodyguard, who pulled out his pistol and quickly shot the quivering man through the head. The guard lay dead on the dirt road, a pool of blood forming beneath his head as the car drove off.

May Ling heard the faint crack of the gunshot that sounded like a car backfiring in the distance. She knew what it was and picked up her pace, pushing the bamboo stalks away from her as she moved deeper into the jungle. The branches scratched her legs and arms and leeches climbed up her legs.

Forty minutes later the jungle thinned and the undergrowth became sparse. Abruptly, sunlight faded. She started to run, hoping that she could find her way out before she lost all sense of direction. As darkness enveloped the jungle, it became alive with noise. The cicadas began their night song, and other creatures joined them.

After struggling through the jungle for an hour in the semi-darkness, she saw a light in the distance and walked toward it. At the edge of a small village, a small house with a white sedan parked in the driveway came into view. A light over the door was on, illuminating the path to the front door. She quietly crept up to the house and stood in the shadows on the side of the door, listening.

She could hear the voices of people talking and eating. Finally, she knocked softly and waited. In a few minutes, the door opened. A Malay man in his sarong was staring at May Ling.

"What do you want?" he said in Malay. "Who are you?" He looked beyond her for a car.

She quickly replied, "I lost my way. I left my phone in the car and have no way to call my friend to pick me up. Could I please usc your phone?"

He closed the door and spoke to a woman inside. In a few minutes, he opened the door and invited her in. She looked bedraggled in the light. The man's wife stared at her, and her appearance immediately made the woman uncomfortable.

The wife became suspicious. "How did you get here? Your clothes are torn. Did you come through the jungle?" She stared at her for a moment and finally said, "Who are you?"

"I got lost, then my car broke down in the rain." She sobbed, wiping her nose with her hand and brushing away the tears.

"I walked through the jungle and was lucky I saw the lights of your house. I don't know where I am."

She continued to sob. "It was a terrible experience being in the jungle alone. I fell several times when I tripped over tree trunks and dead limbs. Thank you for letting me into your home."

The woman calmed and said, "Oh dear, you poor girl. How can we help you?"

"Can I use your phone to call my friend?"

"We can drive you to your car if you would like," the woman offered.

"No, I wouldn't want to put you to any trouble, and besides, it won't run. I'll send my repairman to fix it tomorrow. Thank you for your kindness."

The man handed her his cell phone and she called Sue. She spoke in Cantonese and told her the story, then said, "Sue, please come and get me."

May Ling gave the cell back to the man. He gave Sue directions. He told May Ling she would be at their home in an hour.

In about an hour, there was a knock on the door. Sue stepped into the room, and May Ling ran to her and hugged her. They both started to cry and held each other for a few minutes.

"I was so worried about you. What if something happened to you? Never mind. I'm happy you're all right. Thank God you're safe."

"I'll be fine now that you're here." She hugged Sue again. They turned to the couple, and May Ling said, "Thank you for your kindness."

As they drove away, the couple stood in the doorway, watching them. Sue turned the corner, drove for a few minutes then stopped the car out of sight of the house.

They hugged again.

"I'm so happy to see you," Sue said. "We didn't know what had happened to you and were frantic with worry. Chris and Suhaimi have been searching for you. You can tell me about your experience when we get back, but right now let's get out of here. Lay down on the floor in the backseat. Stay out of sight until we get onto the main highway. I don't want anyone seeing you."

Sue drove on a dirt road that eventually took them to the highway back into the city.

May Ling gave her sketchy details, just enough to satisfy her curiosity. She took Sue's cell and called Suhaimi.

"Suhaimi? It's May Ling. I'm in the car with Sue. I escaped from the kidnappers and am on my way back to KL."

"May Ling! Thank God! We were so worried about you. How did you get away? Never mind, tell us later. I'll inform Chris immediately. He's at the minister's office in Putrajaya. They set up a communications center to assist in finding you. Everyone will be thankful that you're all right."

"Suhaimi, I don't know where to go. Where should I go? It's not safe."

"Ask Sue to bring you back to the hotel. It's too dangerous for you to return home because the kidnappers know where you live. We'll take care of you once you get here."

"We've been using Chris's suite as our operations base. I'll meet you there. Pull off to the side of the hotel and wait for me before you get out of the car."

"Thank you, Suhaimi. I'll wait for you. I thought Chris was in Seattle."

"No, he canceled out on the trip when he found out you were missing."

Slowly, all her tension drained away, like an outgoing tide receding from the ocean's shore. She felt safe and calmed down.

As they pulled up to the hotel, she saw Suhaimi at the lobby door. Before she opened the car door, she turned to Sue. "Thanks for helping me out. You're the only one I trust. I'll not forget that. Please don't mention what happened to anyone. If someone asks about me, just say that I was out of town on a business trip. I don't want anyone to know where I am. I'm afraid they might try and kidnap me again."

Sue held her close. "Don't worry, your secret is safe with me. Keep in touch so I know you're OK too."

Suhaimi opened her door and walked her into the hotel.

Once inside the hotel, he hugged her and said, "You look a little unkempt but a good hot shower will help." He put his arm around her, and they took the elevator to Chris's suite. May Ling took a shower and put on a bathrobe.

They sat on the sofa, and Suhaimi said, "Tell me what happened."

She talked about the ordeal, telling him everything. She talked for an hour without stopping. He occasionally asked questions, but mostly just listened.

"Chris has been beside himself with worry. He hasn't slept, calling anyone he knew and chasing down leads that went nowhere."

She yawned and said, "I'm sleepy. The drugs knocked me out." She leaned her head on the sofa and was asleep in a minute.

Suhaimi carried her to the bedroom, gently laid her on the bed, covered her, and closed the bedroom door.

Just then, Chris rushed into his suite. "Where is she? Is she all right?"

"Yes, a bit shaken up, but she'll be all right. I wrapped her in a blanket and put her in your bed. She's sound asleep and exhausted from her ordeal. Let her tell you about it when she awakens. It will be a cleansing for her to clear her mind, and she will be less traumatized."

May Ling slept until late the next morning. When she emerged, Chris saw her and immediately hugged her and held her tightly, almost afraid that she would disappear if he let go.

"Oh, May Ling! I am so relieved that you're well. I was so worried about you, but we had no clues or information where you were. We roughed up Kwang Li and Jimmy Lee, but got nowhere with them." He still held her in his arms.

She moved away from him.

"I am feeling much better and ready to do some work. I've put all that behind me. I hadn't slept for three days, and that was a big part of my problem. Thank you for trying to find me."

Suhaimi added, "You were lucky and quick thinking to hit the guard with the bucket. He would never have expected that. It gave you enough time to escape. Smart girl!"

"My training came through. I didn't panic and let the guard control me. That was important and what saved me."

Chris agreed. "Now the Triads know who you are, and you'll have to be more alert than ever before. Stay in a defensive mode."

"Yes, Chris, I know. The Americans can do it better, right?"

"No, I didn't say that. You're back to your stubborn self." He laughed.

Suhaimi interjected, "Don't let anyone know you're at the hotel. We don't know who was involved in your abduction."

May Ling nodded as she drank her tea.

"I'll make arrangements for you to stay in a safe house and I'll call the embassy now."

After Chris spoke to Roberts, Suhaimi pulled him aside.

"We should put a watch on her parents. The Triads always hit family members for retribution."

"You're right. Set that up with the police."

"I'll get on it right away."

❧

Zhang Chen was furious about the escape. "You're a bloody fool! You kidnapped a woman who worked for the minister, and she got away!" he screamed over his cell phone at Kwang Li. "How effective is your group in Malaysia? If you're not careful, you will be replaced."

Kwang Li defended himself. "I let a new recruit guard her. I thought it would be fine because she was tied up. Nothing could go wrong, and yet it did. I took care of the guard and no longer have to worry about him."

"That was your first mistake, having only one man guard her. Now you'll kidnap someone from the Wildlife Department. He has been in our way too long. You know who I want. Don't make this your second mistake."

"Yes, Zhang Chen, we will do it as soon as is possible. He won't trouble us anymore."

"Remember, Kwang Li, our shipments have slowed, and there is a bigger demand for the products than ever before," He said. "We must move fast to continue the flow of shipments. We're all losing money!" He continued to yell into the cell phone, venting his anger.

Kwang Li started to sweat. "We'll continue the shipments immediately and will be moving a lorry to Bangkok tonight."

⁂

Chris picked up the morning paper and showed it to May Ling. On the front page was a photo of a man on the ground, covered with a sheet in front of the abandoned house. Police had been informed of the body by an animal control unit that went to the development to capture the numerous malnourished and diseased stray dogs. The police would investigate the murder.

May Ling knew who it was immediately and shivered when she saw the picture. "He was killed because he let me escape."

Chris added. "You were lucky you escaped when you did. I'm

sure the boss arrived to kill you."

He put his arms around her and pulled her close to him. She looked into his eyes and smiled, enjoying the closeness of the moment.

"Stay here. Don't leave the hotel. I am going to meet with Roberts and will return shortly."

"I'm not going anywhere. Not until I know what the situation is outside."

Chris took a taxi to the U.S. Embassy and went through security to the waiting room. John Roberts was CIA's Head of Station in Southeast Asia. At any one time, he had over twenty agents working undercover throughout the region. Roberts' secretary came to the main hall to escort Chris to his office.

Roberts was tall, slightly overweight, with a small paunch forming a bulge in his shirt. A small designer red beard covered his chin.

"Well, well," said Roberts, smiling at Chris, "I wondered how soon you would get in trouble and come running to papa. How the hell are you, Chris?"

"Getting by! And you? You haven't changed since I last saw you, except for the gray in your hair."

Roberts laughed. "Too many close calls does that to you. Anyway, you haven't changed either. How long has it been?" Roberts asked as Chris sat on the two-seat sofa, and Roberts sat in one of the two side chairs opposite. A low table in front of the sofa held several magazines. Two framed watercolors of San Francisco hung on the wall behind the sofa. A modern oil painting of a Vietnamese boat scene hung on the wall behind the desk.

"Five years at least. The last time I saw you was at Langley for my training."

"I enjoyed those years at Langley teaching your class. You were a pain in the ass, Chris, but my best student."

Chris laughed. "I would lie awake at night thinking of ways to annoy you, but you were always one step ahead of me."

Chris noticed that he was neatly dressed in a pink long-sleeve shirt with a black-and-pink striped tie and black trousers.

"You're still as dapper as ever. The embassy hasn't had any effect on your style."

"Nope. I want to keep it that way. I dislike the institutional style of dress in the embassies. Their styles match their jobs."

Chris nodded. "I heard that you had left the training department and transferred into the field. George said that you were in Malaysia and if I needed assistance to get in touch with you."

"I like it here in Malaysia, great food and good people. Not necessarily in that order. I keep an eye on the junta in Burma, the boys in Cambodia and Vietnam, the generals in Thailand, and the terrorists in Indonesia. So far, so good! Usually very peaceful, but every once in a while someone rattles a cage or two. Now what can I do for you? I know you've changed jobs in the past. What happened at San Ysidro?"

"I got burned out quickly; too much traffic and not enough action for me. Every day was the same: intense and overwhelming. I wanted to put a dent in the animal smuggling in this arena and finally got the assignment. This rare animal black market is a big problem. I had no idea how widespread and sophisticated the network is."

Roberts poured them each a glass of water.

"I need a safe house to shelter a local undercover agent that's been assisting me in the anti-smuggling campaign," Chris said. "I'd also like to give safe passage to the U.S. for the agent and her parents. There were attempts on her life. She was kidnapped a few days ago by the Triads, but managed to escape."

"Where is she now?"

"At my hotel suite. She was kidnapped in her flat and can't return there. We haven't any place to hide her so she's with an officer from the Wildlife Crime Unit."

"What's his name?

"Suhaimi Wahab."

"I know him. He's a good man and well trained. You did the right thing by having her sequestered there with him. A safe house is no problem. We have a number in Malaysia. I suppose you want one in this end of town. Makes no sense to put her outside the city."

"Yes, KL. The three of us work together, so we need her close by."

"OK, I'll make the arrangements. You call this number when you're ready to move her and we'll take it from there." Roberts wrote on a card and handed it to Chris.

"Now to the visa, I'll need a full report. You know the drill, and I'll let you know the results as soon as I hear from the U.S. It should only take a few weeks, OK? Pick up the paperwork downstairs from the visa section and have her and her family fill out the forms."

"OK," replied Chris. Both men got to their feet and continued to talk about old times.

Roberts walked to the door with Chris, his arm on his shoulder as he walked him through the outer office and into the main hall.

"I'll require passports, birth certificates, police checks, and references before I can proceed. This is all standard procedure, whether their visas are expedited or through regular channels. However, it'll take less time for them than for normal applications."

"Thanks. You've been a big help. I'll keep in touch."

They shook hands.

"Stay out of trouble."

Chris smirked.

"Tough to do, but I'll try."

May Ling was sleeping, and Suhaimi went to get some clothes from her flat. Chris went to the phone on a side table and dialed the direct line for Idris. The phone rang for a long time but was eventually answered. A female voice answered, "Hello?"

"Hello. May I speak with Idris, please?"

"Who's calling?"

"Chris Johnson."

"From?" Chris thought for a minute ... from where? From KL? From the hotel?

Finally, he replied, "I'm in KL."

"He's not here. He's in the toilet, and he took the newspaper with him."

"I think you have given me more information than I want, but I'll wait." Chris chuckled and wondered how long he would be.

A few minutes later, Idris picked up the phone. "Hello?"

"Good morning, Idris. This is Chris Johnson calling on the animal smuggling issue."

Idris sighed and said, "Let's get together today. I'll notify two other directors whom I can trust and they are probably all I can trust. Come to my house. Let me give you my address."

Suhaimi entered the suite carrying a small suitcase and set it down by the door. They sat on the sofa, and Chris briefed him on Roberts. May Ling quietly sat on a chair facing the sofa.

"I am sure feeling better after the nap. What's up?" She saw the suitcase. "Thanks, Suhaimi. I was getting tired of wearing the same clothes." She rolled the suitcase into the bedroom, changed, and came out smiling a few minutes later. "Now that feels good." She twirled around then sat in a chair.

He looked at her. "Wow, you look so much better now!"

Chris nodded his approval. "May Ling, I've arranged a safe house for you and then a visa to the U.S. for you and your parents."

"Wait a minute, Chris. I don't want to leave Malaysia and am not running away from any battle! What would my mother and father do in the U.S.? No friends, no work? Our whole lives are here, their friends are here, and they will not move."

"I know that, but what is more important, their friends or their lives? You managed to escape this time but what about next time?" He went over to her, kneeled down in front of her, and held her hands and said softly, "It'll be all right, May Ling. I promise."

She nodded. "But who'll be there with me at the safe house? I need to be able to do my job, not sit there like a toad on a rock."

"Two agents will stay at the house with you. You can't leave the house, so any work you want to do will have to be done there."

She started to protest, but he went to the phone, punched in a number, and received his instructions. He looked at Suhaimi and May Ling and said with authority, "We're ready to move. The cars are in the underground garage. I'll be in one car with May Ling. A driver and a police officer will be in the front car. Suhaimi, you'll be in the trail car with two police officers."

He turned to May Ling. "This is the way we transport a principal or run a convoy in the U.S." She looked at Chris, opened her mouth, but said nothing.

Chris grabbed May Ling's bag and the three of them took the elevator to the parking garage. A white sedan pulled up, followed by the black trail car. Chris and May Ling got into the sedan. Suhaimi jumped in the back of the trail car beside one officer. Another officer sat in the front.

They drove up the ramp and exited onto the street. Immediately, a black sedan with dark windows sped toward them, blocking their car from moving forward. The embassy driver hit the brakes and skidded to a stop into the right front fender of the black sedan. The driver of the trail car slammed on the brakes and stopped a few feet behind Chris's car. Chris quickly pushed May Ling down on the floor and yelled at her, "Triads! Stay down until I tell you to move."

He opened the door and quickly jumped out, weapon in his hand. The open door gave him a shield from the gunfire. He raised his head slowly and looked out the window at the black sedan. He saw the silhouette of the driver hiding behind his car door as his head appeared in the window glass. He aimed his weapon at the driver and fired three rounds, which pierced the window, hitting the driver in the head.

Chris scanned the black sedan's passenger side and saw another Triad member drawing his weapon upward toward the windshield. His second shot hit the embassy driver in the shoulder as he scrambled to get out of the car.

A cacophony of gunfire ensued between the black sedan, Chris's car, and the trail car. Chris continued to fire his weapon, watching as the rounds pierced the black sedan's windshield, killing the hit man. He counted down the number of rounds he had left as the magazine emptied. The weapon jammed, the last round chambered in his Glock.

Suhaimi had crouched behind the door, leveling his weapon at the black sedan's rear seat side window. He recognized the distinct toylike plastic look of an M-16 being pointed toward him out the open rear window. The second hit man fired a full-automatic burst, raking the trail car's engine. Chris could smell the lingering odor of cordite, the gunfire deafening as it hit the car.

He waited until he heard the distinct slap of an empty magazine. In a few seconds, the poorly trained gunman had emptied his thirty-round magazine. Chris caught the form of the hit man nervously trying to change his magazine. With a smooth pull of his trigger finger, he fired off three rounds into the hit man's chest. He watched as the third hit man raised his AK-47 to firing position, his hand on the banana clip. Chris next saw another shooter with the AK-47. With his weapon following his head movement, Chris pointed his weapon at the hit man and pulled the trigger, squeezing off another five rounds. The gun fight continued as the police escorts battled with the fourth assassin.

Suddenly, it was quiet. The black sedan was riddled with bullet holes, and four men were dead. Several pedestrians hiding behind cars peered out to see if the gunfire was over. Other people rose from the sidewalk still unsure, waiting behind parked cars to see what would happen next. A crowd began to gather, coming out of hotels and offices.

Chris immediately called Roberts and gave him the news as he looked at the white sedan riddled with bullet holes. He helped May Ling crawl out of the car. Within minutes, police swarmed.

"How did they know I was at the hotel?"

"They knew I stayed here. They didn't know you were here," Chris said as he placed his weapon back into its holster. The sound of sirens wailed.

"They weren't after you, May Ling," Suhaimi said quietly. "They were after Chris."

She looked surprised.

"They wanted to kill me because of the slowdown in the animal smuggling. When they kidnapped you it was because you were close to Tan Sri, not knowing that you were working with me."

She raised her eyebrows. The police set up barricades and ran "Do Not Cross" tapes around the scene. In a matter of minutes, reporters arrived from several newspapers, all wanting photos and stories.

Chris put his arm around May Ling. "Looks as though we'll be here for a while. Go and sit in the hotel before word gets out about your connection to us."

She nodded and left.

The police soon had the scene under control and had taken statements from them. The constable made several calls to the embassy and police, clearing them of any wrongdoing.

Finally, they were allowed to leave. Another car came to fetch them, and they were able to continue to the safe house. They drove through the city to a residential area twenty minutes from the hotel, down a busy main street, and then stopped in front of a small bungalow with a high cement wall and an electronic wrought-iron gate. The new driver pressed his automatic gate button, the gate swung open, and they drove up to the open front door where a man and woman stood, waiting.

⚜

Chris introduced May Ling to Karen Pillai and David Kumar, two undercover agents assigned to look after her until she was ready to leave for the U.S. They were local Tamil Indians, working for Roberts at the embassy.

"We had word that you ran into a bit of a problem leaving the hotel," David said.

"That's an understatement, but yes, there was a slight engagement. Four men dead, one injured, cars damaged, but we're OK. I need to ask Roberts for a new round of ammo. I don't think they expected the firefight, otherwise they would have sent more than just four men."

"I didn't have my weapon with me." She defended herself. "But they handled it well."

They walked into the living area that was decorated simply with a sofa and two chairs, and a small, square rattan table in front of the wicker sofa. A kitchen was off to one side and the bathroom down the hall. The white marble floor tile and the sheer curtains on the large picture window gave the area a homey, comfortable feeling.

"May Ling, I'll return this evening to have dinner with you here," Chris said. "We can talk about the visa and the paperwork required and perhaps get that rolling."

"I'll be all right," she snapped. "As I said before, I'm not going to the U.S. Your country isn't any better at protecting people than mine."

Chris gave her a hug. "You'll be all right. The shootout made us all nervous, but everything is fine now."

As they pulled away, he looked back and saw a forlorn May Ling waving goodbye before the gate closed.

16

AN OLD SHIP WAS MOORED at a long jetty located in a small, secluded cove on the South China Sea. It was midnight, and ten men worked beside the small vessel. Two men stood on a platform on the stern of the vessel, just above the water line, repainting the ship's name.

Pirates had boarded the ship in the Straits of Malacca in the early morning while the crew slept. They shot and killed the crew, dumped them into the ocean, then sailed the ship to Sarawak and sold it to the Triads. The ship was originally from India, laden with goods for the Philippines. Spices, food, jewelry, pottery, clothing, and fabrics were bound for the Southeast Asian markets. The stolen cargo was sold to night market traders in Kuching, Sarawak.

The vessel registry and flag had been changed to Libya. The final touch in the disguise was changing the name of the vessel to New Sun.

Ten lorries carried crates of animals to the jetty. Six men unloaded the crates and stacked them near the gangplank. Lorries waited in line to unload their cargo. By the time unloading was finished, over four hundred crates waited to be loaded onto the vessel.

One driver backed his lorry into a stack of five crates. They tumbled onto the jetty. Three lids flew open. Several lizards quickly scrambled out and over the side of the jetty into the water. A large pangolin from another crate lumbered down the jetty and escaped into the underbrush. One crate sat on the edge of the jetty, teetering on the edge. The top fell open as the crate fell into the water. Several turtles slid out and swam away.

The cargo loaders quickly closed the lid of another crate before the snakes could escape. The boss yelled at everyone to be more careful. He had to change the count on the manifest.

Four hours later all the crates were loaded into the hold of the ship. The tide was starting to turn, and the ship was ready to sail. It would take them several days to sail to China and the captain knew the consequences if too many animals died on the voyage. A previous careless captain's fate was a lesson for all. The captain sent a fax to Wang Ju telling him the ship had left and the approximate arrival date.

Chris checked his e-mails and had three messages from his supervisor in Seattle. All made the same demand.

Johnson, get your ass back here! You have been in Malaysia too long. This is not, I repeat, not a vacation. The Malaysians can solve their own problems. I expect you back next week. Don't give me that message about how you are needed there to help out. Your job is here, not in Malaysia. If you want to keep it you will return tomorrow. George.

Chris muttered under his breath and replied to the message:

We are making progress with a slowdown of the smuggling here. My work is making a dent in the problem at hand, and

I will be staying longer to finish what I started. However, with my excellent progress, you will be commended for your assistance. The Malaysian government is appreciative of your efforts.

That should feed his ego and get him off my back for a while, Chris thought.

They drove to Bukit Tunku, to Idris's house. The director lived in a gated community with security guards stopping everyone who entered. Ministers' families and the very wealthy lived in this exclusive suburb. The director's house was a large two-story white stucco house with a red tile roof. The house was barely visible behind the eight-foot wall surrounding the property.

The circular driveway was lined with tall umbrella-shaped trees that spread their branches into a canopy shading the driveway. An Indonesian maid opened the door and waited for them to enter the house. The dramatic rectangular-shaped reception room had two entrances into the living area. Highly polished black marble floors were spotlessly clean and held many antique pieces from Malaysia's past. A six-foot tall black marble vase stood next to the back wall surrounded by orchids in various colors. Two large Indonesian daybeds made from beautifully carved teakwood with red cushions and gold pillows sat against both walls on either side of the entryway into the living area.

A narrow hallway opened into an impressive living room with fifty-foot high ceilings and a transom that opened to the sky, allowing air movement to keep the room cool. Slate floors and antique tables stood against one wall with two Malaysian carved settees opposite one another.

The maid led them into another great room off the living room where the two directors were chatting and sipping tea at a round marble-top table. The seats of the old Malay chairs were covered with rich green brocade silk fabric and the wooden back, legs, and arms were ornately carved. Full-size palm trees grew in the room, forming a divider between the two areas. Orchids in large vases added to the distinct tropical flavor of the house.

Chris shook hands with the two directors from customs and immigration. Idris then motioned them to sit at the table. Suhaimi sat next to Chris and Idris. The maid poured tea and served small Malay cakes.

"Thank you for coming," Idris said. "We are just waiting for Abdullah Razak to arrive. He wanted to join the meeting but is a bit late … quite unusual for him."

Idris continued: "We have been discussing the animal problem, waiting for everyone to show up. We must take responsibility for the losses of the endangered animals."

"I remember what happened in the rice fields of Vietnam," Suhaimi said. "The Vietnamese caught all the snakes that lived in the rice paddies to sell the meat for food and blood for health. When the snakes were depleted, the rats overran the fields eating the rice. Rice production dropped, and people had little rice to eat so they ate the rats. The Vietnamese finally reintroduced snakes into the paddy fields to control the rat population. The people had more rice to eat and the balance of rats to snakes returned to normal. The same thing will happen in Malaysia if we don't monitor our flora and fauna to protect it."

Idris nodded in agreement and said, "Greed is a terrible thing. A few people are controlled by their own weaknesses and will ruin the environment for the rest of the population." He looked at his watch. "It's strange that he hasn't arrived. He should have called to let us know he would be late."

At that moment, Suhaimi's phone rang. He listened for a second then passed the phone to Chris. "It's Tan Sri."

"Yes, Tan Sri?" Chris listened for a moment, then motioned to Suhaimi. They moved to a corner away from the table. "Deputy Director Abdullah Razak has been kidnapped!"

"Oh no, not another kidnapping! Dear God, what happened?"

Chris related what he was told over the phone. "Abdullah was on his way to a downtown hotel last night about nine where he goes for his weekly massage. His driver stopped the Mercedes in front of the lobby door. A man, who appears to have been waiting, wore a ski mask and rushed to the driver's side of the car, jerked open the door, dragged the driver out, stabbed him in the chest then pushed him away from the car. The driver fell to the ground at the side of the driveway. The kidnapper jumped into the driver's seat.

"At the same time, another man yanked the back door open and jumped in beside Abdullah. The car sped out of the driveway and onto the road before anyone was aware of what happened. This all took place in less than five minutes and was well planned out.

"The driver was lying on the road, blood spurting from his wound. It was several minutes before the ambulance arrived, and he died on the way to the hospital, stabbed in a major artery. The emergency medical team couldn't stop the bleeding in time. The hotel doorman was missing. A hotel guest saw the killing through a lobby window.

"By the time the police arrived on the scene, the Mercedes was long gone. They found the doorman tied up in a closet. We have no idea where they took Abdullah."

Chris was stunned and after a pause, he said, "This is terrible! Poor Abdullah! It has to be the gang making another move to stop us."

Suhaimi immediately called the police and got the information. As soon as he ended the call, Chris asked, "What did you find out?"

"An APB went out on the car but no one saw it. The police have no new information."

The directors were now standing near Chris, listening. Everyone was stunned and started to talk at once. Then Chris said, "We have to leave immediately!"

On the way, Chris called John Roberts and told him what news he had.

◆

One week passed without any word from the kidnappers. Suhaimi had daily contact with the police. They continued their search and talked to anyone who may have had contact with Abdullah. No word on ransom, no phone calls, and his car had vanished. The trail was growing cold.

Finally, the police received a call from a rubber tapper, an older Indian man who worked on a plantation two hours west of the city. He asked the police to come to the plantation as he had discovered something he thought they should see.

The inspector and the forensics team drove to the plantation and met the tapper at the highway entrance. They followed his motorbike down the dirt road deeper into the plantation to an area near a small lake. The tall rubber trees blocked out the sunlight as they went farther, causing a foreboding sensation as the darkness set in.

The tapper parked his bike and waited for them to park the cars, then they followed him on foot to a newly turned dirt area on the side of a small lake in the midst of the rubber trees. He pointed to the area where the ground had been disturbed.

The inspector nodded. "Please continue. Tell me again what you saw."

"I followed my usual route, checking out the rubber pots to see if they were full. Down by the lake I saw something sticking out of the dirt. A civet cat was pulling it out of the ground. I chased the cat away. I saw an arm, covered with dirt, hard to recognize until I saw the fingers."

"Did you disturb anything in the area?" The inspector asked.

"No. I was scared to touch anything. Bad spirits."

"You can go now, but don't mention what you found to

anyone." The tapper got on his bike and left in a hurry.

The forensics team used their flashlights, shining them on the disturbed dirt and very carefully moved the dirt so as not to disturb the decomposed arm, then gently lifted it from the hole, placing it on a stainless steel tray, covering it with plastic. They dug deeper into the hole, but it was empty. They looked around the area and discovered several areas of fresh-turned earth several yards away from the arm. They went to each area and dug carefully. Each mound held a body part. By the time they were finished with the last mound, they had an entire body except for the head.

In Malay folklore, the head is buried separately from the body to prevent the spirit from returning to haunt the murderer. After several days of digging, they found the mutilated head, buried two hundred feet from the body. It was Abdullah Razak.

Every newspaper and news website in the country printed the story with photos of the area where he was found. According to the forensics lab, he was shot in the back of the head execution style, then his body was chopped into several pieces.

Follow-up stories speculated on why he was killed. There were no witnesses and no physical clues. The police suspected he was killed elsewhere, then transported to the plantation and dismembered.

He was buried as soon as the autopsy was completed. The prime minister and his cabinet attended the funeral along with several hundred people who came to pay their respects and gave their condolences to Razak's wife and children. May Ling was accompanied to the service by an undercover agent. She wore dark sunglasses and covered her head with a scarf.

Chris talked to May Ling as they watched the funeral cortege.

"I am so sorry for what happened. He was the only one who stood up for what he believed. He was dedicated to saving the animals, even though he appeared not to want to change anything. I know that was all an act."

"He was like an uncle to me, and I'll miss him. The gang will pay for my brother's death and Abdullah's death. I'll get that syndicate leader and kill him."

Chris grabbed both her shoulders and looked into her eyes. "You can't do that. Work within your office to get the killer. Don't do it on your own. It's too dangerous. I don't want anything to happen to you." He gave her a hug and held her tightly.

She looked surprised and knew that something had changed. "Chris?"

"I know. You mean more to me than just as my partner. I love you, May Ling, even though you are very stubborn."

"Does that mean we can't fight anymore?"

He gave her another hug.

May Ling and Chris talked every day, and Chris tried to see her in the evenings when possible. He was careful to ensure that he was not followed. He felt different—happy and had a warmth in his heart. It was different than the feeling he had for his former fiancé, who he would have married if she hadn't turned out to be a money grubber.

⋲⋊

Chris received a call from Roberts the next morning.

"Meet me at the MiCasa Café near the embassy, as soon as you can get there."

Chris looked at his watch. "Give me twenty minutes."

Roberts was already seated at a table facing the door when Chris walked in and ordered coffee at the counter, then sat beside Roberts. There were few customers sitting in the small coffee shop at this time of day.

"Morning, John. It's early for you, isn't it?"

Roberts nodded. "I may be at the office at eight, but I don't wake up until ten o'clock."

"What a turn of events over the past few weeks!" Chris

replied. "Are we gaining on the problem or is the situation worse than before?"

"Hard to tell at this point, Chris. I know you're making a dent in the smuggling. The Triads are trying to stop your efforts. Your friend must not leave the safe house under any circumstances. Here are the visas." He handed over a brown envelope.

Chris took the envelope and said, "The drug sniffing dogs arrived from LA and I'll be making a trip to the border tonight to see them in action. I called to set it up. The dogs will work at the ports as well. The Maritime Enforcement Unit is helping us at the ports and are catching a few poachers and smuggled animals.

"It will take time but with everyone's assistance we can make the smuggling of animals a nonprofit business. The prime minister is giving us total support. The Triads made a mistake when they murdered Abdullah. The public is calling for new laws and amendments to old laws."

"Well, let's hope we see some changes," Roberts said. "Let me know when your people are ready to leave for the U.S. and my people will make all the arrangements."

Roberts gave Chris a warm smile and shook his hand.

"We'll use our energy to stop the smugglers, and that's where we will make a difference."

Chris's cell phone rang as he walked to the hotel. It was Riley Logan from the embassy.

"Everything is set. I'll pick you up at three. Pack a small overnight bag."

Chris looked at his watch. It was close to two o'clock. When he got back to the hotel, he packed his Glock in his bag. His phone rang.

"It's May Ling. I haven't moved outside, seen anyone, or done anything. I am getting bored. Can I leave for a while with David? I need to get out of here. I feel like a caged lion pacing back and forth, waiting for a way to escape."

"Stay put. Don't leave. There are too many people wanting to know where you are. I have your documents so it won't be long before you and your parents are out of the country."

"Well, we shall see."

Chris quickly showered, changed into his black clothes, and went down to the lobby with his bag.

Suhaimi was waiting in the lobby as an embassy car drove up to the lobby door. Chris and Suhaimi stepped into the backseat and drove off to the airport. Riley gave them a run down for their plan of action at the border. The car and driver were waiting when they came out of the airport in Alor Setar.

Forty-five minutes later the driver slowed the car, searching for a dirt road three hundred yards from the border. The road led to a pineapple plantation and was hidden by the trees, barely visible as the driver turned off the main highway onto the road and stopped underneath a tree. They were hidden from the highway but the half moon gave off some light through the trees, enough to spot the lorries on the highway driving toward the border. They were near enough to the well-lit border to watch the activity through night glasses.

By prior arrangement, a police surveillance van was waiting for them on the dirt road. They had pulled off to one side and backed the surveillance van up to the edge of the field. Surveillance equipment and two technicians sat inside the van monitoring the highway. A small van carrying six army personnel parked farther up the road. They had turned the van around and were facing the highway, ready to make a move.

Inspector Azmir Zulkifli stepped out the side door of the surveillance van and welcomed Riley, Suhaimi, and Chris as they approached. They stepped inside the van and watched the technicians seated at their dimly lit monitors, checking on the highway activity.

"An informer passed information to us about a lorry crossing the border but didn't know when," Azmir said. "This border is busy and the checkpoint understaffed, but they are using the dogs."

Chris looked through the night vision glasses and watched a handler and his dog approach a small lorry. The handler used a hand motion to direct the dog into the back of the lorry. It leaped onto the tailgate then disappeared into the interior.

About five minutes later it returned, jumped down, and went to stand at the side of his handler. The handler patted the dog, then snapped on his lead and motioned to the customs officer that the lorry was clean. The customs officer waved the lorry through.

Over the next few hours, Chris and the surveillance team watched twenty lorries clear the checkpoint. The dog checked the lorries, while customs officers inspected small vans and cars.

Suddenly, a lorry slowed as it passed their lookout point heading for the border. It was an eighteen-wheeler with a large load covered by a gray canvas. A pale light in the cab gave a glimpse of the two men as the lorry passed their observation point. Azmir focused the night glasses on the men. They were both Chinese, one man talking on his cell phone, the other driving the vehicle.

Azmir said to the technician, "Can you pick up the conversation?" He nodded, listening to the man talking in Malay to someone at the border. He put the conversation on speaker. The man on the other end of the call was giving the lorry driver information on the border traffic and which lane to use at the border.

Azmir radioed the other police van. "This may be the one. Move out and block the road."

The van with the army unit pulled onto the highway with headlights off, followed by the second van. The lorry slowed to a crawl and pulled into the far right lane. The two vans pulled into the left lane nearest the office. The technicians watched their computer screens. Speakers picked up the conversation between the customs officer and the driver.

Documents were passed to the officer, who gave them a cursory look. As he motioned the lorry forward, the inspector left the office and walked to the lorry, flashlight in hand.

He untied the canvas, lifted it, quickly looked inside, and motioned to the dog handler that he was not needed. The dog and his handler had already approached the back of the lorry. The dog was excited, looking at the lorry then back to the handler.

Azmir gave a command: "Surround the lorry, arrest the men in the cab, and place the customs officer in custody."

One van pulled behind the lorry and blocked the lane. The unit quickly jumped out carrying semi-automatic M4 carbines. They stood outside the cab doors and ordered the men to step out. The Chinese men slowly opened their doors. Two officers grabbed them roughly and dragged them out of the cab. They had revolvers, but dropped their guns when they saw the assault weapons and they held their hands above their heads.

"Facedown on the ground, hands behind your back. Now!" Azmir ordered. They were swiftly flex-cuffed. One officer pulled the cuffed customs officer to the front of the lorry and put him on the ground near the Chinese men with two army officers guarding them.

Chris, Riley, and Suhaimi walked to the back of the lorry and lifted the canvas. It was loaded with the usual boxes and crates carrying garments. The handler motioned the dog into the lorry. He leaped into it and slowly walked between the boxes, sniffing each one. He sniffed another large box and sat on his haunches and looked at his handler, whining.

Two of Azmir's men climbed inside the lorry and began opening boxes as they worked their way toward the cab. A few boxes closest to the back of the lorry were half-full of garments. Suhaimi pushed them onto the roadway. The boxes opened as they fell to the ground and the clothing spilled out onto the road.

They could hear noises coming from other crates. One of the men had a crowbar and started opening the crates.

Live pangolins, lizards, turtles, snakes, and civet cats were in the containers. One hundred crates were stuffed with animals of different sizes, from very small to large pangolins and two six-foot monitor lizards. Star turtles from India were packed one on top of the other between black cloths. Two burlap sacks of snakes were stuffed between the crates, and twenty-five bear paws in plastic bags were kept cold on ice. There were more animals than they could count, some dead from dehydration, others in states of shock.

Chris and Riley went to the front of the lorry, where the Chinese men were lying on the ground. The police were interrogating them in Cantonese and Malay. Suhaimi continued to assist with the crates.

Azmir addressed the prisoners: "You understand that you will be sent to prison for smuggling? Do you know how serious this is? Your gang will let you rot in jail. They won't rescue you. Why would you want to take the blame for someone else that is making much more money than you are?"

The driver was frightened and he broke down. "OK, OK," he said. "I was hired yesterday by a gang member to drive the lorry. His name is Ben Joh. Please let me go! I have a family. But my life is in danger if they find out that I ratted on them."

"It won't get out that you told us anything." Azmir wrote down the names and addresses.

The police loaded the three men into the van and sped off for Alor Setar. Another officer drove the lorry to the army base, where the animals were put into cages.

Chris went inside the office. "I want to see more arrests. The dogs did a good job and have proven how valuable they are to this operation."

"They have made our job easier," Azmir said. "Fortunately, it was a clean ops, no firefight. The two men were frightened and will probably give you more info tomorrow."

Azmir nodded in agreement. When the cleanup was finished,

they went back to Alor Setar. By the time they got to the hotel Chris could see light in the east as the sun was beginning to rise.

17.

KWANG LI SAT IN A small suburban Chinese restaurant early in the morning. His two bodyguards stood by the entrance. The short street was busy this time of day, serving breakfast to workers and the owners of the hawker stalls busy serving up plates of local food: noodles (chee cheong fun), curry noodles, nasi lemak (fat rice with egg and anchovies), and teh tarik (pulled tea with sweetened milk).

Kwang Li looked at his watch as he nodded to Kiow, who pulled up a chair and sat across from him. Both men were eating noodles in soup and steamed buns, discussing the shipment that was on the way to China. They didn't know it had been confiscated.

They also didn't know a taxi driver was sitting down the lane watching the restaurant. He was an informer and knew that the Triads leader ate breakfast there. It was no secret that it was their meeting place.

He watched the two Triads walk into the restaurant, and he immediately text messaged the officer leading the raid. The police vans were parked two blocks away at a petrol station.

Two large white vans drove into the parking strip near the restaurant. The company name, Fatt Painting Contractors, was splashed on the side panels. One van with three officers drove past the restaurant and pulled into a parking spot on the crowded road. The second van with three officers and the lead investigator parked along the entrance to the parking area.

The bodyguards watched the van as it drove by, paying little attention to it. They closed their eyes again and napped in the sun.

The plain-clothed police in the vans watched the men doze off and then opened the side doors. Seven men made their way silently toward the restaurant; three men entered the back door on the left-hand side behind the fish tanks. At the same time two others entered and grabbed the bodyguards before they could get to their semi-automatic weapons, while the lead investigator and another officer went for Kwang Li and Kiow.

Kwang Li saw the action and in a split second, he jumped up from the table, quickly spilling the tea and knocking over his chair. He screamed, "Kiow, get out!" He made a dash for the back door, Kiow behind him. The two police officers grabbed them, pushed them against the wall and flex-cuffed them.

The restaurant owner watched, a slight smile on his face as they put them in the van. Another paddy wagon pulled into the lane with the bodyguards locked inside.

They took the men to the main jail in KL.

The police couldn't hold Kwang Li and Kiow for the animal smuggling. There was no evidence that they were involved. Nothing was found in the restaurant.

That night, there was another arrest made at the Singapore crossing. A dog detected animals in the trunk of a car trying to cross the border. The animals had been slaughtered, including a rare black leopard, and the meat was found in plastic bags covered with ice and blankets. The car was headed for restaurants in Malaysia. The driver was arrested.

The Malaysian government was stepping up the anti-smuggling campaign. Four more dogs were expected to arrive by the end of the month. Photos and articles on the dogs had been in the newspapers. One picture on the front page showed the police inspector shaking the dog's paw. The Triads put a ten thousand dollar contract out on the dogs. They wanted them dead and the American responsible for bringing them to Malaysia.

Chris woke early and sent his report to Seattle. He received a phone call almost immediately from his director.

"Well, Chris. I have tried to get you to come back to Seattle, but you are very stubborn and persist in staying in Malaysia. It's difficult for me to justify your length of stay. On a positive note, you are helping the government to see what needs to be done to protect their environment. I sent your report to my supervisor in Washington. He has given you the green light to continue to work with the Malaysians, but not for an extended period. Do you understand me?"

"George, the only thing I can tell you is that I have to complete what was started. My work will soon be finished here, and the government has begun to implement changes. It will be a good mark for you at the end of the day. They are making progress in controlling the animal trafficking, and that is really a good step in the right direction."

"You must return as soon as possible. I am giving you some room to make that decision. Just keep me informed of your activities so I can justify it."

"Thanks, George. The government is willing to spend more money on additional dogs and training for their handlers."

"We're requesting more funding for the training program," George replied. "We'll get at least another two hundred grand for the Malaysian operation so you can send out more people for training."

"Right on, sir. The dogs are doing outstanding work. Imagine, a hit contract on dogs! I'll keep you informed as things progress."

"Chris, I'm not such a bad guy after all, am I? I understand completely what you are trying to accomplish, but you must understand that I am also caught between your request and what our government will allow us to do. Fortunately, my supervisor is on the same page."

Chris put his cell down and sat for a moment on the sofa. He thought through the conversation he just ended and was overwhelmed by the change in his boss. He finished his report to the U.S. Ambassador and e-mailed it to him. He finally shut down the computer and dressed in jeans, T-shirt, and sandals. He decided to call May Ling at the safe house, pick up a Chinese dinner, and spend the evening with her.

☙

As he punched in her cell phone number, the door chimes rang. He opened the door and May Ling was standing there in a low-cut black dress—short, sexy, and stunning! Chris was surprised to see her.

"How did you get away?"

"Easy. David and Florence are no match for me." She laughed.

At that moment, his cell phone rang.

"David here. May Ling slipped away from the safe house."

"She showed up here. I'll drive her back later."

Chris gave her a hug and smiled. "Well, May Ling, now that you're here we might as well have dinner in the suite."

"That's good. At least I can catch up on the news and the progress at the borders. Order me curry noodles."

They sat at the table, eating and talking. "Chris, the other night I told you about my brother. What about your relationship in Seattle? Is it still off-limits?"

He looked at her. "I guess I owe you that much." He took a sip of wine and started to talk.

"I met a beautiful girl last year. We dated for one month and then I asked her to marry me. She was what I wanted in a partner. We were meant for each other or so I thought."

"So what happened? Did you come to your senses?"

"I probably should have. She wanted to pick out a ring so we went to every jewelry store in town. She must have tried on every ring. I should have thought twice about what I was doing. But I was blind to her faults. I loved her."

"The ring must have been a stunner."

"You think I'm a jerk, don't you?" Chris stared at May Ling. She simply smiled. "A lovesick one at that."

"Anyhow, it was a beautiful round diamond, three carats, best quality and color. The salesman literally drooled over the stone and over her. I bought it. Cost me six-months' salary. I almost fainted at the price, but she wanted the best. We walked out with the ring on her finger, sparkling in the sunlight.

"She flaunted the ring among her friends and family and spent the rest of the time planning this enormous wedding, inviting everyone she ever knew—five hundred on the guest list including former boyfriends as well. That was a sore point with us. I had ten guests—my family and a few friends, that's all."

"That's the size of the weddings here. They are large affairs with a lot of ceremonies. The groom just shows up with his family. ... So what happened then? "

"Well, three weeks before the wedding, I was notified about the assignment in Malaysia. We argued about it because she didn't want to leave her precious modeling job. We didn't speak for several days. I thought we were in love and would go anywhere together. Guess I was too naive."

"Well you can't blame her for wanting to stay in the U.S. and keep her job."

"That's true, but I thought I meant more to her than her job. I guess I was a jerk and expected too much. Anyhow, the following week I got a text message from her."

He pulled out his smartphone, scrolled through the messages, found the right one and showed it to May Ling.

She read the message aloud: "Dear Chris, I'm calling off the wedding. I'm going to Las Vegas with someone I met recently and won't be back. I pawned the ring for the cash. You were great, and ... thanks for the ring."

Chris had tears in his eyes. "That really hurt."

"Oh, Chris. I am so sorry for you. She scammed you for the ring. You said the salesman got involved in selling you that ring, didn't you? Well, he was probably the guy she left town with. She never planned on marrying you, just wanted the cash."

"I know that now. It was a setup. I wanted to give her everything, and she took advantage of it and besides that, I'm still paying for the damn ring. I won't get involved with anyone else again, at least not for a very long time. If I ever do, they'll get one small gold band as an engagement ring and that will be all. I'll probably make them pay for it too."

"It was she who called when we were at the tower? What did she want?"

"You really want the whole story. Is this your entertainment for the evening?"

"Come on, Chris. It's time you got it out of your system. You're still hurting. Tell me the rest of the story."

"The guy used her in Vegas and spent all her money on the tables. She said she was sorry and wanted to make up with me. The girl has no conscience. She thought I would be mooning away, waiting for her to come back. Can you imagine that? Maybe I am a complete jerk."

"No, you've been hurt badly. It'll take time for you to heal after that affair."

She held his hand. "We have both been hurt deeply; mine, the death of my brother and you, the engagement. Does that make us kindred souls? Perhaps we can work together now that we know each other better. What do you think?"

He hugged her and gave her a kiss on her cheek.

"I actually feel better getting it out of my head. It's been eating at me. Thanks for being a good listener."

"You'll get my bill in the morning. Or you can pay the bill tonight." She smiled.

"I'm not ready for that yet."

The doorbell rang, and the waiter wheeled in the table and food. They continued to talk as they drank the wine and finished their meal.

"You don't seem to know much about the animals," May Ling said. "Is this something new for you? I love animals and want to protect them. That's why I got into this job. Were you only involved with drug smuggling?"

"Hey, wait a minute. I hate to see an animal abused or hurt in any way. I grew up with dogs and cats around our house and volunteered at the SPCA for years. Animal abuse is nothing new to me. I want it stopped, and I want people that abuse animals to get treatment. It makes me sick when I see a beautiful animal abused by a callous person. What makes you think you're the only one that likes animals?"

She looked at him, eyebrows raised. "I thought you were only involved in drug smuggling. No one ever told me that you had a background of helping animals. How was I to know? I thought you were just another foreigner sent here to write a report and return to the U.S."

"Well, you got that wrong, didn't you? I thought you were just a frustrated undercover agent trying to make a mark for yourself, so I guess we're even."

She stiffened but then relaxed, and said calmly, "Look Chris, we both got off on the wrong foot. Let's start over, OK?"

He calmed down and nodded. "OK, that's a good idea. Let's forget all the pettiness and work together."

They shook hands and smiled.

"I'll drive you back to the safe house."

"Can't I stay here for the night? I can sleep on the sofa. I don't want to go back to the safe house. It's too boring. Please let me stay."

"You can sleep in the bedroom, and I'll sleep on the sofa. I'll call David and let him know."

She hugged him. "Thank you. I just don't want to return to the house. David and Karen are nice people, but they're guards and do their job too well. I wanted to be here. It's more comfortable right now."

"OK, but don't expect anything else. This is just a sleepover for you, and I have work that I must finish."

"Understood, sir." She saluted him, and he gave her a hug.

May Ling went into the bedroom and closed the door. Chris relaxed and thought about the evening. He put his old girlfriend away and decided it was time to forget and move on. He thought about May Ling sleeping in the bedroom as he sat sipping his wine. Finally, he turned out the lights and went into her bedroom.

⚜

Wang Ju faxed the ship's bill of lading to Zhang Chen. The new shipment was due from Malaysia later in the week. He shut down his computer, left the office, and bicycled to the teahouse, parked his bicycle near the door, locked it, and nodded at the two guards standing outside.

Zhang Chen was sitting alone; his other two bodyguards sat at another table watching the kitchen and the front doors. They nodded as Wang Ju sat opposite him. A waiter poured him tea and then left, avoiding eye contact with anyone.

He took a sip of tea and put the cup down on the table. He gave Wang Ju a hard look. "I have read your report, and I do not accept it!" He slammed his fist on the table. The teacups jumped, and the tea splashed onto the table.

Wang Ju, startled, jumped in his seat, looking like a cornered rat waiting for the axe to fall. He finally spoke: "The dogs brought in have been very effective in detecting our cargos."

"Kill them! They are only dogs," He said savagely.

"Not possible. We have tried poisoned meat in the lorries and offered higher bribes to the customs officers, but everyone is afraid. The dogs are heavily guarded. Even the ministers are not cooperating with us. Perhaps we should kill the American?"

"Don't be stupid! Kill one American agent and it becomes an international incident. You'll have a hundred in his place. The answer is in our control over the officers working for us. I thought the elimination of the Wildlife deputy director would be an example to others that no matter how high their office, they were not immune from our reach. After all, we have made them rich." He gesticulated with turned-up palms to emphasize his point.

"So what do we do?" Wang Ju waited for an answer. He took another sip of tea, hands shaking as he held the cup.

"We make an example of those that go against us," He spewed, "not the ministers or the customs officers themselves but those that are close to them." He passed over a slip of paper that held a list of names. Wang Ju read it and put it in his pocket.

"See that they do not wake up to the sun. Perhaps all informers will finally get the message." He pushed himself away from the table, stood, hiked up his pants, gave Wang Ju a stern look, then left, surrounded by his bodyguards.

◆

Over the next two weeks, the smuggling of animals at all the border crossings slowed to a trickle. No more huge shipments of live animals in the big lorries. The dogs were on duty and sniffed out any hidden animals.

The rumor going around said Malaysia government informers, immigration, police and custom personnel formerly in the pocket of the Triads were now refusing to cooperate with them. The Triads were desperate and ready to kill anyone who stopped the animal shipments from reaching China.

May Ling took Chris to meet her family on Saturday. The police van was parked in front of their house with two policemen on duty. Chris gave his ID to the officer at the van window. The officer opened the gate, and they drove into the compound. Her parents were waiting at the open door to greet them.

Her father, Kang Ang Yu, was a handsome man in his early sixties who loved gardening. The gardens surrounding their house were spectacular, lush flowers blooming throughout. May Ling's mother, Kong Ping Chin, was still a beauty with a simple smile and sparkling eyes. Her gray hair was pulled back into a bun. Chris looked at the mother, then at May Ling and decided that she looked like her mother, inheriting her good looks and figure.

Over tea, Chris explained to them why they had to leave Malaysia.

"It's for your daughter's safety. You are in danger too. There's no other choice."

Her father spoke. "We understand, but it is difficult for us to leave. This has always been our home, and our friends are here. It would be difficult for us in a new country. We are too old to make new friends, and we also live by the old ways, not like the young people today. We will give you our decision in two days."

"Please decide quickly before it's too late."

They nodded but said nothing. They finished their tea and cakes. May Ling hugged her parents, and she and Chris walked together to the car. As they drove away she waved to them.

"I have a strange feeling about leaving them alone in the house. It's a feeling of dread that I have never experienced before."

"It's probably because you haven't seen them in a while."

"Yes, I'm sure you're right."

Chris kissed May Ling when they returned to the hotel. "I have ordered a special dinner for tonight. I think you'll like it."

"What's so special about this dinner? Why are you being so mysterious?"

He smiled. "Wait and see."

The bell rang, and he opened the door to the waiter behind a food trolley. He pushed the trolley into the room and set up the table, lit the candles, and quietly left. The candlelight dinner was prepared especially for them by the hotel chef. There were different wines for each course—appetizer, soup, salad, and grilled local fish.

Chris took her by the hand and led her to the sofa, where they had their dessert. As they sipped their cognac and coffee, he leaned toward her and kissed her gently on the lips. She looked at him in surprise.

"May Ling, I love you. I want you to be my wife. I can't live without you." He held her hands and kissed her again. "I said I wouldn't get involved with another woman again, but you came along and everything changed."

She hugged him tightly. "I love you, Chris, and I thought you would never propose." She kissed him passionately, then said, "But Chris, I can't marry you, not just yet. I don't want any attachments. I have a job to do and until that is done I want a clear head."

"You have to let go, put that aside and forget it. It will haunt you forever if you continue to brood on it. I want you to be happy. Your brother would want the same thing for you. I have put aside my unhappy relationship because of you. Can't you do the same for me? I love you and want you, not just now but forever."

She saw the hurt look on his face, kissed him tenderly, then took him by the hand and led him to the bedroom. He sat on the bed as she took off her clothes then undressed him.

He put his arms around her and pulled her to him as they lay on the bed. He kissed her on her neck, her breasts, then his mouth and fingers worked their way downward until they reached her pleasure spot. In the space of a few minutes she exploded, gasping for breath. It was her turn to kiss him, lingering between his thighs until he was ready to meet her needs.

They held each other resting with his head on her breasts. She wrapped her arms around him. Chris sat up and looked at her. He gently ran his fingers over her face.

"I won't take no for an answer." He stroked her hair as he spoke. She smiled at him and softly said, "Yes." He kissed her gently and held her as they both fell asleep.

⁂

His cell phone rang at six-thirty.

"Chris, I have some bad news for you." Suhaimi was somber.

"What news?" He was fully awake now and sat on the edge of the bed.

"May Ling's mother and father are dead! They were brutally murdered last night."

Chris felt the cold hand of fear grip his heart. "What happened?"

"They were found a few minutes ago in bed, lying faceup with their hands tied behind their backs and their throats cut."

"Oh my God! How did that happen? The house was guarded! Where were the guards?"

"One of my colleagues called me. The police received an anonymous call about the murder. When the police arrived at their home, they found U.S. visa forms scattered over the bodies. Their passports and wallets were missing along with jewelry, cell phones, and a laptop. It looks like a robbery/murder case. The guards were asleep in their trailer outside the house. No one was patrolling the area. The guards left their posts during the night. They were arrested this morning, and police are looking into their dereliction of duty.

"The killers broke into the house through a back door. They climbed over the fence from another yard. The guards in front didn't check the back of the house. It was a major error on the part of the guards, and they will be severely reprimanded."

Chris was stunned. "It wasn't a robbery/murder case. It was a Triads killing. It's my fault for not moving them to a safe house. I thought the police were monitoring their house. The guards can be reprimanded to hell and back. Now it's too late, and I have to tell May Ling. How will I ever do that?" He ran his hand through his hair. The voice on the phone brought him back to reality.

"Do you know where May Ling is? She must be told what has happened."

"Yes. She's here with me."

"Thank God you're with her. I don't know what to say, Chris. She has faced too much tragedy—her brother's death, her kidnapping, and now her parents' murders. She'll need your help. I'm heading for the house. If you need me, call."

Chris put his cell phone down and went to the bedroom. He sat in the chair next to the bed, looking at the sleeping form of May Ling, a slight smile on her lips. The pain in his heart was almost too much to bear. At seven o'clock, his phone rang. Chris walked into the living room to take the call.

"Roberts here. Have you heard the news?"

"Yeah. I just got a call a few minutes ago. It's terrible what they did to the old couple."

"Don't go to the house, don't be seen with your informer, and stay out of sight. We will explain the visa forms to the press. Is your friend in the safe house?"

"No, she's here. She didn't want to stay in the safe house so I let her stay here."

"Have you told her yet?"

"No, she's still asleep."

"You poor son of a bitch! I wouldn't want to be in your shoes right now."

Chris walked back to the bedroom, sat in the chair facing the bed, put his head in his hands, and waited.

May Ling slowly opened her eyes then sat up, startled to see Chris sitting in a chair watching her. She rubbed her eyes.

"How long have you been sitting there?"

The sad look on his face was an alarm bell.

"What happened?" She got up quickly and wrapped a blanket around herself, then stood in front of him. He wrapped his arms around her.

"Tell me what happened? Tell me."

He hesitated then finally spoke. "Your parents ..." Her blanket fell as she pulled away then grabbed him by the shoulders and yelled, "What about my parents?! What happened?!"

"They are dead ... murdered!"

"Dead? How?"

Chris caught her as she collapsed. He held her close.

"Oh God! I'm so sorry," he whispered. May Ling pushed him away.

"How?"

Chris looked at her but couldn't tell her. He was overwhelmed with grief.

"Tell me! Tell me what happened!" she screamed.

"They were murdered ... early this morning ... in their beds! Oh, May Ling, I am so sorry! I don't know what to say." Tears filled his eyes as he held her close. She shoved him away.

"Murdered? How ... how were they murdered? Tell me now!" She screamed at him again and beat his chest with her fists, then shook him. Tears rolled down her cheeks. Deep sobs came from her throat. She started to crumple. Chris grabbed her as she fell and took her in his arms to comfort her.

She shoved him away and yelled, "I must go to them! I have to see them! You tell the police not to take them away until I get there. Do you understand me? I need to be with them!"

She grabbed her clothes. He followed her as she went into the bathroom.

"I can't go with you. I can't be seen with you. It would be a big mistake," Chris said quietly. "Suhaimi will go with you."

May Ling gasped. "What?" she sneered.

"My parents' murder was a tragedy," she continued. "They were kind and generous people and wouldn't hurt anyone. You think your coming with me is a mistake? Who do you think you are? Are you so high and mighty that you can't help me? You have no feelings! You're just a dumb foreigner that has no business being here!"

She pushed him out of the bathroom and shut the door. A few minutes later she walked out and grabbed her small bag. She opened the front door, turned to look at him, and said harshly, "It was your fault that they died." She gathered her clothing and walked toward the door. She turned again and said to him, "It is now my responsibility to take care of my parents and their funeral." She walked out, and the door closed behind her.

He slumped into the bedroom chair, took his cell phone, and dialed Suhaimi. "May Ling is on her way. Keep an eye on her!"

"Don't worry. I'll call you later."

He sat without moving, staring at the door. He felt guilty and useless.

Perhaps she is right. I am just a dumb foreigner that can't do anything right. I should have gone with her ... to hell with everyone else.

Another voice argued: *No, you were right to stay out of the way and let her grieve. She needs to be alone with her parents and not have you hanging around. You are a dumb foreigner.*

The police sealed off her parents' house, and no one was allowed to enter except the forensics team. The news of the double murder was headlined for the next week in the newspapers and the media. Speculation was rife among the general public.

The U.S. Embassy explained the visa papers found in the bedroom as routine visa forms for tourists wanting to visit America.

Chris knew otherwise. It was a message to all of those involved in the smuggling of animals that even if you could escape their punishment for informing or not cooperating, your family could not, and they would pay the ultimate price.

Roberts had used his influence to have the police release the bodies after the second day and the Minister of Natural Resources and Environment was ensured that there would be no autopsy. There was no need. The slit throats were the cause of death. The Chinese believed it was bad luck for the body to be cut open and parts removed for examination. The body had to be intact for the journey into the afterlife.

The funeral was covered in newspapers, websites, and on TV. Pictures focused on the overwhelming number of funeral wreaths sent by sympathizers.

Six Buddhist monks chanted prayers over the deceased during the three days when family and close friends filed past the closed coffins paying their respects to the couple.

Chris went to the funeral with Suhaimi. They joined the long procession that left the Kang house. A funeral band of eight musicians led the cortege, followed by the oldest family member carrying a picture of the deceased couple. The band played contemporary happy music, marches, and Chinese songs. The hearse came next with the two caskets. Chris saw May Ling walking behind the hearse, followed by the rest of the family members in order of their relationship to her parents. Each family member wore a piece of burlap sacking pinned to their shirts to remind them of their origins. Friends of the family walked at the end of the cortege. Three lorries followed the cortege carrying the wreaths and bouquets of flowers.

The procession made its way to the waiting cars that would

take the mourners to the temple, then continued to the cemetery at the back of the temple. When the coffins were lifted out of the hearse the mourners turned away, not looking at the coffins. It is considered bad luck to look at the coffins as they are being removed from the hearse. The band played while the coffins were placed in the family's area facing east. Each family member threw dirt on the coffins. Food in containers was placed near the gravesite so the deceased would have nourishment when they crossed over the Yellow River.

The Buddhist monks began to chant prayers. After seven days of prayer the souls of her parents would cross the Yellow River and be greeted by their ancestors who were waiting for them. Chris looked for May Ling at the mausoleum, but she was nowhere in sight. When the funeral was over, the people walked away without turning to look at the gravesite.

Suhaimi whispered to Chris, "I talked to the police that were at her parents' home. A corporal escorted her into the bedroom and left her with her parents. She was there for over an hour. We started to worry that she may have had thoughts about joining them, but she came out of the bedroom looking calm and at peace. The bodies had been cleaned, clothes changed, and the neck wounds hidden by scarves. She got into a car with family members and was taken away."

"I expected as much from her," Chris said. "She was so overwrought over her parents' death that she didn't want to see anyone. We will just have to wait until she surfaces."

On the eighth day after the funeral, May Ling called Chris.

"Where are you? I've been so worried about you! Are you all right?"

"Yes, I'm OK. Just listen to me. I'm sorry about what I said to you that morning. But I don't want to see anyone just now, so please give me space and don't try to find me. I saw you at the funeral. Thank you for coming. I needed your support. Just your being there helped me."

"I will continue to support you because I love you. Come back to me now so I can protect you. The longer you're in the open, the easier it is for the Triads to get to you."

"The Triads only know that I am Tan Sri's personal aide. They don't know anything else. No one knows what I really do. Tan Sri is not corrupt and will not give in to their demands. That's the only reason they kidnapped me and murdered my parents. It's to get to him."

She continued in a monotone voice: "Yes. I am in danger because Tan Sri sent me to you, and Abdullah is dead. They kidnapped me and now my mother and father have paid the highest price. You and I are not meant for each other, Chris. You're yin and I am yang. We can never be together. Lead your own life and forget me! Go home to your country."

"No! Don't say that. Come back. I'll be here for you. Don't stay away."

Suddenly, the phone went dead. Chris continued to call her phone but it went to voice mail. He sat on the sofa, looked at his phone, then tears flooded his eyes. He thought about his assignment. It was a grave turn of events, but the best plan of action was to continue with the project and see it through. He would be here for her, and that was important. He thought about his next move and called Suhaimi.

1.8

MAY LING GAZED AT HERSELF in the mirror. Her disguise was complete. Her short hair was in tufts, and each tuft was dyed blond, red, or brown. She wore tiger-striped brown contact lenses, artificial eyelashes, scarlet red lipstick, a sleeveless scoop neck top, and a tight pair of jeans low on her hips that showed at least three inches of bare skin. She looked cheap, trashy, sexy, and dangerous. She was ready.

Chris missed her. The emptiness he felt was almost too much to bear. He was under no illusions if the Triads found her. She was right in one sense. If Tan Sri hadn't sent her to him, none of this would have happened. But if ... if ... if ...

All he could do now was immerse himself in his work and pray that she was all right. He felt useless and helpless.

Suhaimi tried to find her. Roberts spread the word on his network, but so far there was no response. None of her friends knew where she was hiding. Chris lay awake at night thinking of her, calling her name, hoping that she could hear him. No matter where he looked or whom he talked to, the response was the same. No one knew anything.

May Ling thought she had identified her parents' murderer. She had searched through the archives of the local newspapers and the Internet for any information about the Triads operating in Malaysia. There were almost two hundred thousand websites with Malaysia Triads mentioned. The information pointed to the leader of the Tiger Triads in KL as the one with connections to the Triads in Guangzhou. The name Kwang Li kept popping up in animal smuggling, prostitution, and drug crimes. She knew he murdered her brother. Her gut told her Kwang Li killed her parents too. She called Bette Lim, her closest friend since childhood, who was beautiful, sexy-looking, and known as a high-class party girl about town.

"Bette, it's May Ling."

"Oh, May Ling, I'm so sorry about your parents. I was at their funeral. It was a beautiful ceremony, but I didn't get a chance to talk to you. Please let me know if I can help you in any way."

"Yes, you can help me now, Bette. You know the Tiger Triads very well. Where does the leader hang out? Does he hang out with his group or by himself?"

"Evergreen Bar. I've been there several times. That's where they party. Their office is located in a building in town. They all hang out together—safety in numbers, I guess. Why?"

"I would like to meet the leader."

"Are you serious? What in the world for? He's mean and a real playboy. I've heard he beats his women. Don't know how true that is, though. He has a girl who is very jealous of any woman that comes near him. She has been on his arm for a while."

"Could you take me to the Evergreen? I want to meet him."

"Sure, but I don't know him personally. I know his lieutenants."

"Let's say I am a new girl in town, and you're showing me around. How about tonight?"

"OK, I'll pick you up at nine. I sure hope you know what you're doing. They're a very dangerous group, May Ling. I don't know why you want to meet him. He'll bring you nothing but grief at the end of the day."

"Thanks for the warning, Bette, but I can handle myself. Just keep it quiet!"

That night, she was dressed in her "trashy clothes" as she called her outfit, long artificial eyelashes, neon red lipstick, and revealing clothes that screamed, *I'm available.* Her five-inch heels and tight miniskirt showed off her legs to good advantage.

When Bette picked her up at the cheap ground floor apartment she had rented, she just gawked at her with an open-mouth.

May Ling said, "My name is Leona Lee if anyone asks." She stood in a sexy stance, hand on her hip, the other hand holding a cigarette, and chest stuck out.

"Are you sure you know what you're getting into? Those guys are going to eat you up." Bette put her hands on her hips in a motherly style. Her short skirt was moderate compared to May Ling's, but Bette's heels were just as high and her top just as tight.

"Don't forget my name."

Bette shrugged her shoulders. "OK, Leona Lee! Let's go!"

Petaling Street was well lit with a large night market filling the street. Tourists and locals were perusing the goods in several stalls while Chinese traders were touting their goods. Chinese hawker stalls served a variety of local food.

Halfway down the road they turned onto a quiet side street and walked toward the bar that was in the middle of the block surrounded by closed shops. Garbage stacked on the roadside and several cars were parked near the bar.

A large brown rat scurried across the street. Bette jumped as it ran into a drain. A single light hung over the doorway and lit the wooden Evergreen Bar sign. They pushed the ancient wood door open and walked into the crowded, darkened room.

Silence filled the room when Bette and May Ling entered. Several men seated at the bar turned and stared at them, then whistled as they strutted to the bar, sat on barstools, and crossed their legs so that their short skirts rode up their thighs.

May Ling scanned the room. Several tables were occupied with men and their girlfriends. The girls were smoking and laughing while the men drank and talked. Conversation was mostly in Cantonese. The waiters brought hot steaming food to two tables and cleared away the dishes from other tables.

They had hardly settled onto their stools when six men surrounded them. Each one insisted on buying them a drink. They both opted for red wine and within minutes there were six bottles of wine standing in front of them.

Tong, one of the lieutenants, was at the bar. He smiled when he saw Bette and said, "Hey Bette, who's your friend?"

"Hi, Tong, this is Leona Lee. She's new in town." She smiled coyly at May Ling. Tong nodded in greeting, and they all moved to a table. Extra chairs were brought over and Scotch poured for the men. The men quizzed May Ling. She was different from their regular girls and more exotic.

Bette and May Ling just smiled and sipped their wine, nodding every once in a while and not saying much.

Finally, May Ling stood up, hands on her hips, and looked at the men. "What are you guys ... the police? Is this an interrogation? If so, I want a lawyer now!" The men laughed and drank. No more questions.

The evening progressed with more bottles of wine and food. They all ate, drank, and talked.

Close to midnight, the leader of the Tigers walked in accompanied by a beautiful woman in her late twenties. He had an air about him as he entered the room. The crowd immediately made space for him and his girlfriend at the table. He introduced himself as Kwang Li and his girlfriend as Liza Chin. He leered at May Ling as she watched Liza, who glared at her. She smiled sweetly at Liza as imaginary daggers flew back and forth between the two women.

As the night wore on, the noise got louder and the Triads got drunk. Kwang Li shouted, "Gan Bei!" All the members shouted back, "Gan Bei!" as they drained their glasses. It was then, as Kwang Li raised his glass, that May Ling saw the gold dragon cuff links. The dragon's tiny ruby eyes flashed in the light. She had them made for her father's last birthday as he was born in the Year of the Dragon.

She felt dizzy, her heart hammered in her chest as cold shivers radiated throughout her body. Bette and May Ling refused offers of rides home and left, quickly disappearing down the dark and deserted street to their car. They drove to her flat, and Bette stayed the night.

Over the next two weeks they became regulars at the Evergreen Bar and were accepted by the gang members. It was obvious to everyone that Kwang Li was interested in May Ling. She indirectly mentioned her business skills in conversations with men at the bar. She spoke Cantonese to communicate with some of the gang and read the Mandarin language newspaper to them as most only spoke the dialect but couldn't read or speak Mandarin.

One night when they were at the Evergreen Bar, Kwang Li asked her to visit his office. She agreed and went the next morning. The office was on the eighth floor of a bank building on Ampang Road. The sign on the door said *Chung Kang Exporters*. The receptionist, a young, pretty Chinese woman, was seated at a desk in the small waiting room. She smiled as May Ling moved toward her. "I have an appointment with Kwang Li." The receptionist looked her over then, without a word, buzzed him on the intercom.

A few minutes later he came to the reception area and welcomed her. They walked down a narrow hallway to the main area of the office where several staff sat, busy working on their computers. She was introduced to the five people, all Chinese— one man and four women seated at their desks. The women were young, very pretty and didn't look too intelligent. The man was in his early thirties and supervised the women. After the introductions, Kwang Li led the way to his private office, bare except for the desk and two chairs. He shut the door behind her then walked to his desk. She sat on a straight-backed chair in front of his desk and could barely see him over the piles of folders on the desk, not a clean space anywhere.

"Tell me about your work experience. I heard that you worked in an office previously."

She ignored his gaze and spoke professionally. "Yes, I've had several years of office experience. I understand the programs necessary to run a business office and know how to keep it organized."

She glanced at the mess on his desk. "I am fluent in using computers and the software."

"You noticed my desk and the disorganization. I desperately need someone to help organize files. Would you be willing to work for me?"

She hesitated a moment. "Well, I didn't expect an immediate offer. You don't know anything about me. Here's my resumé. I do have the qualifications you require."

She pulled two sheets of typed paper from her handbag and placed them on his desk.

He glanced at the paper. "You definitely have the qualifications I want." He leered and nearly salivated.

He continued: "I know enough about you. You're pleasant and play a mean game of darts and the members like you. You live in a small condo and give private massages. I have one of your cards." He showed her the business card she had printed and passed around at the bar. Leona Lee was printed in large black letters and the card also said, *Massage for Ladies Only.*

"Ladies only? Does that mean you don't like men?" He leaned forward on his desk as he peered at her. "What a waste! Perhaps one day I can change your mind." He grinned.

You will be dead before that can ever happen.

She and Sue spent days trying to decide on an occupation in case the Tigers checked on her and they decided on the ladies massage idea. She outfitted her other bedroom into a massage room, with massage table, mirrors, wardrobe, soft lights, towels, lotions, and oils. She had purchased a number of DVDs on the art of massage and spent hours watching them and practicing on Sue.

May Ling explained her new occupation to Bette before they went to the Evergreen Bar.

"Why the cover? What's going on, May Ling? I want to know in case you need help." Bette put her arm around May Ling's shoulder. "Does it have something to do with your parents?"

"Don't ask. The less you know, the better. I don't want you involved."

"I'm already involved, but I understand. You can tell me when you're ready to talk about it."

"I know. Thank you." She hugged Bette.

Bette sometimes stayed over on weekends with May Ling sleeping on her sofa. Many nights they sat up talking about her parents. May Ling slowly overcame her grief.

Chris was constantly on her mind. His image and the sound of his voice would intrude into her thoughts, mostly at night when she was waiting for sleep to come. She couldn't do anything about it yet. Chris would have to wait until the fear of the Triads had passed and life was more normal for her. Until then, Chris would be in her dreams.

She accepted Kwang Li's job offer. "Do you have a contract for me to sign?"

"Very good. I was hoping you would take up my offer. No need for a contract. You can start tomorrow, and you can have your own desk and computer right in front of my office so I can watch you."

"That won't be necessary. I'm well trained and don't need supervision."

She arrived at eight the next morning and took further instructions from him.

"You'll track my mail and answer it. If you have any difficulty, I'll be in my office." He put his arm on her shoulder, and he grinned as she moved away.

She tracked e-mail and sent messages received from respective members and e-mailed replies and instructions, if any. All incoming mail was coded. It took her awhile to understand their routine. She asked him questions and typed his responses. Most mail was typed in Chinese characters. She was tempted to send Chris an e-mail, but resisted the urge to communicate with him. If Kwang Li found that e-mail it would be difficult to explain.

※

Chris went about his work, his thoughts on May Ling. *Is she all right? What is she doing? Where is she? I must find her.*

Suhaimi had a folded newspaper in his hand as he entered Chris's suite. He opened the paper to the front page and handed it to him.

"Chris, look at the headlines. The ministry is committed to curbing the wildlife smuggling. They will work through the department of Wildlife and National Parks. They want to stop the corruption and plan to arrest anyone involved in it. The department has successfully caught smugglers in forty-three cases since 2005, and the list is growing."

"That's not a lot of cases," Chris said. "That means that more smugglers were successful because of corrupt officers. Now, if they arrest the corrupt officials, then you should see a decrease in the smuggling. I think we're making a difference. We're putting the officials on notice that something has to be done."

Suhaimi nodded. "Yes, our efforts are working. Finally we are seeing the progress. The government moves at a snail's pace, but it's moving in the right direction."

They traveled to a Malaysian border crossing for a check on lorries entering from Singapore. Chris briefed the Malaysia immigration and customs personnel on better inspection techniques. Suhaimi acted as his interpreter when required.

Later in the evening, a black Toyota sedan pulled into the Singapore checkpoint. The Singapore customs officer motioned the driver to pull forward for inspection.

"Open the trunk." The driver stepped out of his car and lifted the lid. Suddenly, he sprinted across the border into Malaysia. The Malaysian police moved swiftly to track the man. He ran down the main road heading into the city. A police car with two officers blocked the road in front of him. One officer jumped out.

"Halt!" His weapon was drawn, safety off. The man stopped in his tracks, looked at the officer, then at his weapon and bolted to one side of the road like a scared jackrabbit.

The police officer gave chase and yelled again, "Stop now! Put your hands behind your head." The man continued to run. The police officer fired his weapon in one burst. The man quickly stopped and put his hands in the air. The officer flex-cuffed him and hauled him back to the border in the police car.

The trunk held a large burlap sack containing the corpse of a rare black panther. Another bag held the organs and was resting on ice covered with a thick quilt. The specimen measured more than six feet from nose to tail and weighed in at almost seventy pounds. It was the most beautiful creature Chris had ever seen. He could barely speak.

"I didn't know there were any black panthers left in Malaysia! It's a crime to see an animal so beautiful, dead and gutted. I feel sick looking at this butchering."

Suhaimi nodded. "Yes, there's still a few in the jungles, but you rarely see one. This smuggler will go to jail and face a heavy fine. The government is very fond of black panthers and woe to anyone that poaches one." The driver was a gang member and the car was stolen, license plates changed.

The next morning after breakfast, while Chris was typing his e-mail report, a message from May Ling came in on his cell phone: *I'm OK, don't worry about me.*

Chris immediately tried her number but got the same response he had received so many times since she had disappeared. At least she was safe.

He saved the message and sent back a message pleading with her to call him. He had sent so many of them over the past weeks.

Chris thought, *I can call the police and have them trace the chip in her phone but it wouldn't tell me where she is and a corrupt police officer may rat on her to the Triads. I'll just have to be patient. Besides, it would blow her cover. I'll find her my own way.*

⁌

It didn't take May Ling long to break the Tigers' communication codes. She discovered how involved the gang was in illicit activities: gang rape to keep the trafficked girls in line; animal smuggling; bribes of low-level police, immigration and customs officers, and other government officials; drugs, murder, and kidnapping.

Every time a Malaysian official was bribed to let a smuggled animal shipment out of Malaysia, a Thai border official was bribed to let the shipment into Thailand and then once again when it left Thailand for China or elsewhere. Usually, border crossings were in isolated areas and each unit almost a law within itself. The Triads would also threaten customs officers if they didn't cooperate.

May Ling formed a plan of how she would extract her revenge on Kwang Li and the Tigers. Her opportunity came two weeks later on a Friday afternoon while she was at her computer receiving coded messages for Kwang Li. She was able to decipher the messages as they came up on her computer. Most were routine: arrival of other Triads, money requests for operations, drug payments and bar money from guest relations officers (GROs), a fancy name for prostitutes.

The coded messages read: *20 boxes of ladies underwear delivered to Penang* translated as *20 women had been delivered to the clubs and bars to work as GROs. Five cases of whiskey* translated as *fifty kilos of heroin. Five cases of vodka* meant *fifty kilos of cocaine.*

She read the latest message: *750 kilos of pet food to be exported to Thailand for China destination. Invoice total $270,000, delivery this Sunday via Bali 11:00 p.m.* Bali was the code name for the Malaysian-Thai border crossing.

Pets will be sleeping, meaning the patrol dogs would be out of action. So, seven hundred and fifty animals would be smuggled across the border into Thailand on Sunday and not to worry about the dogs. She printed off the message and took it to Kwang Li's office. He was talking on his cell phone. He motioned her to place the printout on his desk then blew her kisses as she left. She stared at him in disgust. She left his office for the washroom and into a stall.

She quickly sent a text message to Chris's cell phone: *Shipment Friday 11 p.m. Thai border.* She then deleted the message.

Chris and Suhaimi had finished their inspection and training at the main border crossings when Chris received May Ling's message. He immediately tried to call her, but there was no answer.

"Listen to this, Suhaimi. May Ling texted there will action tonight at the northern border. How did she get this information?"

"Must have come from a Triads member, where else?"

"If we only knew where she was, we could at least try and protect her. Her friends don't know where she is either."

"She blames herself for the death of her parents."

"She blames me too, but what can I do? Nothing at the moment."

Suhaimi disagreed. "She's too intelligent to hold the murder of her parents against you. This information means she has a good source. I just wish she wasn't involved."

Once they had reached their hotel in Alor Setar, Suhaimi called the director of the Anti-Smuggling Unit. "Idris, it's Suhaimi here. We received a message on activity at the border tonight. It appears the dogs will be out of commission. Can you check on that?"

The director called back. "The dog handlers reported in sick with food poisoning and there'll be no dogs working tonight. I'm preparing a team for tonight, and they'll meet you at the hotel in an hour."

Both checked their weapons and dressed in loose-fitting black clothes, black caps, and military boots. By eight o'clock, the sergeant and his team of five men in two nondescript vans arrived, picked up Chris and Suhaimi, and drove to the border.

The sergeant directed one van with the task force to stop one mile from the border, pull off the road, and watch for a large lorry. The communication van with Chris, Suhaimi, and four technicians pulled off onto the small dirt road one-half mile from the border. The technicians monitored the activity on their computers; only a pale green light lit the back of the van unseen from outside the van.

At about eleven-thirty a call came in from the van behind them.

"A twelve-wheeler is speeding toward the border. Can you monitor its activity?" the sergeant said.

The technician reported, "The lorry just passed us with two

men in the cab, both Chinese. When they saw our van parked by the side of the road, they slowed down, looked at the van, and then drove on."

The sergeant acknowledged the transmission, and their van pulled out and drove toward the border. As the lorry pulled up to the booth, the van pulled in behind it, blocking the road. The communication van pulled off to one side at the border. The team jumped out of the van, semi-automatic rifles ready. The men took cover behind the van and waited. The sergeant spoke through a megaphone.

"Step out of the cab with your hands in the air." The command also crackled over the lorry's two-way radio. There was no movement from the occupants. He repeated the command.

The cab door on the driver's side slowly opened. The driver stepped down, hidden from sight by the cab's door. An officer saw him and shouted a command to stop. The Chinese driver fired wildly at the police officer to cover his escape.

Chris and Suhaimi were on the side of the lane, crouched and slightly hidden from the driver's view, their weapons drawn, waiting. Chris had an open shot at the driver and fired. He caught him in the right shoulder. The driver ran for the trees on the side of the road.

Suhaimi yelled and waved his hands. "Cease fire! We need him alive!" But no one heard him over the noise. At the same time, the rider opened his door and quickly stepped down on the pavement. He fired at the van behind him, hitting the windshield, shattering the glass.

He ran in front of the lorry, firing his automatic pistol wildly. The officers returned the fire, hitting the second man in the leg and the left shoulder. He fell to the ground and rolled onto the dirt and tried to crawl away. Another flash of fire from the armed police and the man was hit in his head, his weapon now silent.

The driver continued to crash through the underbrush and the trees. Two officers ran into the jungle and fired blindly where they heard the noise. The driver fired back. The officers followed his trail and rapid gunfire ensued from both sides in the darkness. Chris's eyes were drawn to the muzzle flashes that lit up the jungle for a few seconds, then, all was silent. The driver was critically wounded and nothing more was heard.

They walked with the sergeant and two of the police officers to the first body. He lay face down, blood seeping from his wounds. The sergeant checked his pulse and shook his head. The man was in his mid-twenties.

One of the officers went through the dead man's pocket, found a wallet along with a Malaysian passport, and handed both to the sergeant. The other dead man lay further into the jungle, bleeding from a fatal chest wound. A few more feet and he might have made his escape. His wallet and passport were also handed to the sergeant.

The sergeant looked at the passport and commented to Chris, "He's a Thai national. He has a Thai passport. He was only twenty-two. What a waste."

Chris nodded as he continued to watch the action at the back of the lorry. By this time, the tarpaulin cover had been untied and pulled off. The men started searching through the cartons stacked one on top of another. As Suhaimi and the sergeant approached the lorry, they could already hear cries of frightened animals.

"It's loaded!" one of the men shouted. "Must be hundreds of animals here."

"OK! Looks like we hit paydirt," the sergeant said. He pointed to three team members. "Drive the lorry back to Alor Setar to the animal shelter, see that they are fed, watered, and looked after. Count the animals, list the species, and have your report on my desk first thing tomorrow morning."

The men saluted, jumped into the lorry, and drove away.

The coroner arrived to transport the bodies to the hospital morgue. A coroner's staff member took photos of the dead men as they lay on the road. Weapons were placed in plastic bags, measurements taken of the crime scene, and bodies placed in black bags and loaded into the coroner's van.

The sergeant put the wallets and passports into a plastic bag, and he, Chris, and Suhaimi jumped into his van and drove back to Alor Setar. No one spoke on the return trip. There were two deaths that night, but there could have been more—one of their own, if a bullet from one of the criminal's weapons had hit its mark.

"That information was spot-on, Chris," said the sergeant. "A good night's work! This will make the smugglers take notice!"

"It should. This shipment must be worth several hundred thousand dollars."

"Much more when it reaches China," said Suhaimi.

"There'll be a few disappointed diners next week. Too bad they won't be able to enjoy their dinner. They'll have to eat vegetables!" said the sergeant. They all had a good laugh at the expense of the gang.

Chris and Suhaimi were dropped off at their hotel. Chris labored over his daily report to George. As he gave a description of the day's events, images of men dying and animals crying to be rescued filled his thoughts.

19

MAY LING WAS GETTING READY for bed when she heard a knock on the door. She looked through the spyhole and shuddered, then quickly checked herself in the mirror. She heard the knock again, louder this time, and opened the door. Kwang Li was standing in front of her, smiling and holding up a bottle of champagne. She was immediately conscious of two things: *Does he know I sent the message to Chris? I haven't anything on under my robe.*

"Busy, Leona? You took your time answering the door." He pushed past her into the room, kicking the door shut behind him. She could smell the alcohol on his breath.

"I was just going to bed." She immediately regretted her response.

"Alone?" He walked past her and looked in her bedroom and the massage room. "Pretty professional massage parlor! Do you do many women?" He guffawed as he leered at her.

She was abrupt. "What do you want? It's late, and I'm very tired." She looked at her watch.

He moved closer. "What do I want, Leona? I want to have a glass of champagne with the most beautiful and sexy woman I know!" He gave her an exaggerated up-and-down look.

She held her ground. "I don't drink champagne! You can take it back." She stepped back a few paces, but he moved toward her again, and she could smell the whiskey on his breath.

"A good time to learn! One glass won't hurt you!" He went into her kitchen, rummaged through the cupboards, found two wine glasses, brought them into the living room, and put them on the table next to her. She was still standing in the same spot.

A loud pop and then two glasses were full of the foaming liquid. "This champagne cost two hundred and fifty U.S. dollars. Only the best for you, beautiful Leona!"

She cringed at his words.

He put the champagne bottle on the table in front of the sofa, walked to May Ling, and handed her one of the glasses.

"Drink up, Leona! This is good stuff!" He gulped his drink with one swallow. "Come on, drink up. I'm your boss, remember?"

She tried another tack. "What about your girlfriend, Liza? Wouldn't she like to have some champagne?"

"What about her?" he groused as put his glass down and waited for her answer. When she said nothing, he poured himself another glass and moved next to her, touching her arm with his fingers, then whispering into her ear.

"Drink up now. Don't be a tease." He touched her cheek and she pulled away from him.

"I'm not a tease, and I don't want the champagne!" she yelled.

"Oh no? How come you wear those trashy clothes at the Evergreen? No bra, your tits hanging out, and that short miniskirt that shows the cheeks of your ass every time you throw darts? That's a real come-on. You drank red wine that night and now you don't drink?"

He gulped his drink, then put the glass on the table, and moved in front of her, breathing on her face. He raised his voice.

"Now drink, or I'll pour it down your beautiful throat!"

She stood still, staring at him. Her heart hammered in her chest. Then, suddenly, she tossed the champagne into his face and quickly darted behind the sofa.

He stood there in disbelief, wiped his face with his hands, and said "I always wanted you, you little tart."

He jumped over the sofa, grabbed her in a bear hug, pushed her arms behind her back, and pinned her against the wall, and then forced his mouth on hers. She tried to turn her head, but he continued to hold her still. He spread her legs, holding them open with his feet and moved his body against hers so she couldn't knee him in the groin.

She struggled as best she could, but she was no match. One hand loosened the belt of her robe, and the other hand was on her breasts and then in between her thighs.

"Please! ... Please don't! I'm not interested in you. Liza loves you and would be upset."

Still holding her pinned against the wall, he unzipped his fly and reached into his trousers.

"Suck it, and I won't screw you."

He pushed himself against her. She squirmed as she tried to escape. Suddenly, his cell phone rang. Using his other hand he pulled out his phone and said while breathing hard, "Yeah, what is it, Kiow? I'm busy." He listened for a minute, suddenly sobered up. "When?" He listened again. "Damn, I'm on my way."

He turned to her and said, "Saved by the phone!"

He zipped up. "Enjoy the champagne! We'll do this again real soon, but I have a pressing problem right now."

He tried to give her a kiss on her cheek, but she turned her head. He leered at her and walked out. As soon as the door closed, she ran and locked it, ran into the bathroom, knelt in front of the toilet, and heaved until there was nothing left. She rose to her feet, went into the shower, and scrubbed herself. She poured the champagne down the sink and threw the bottle in the garbage. Finally, she relaxed and fell into bed.

❧

Monday morning papers and the TV news headlined the shootout at the border crossing and the animals discovered in the lorry. The chief inspector was smiling and holding a large python with both hands.

Chris received a call from Tan Sri congratulating him on the success of the operation. Suhaimi received a commendation letter from the chief of police.

One smuggler was identified as a Malaysian and suspected member of the Tiger Triads. The other was an unidentified Thai National. Their passports were forged, and the lorry was stolen. The value of the cargo of animals was put at one and a half million dollars. It was not the value of the animals or the discovery that made the headlines. The smugglers had fired at the officers. The fact that both smugglers were killed in the exchange was a direct message to the gangs that the police and the Wildlife Department were prepared to stop the smuggling at all costs. The government was clamping down.

This message was not lost on Kwang Li and the other leaders of the Triads.

❧

May Ling wondered what her reception would be from Kwang Li as she walked into the office the next morning. She was nervous and worried that they had somehow discovered she was the informant. *Was he still angry at her refusal to have sex with him? Would he become violent?*

She quickly sat at her desk and opened the e-mail. She saw several messages from other Triads. So far, the messages were ordinary mail. Each one concerned about the border.

Kwang Li had five of his lieutenants in the office, and she could hear him shouting at them. She was a bundle of nerves as she watched him waving his arms. Finally, when he was finished, the men almost ran out of the office, and he stood at the door, leering. He called May Ling into his office, shut the door, and sat down behind his desk.

He was contrite and talked softly. "About last night, Leona, I didn't mean to come on so strong. Maybe I had too much champagne. So let's forget it happened, OK?"

"All right, but don't let it happen again. Let's keep it strictly business, OK?"

He nodded. The silence was heavy. She turned toward the door, waiting.

"Oh, by the way!"

"What?" She continued to face the door.

"You got great tits!" he chortled. "Close the door on your way out."

She went to her desk, sat quietly, and thought: *I'm still safe, but for how long? They will find out sooner than later, and I'll be dead meat.*

She knew he would try again, that was obvious. If she wanted her revenge, she would have to work fast. During her lunch break, she bought a new cell phone, transferred her SIM card to the new phone and bought another SIM card for her old phone. She would use the old phone with the new SIM card to send messages to Chris. The new phone carried her old number so Kwang Li would not be suspicious.

Over the next several weeks May Ling sent Chris text messages concerning the smuggling of animals out of Malaysia through border crossings, ports, and airports. All of the information proved accurate, the cargos were intercepted, and smugglers arrested.

She left her old phone hidden in her flat. If Kwang Li or another member wanted to check her messages on her cell phone and the telephone numbers she called, they would find nothing but exchanges between May Ling and her girlfriends. She told her friends she had taken an English name and to call her Leona.

·b·

The room was full of cigarette smoke, so thick it was difficult to see the men seated around a long conference table in the Moral Uplifting Society building. Everyone was smoking and ashtrays placed in front of each man were full. The meeting had been in progress for more than one hour, each man reporting on his activities in his area.

Wang Ju's eyes were watering and his hands shaking as he finished his report to the senior members of the China Triads.

There was a long moment of silence after Wang Ju sat, and then Zhang Chen erupted. "Four shipments lost in one month. Our loss is over six million. Our customers are screaming for supply, and we can barely give them anything but a few lizard tails and bat wings. We have increased shipments from Indonesia and Vietnam, but without the Malaysian supply we can never meet demand. We are losing millions. There's an informer somewhere in the Malaysian operation. Besides losing the shipment, a Malaysian Triad soldier and one Thai Triad soldier were killed by the police."

"Who runs the Malaysian operation?" one of the men seated at the table asked.

"Twenty-year member," Zhang Chen said.

"What has he been doing to find the informer?" another member asked.

"He has changed the codes, controlled the members who sign into headquarters, and limited the information on shipments to only those involved."

Another member spoke up. "The informer could be from the Thai side."

"Two of the four shipments were caught at the Thai-Malaysia border crossing."

"It has to be someone at the top who has access to the information," the second Triad member said.

"We have sent our own men into Malaysia without the Tigers knowing," Zhang Chen said. "They will report back to us as soon as they have information."

"Does Kwang Li know?" the member continued.

"Yes, I had to tell him. He was angry that we sent our men into his territory. He said they could handle it themselves. If it's a Malaysian informer, they will find him."

"What are our men doing?"

"They are following all of the senior members of the Tigers, watching where they go and who they meet. There has been nothing to report so far. We are still waiting for any news."

"So what do we do in the meantime? Do we sit and wait until they are caught and killed or do we keep shipments coming through the usual channels?" another member complained.

Zhang Chen cleared his throat. "We changed the main focus of our Malaysian operation to Sabah and Sarawak, and we increased our shipments from Myanmar and Vietnam. In the meantime, keep looking for the informer, and when we find him, we will make an example out of him that no one will ever forget!"

One man stood and shouted, "Kill the American! He's the one causing the problems. Forget about everyone else. Kill him, and we will be back in business."

Zhang Chen slowly made eye contact with everyone and then sat down. Silence again filled the room.

He spoke quietly. "Killing an American is dangerous. Kill him and several more will come here looking for the murderer. However, if the American is killed in an accident, that's something else. There's a large reward for anyone who can do the job. But it has to be handled professionally."

"How much of a reward?" One member asked.

Zhang Chen thought for a moment. "Five hundred thousand U.S. dollars." He clapped his hands and a line of waiters entered the room carrying trays of steaming food, glasses, water, and Scotch. The men settled down to eat and drink.

⁂

Chris and Roberts sat drinking Tiger Beer at the Westin Hotel lounge. A Cuban band played salsa music with several drums beating out the rhythm. It was difficult to carry on a conversation above the noise.

"You've done a good job," Roberts yelled over the music. "The smuggling from Malaysia is down to a trickle, thanks to you."

"You mean thanks to Suhaimi and my undercover agent. They are the ones who keep the operation going."

The Cuban group ramped up the drums and the dance floor was packed, everyone gyrating to the hot salsa beat.

Roberts listened to the music for a moment then responded, "Yes, they have, but together all of you may have broken the back of the Triads smuggling operations. My contact tells me they're changing their concentration and looking more at Sabah and Sarawak. That's going to be tougher to control than the borders on Peninsular Malaysia. That would be the obvious move for them. There are so many places where they can load a ship unseen by the police." Roberts sipped his beer thoughtfully as he watched the conga drummer beat out the fast rhythm.

"I'm very worried about our agent," Chris said. "They must know they have an informer in their group, and they are probably searching for that person. It won't take them long to figure it out. Our agent has to get out now and not wait too much longer or they will be dead meat."

"You're the one that they'll be gunning for," Roberts said.

"I know what you're saying, John. Suhaimi and I are aware of the problem. We carry our weapons all the time now and are on red alert. I don't like the alternative."

Roberts was silent for a moment. "I can give you an extra bodyguard."

"Not right now. Let's wait and see what happens. Suhaimi has me covered."

"Where is he now? I don't see him here."

"That's good. Somewhere in a dark corner there's a person watching us. I don't know who it is, but I know who it isn't."

Roberts looked around but didn't recognize anyone. "I'm glad to hear that. By the way, Malaysia immigration picked up one Tiger gang member entering the country yesterday with a tour group and when they entered Malaysia, immigration identified him from their watch list."

"They let him in?"

"Yes, but they're keeping him under surveillance. They know why he's here. He's a hit man for the Tigers. But they don't yet know his target. Keep your weapon close and watch your back."

"Thanks for the info. I'll be careful."

Roberts left and Chris stayed to enjoy the music. A beautiful, young Chinese girl approached him in a tight red dress that left nothing to the imagination.

She smiled sweetly at him. "You look lonely. Buy me a drink?"

Chris looked at her and smiled. "No thanks, not tonight." She looked disappointed when he paid his bill and got up to leave.

He walked out of the lobby onto the street. As he did, a man followed behind him. Chris turned to watch the traffic, then nodded slightly, and continued walking. The streets were crowded with young people, mostly Chinese, hanging around looking for mischief. He kept one eye on the crowd and a hand on his wallet as he headed toward his hotel.

20

MAY LING HAD LOST WEIGHT and looked haggard. Being undercover, and the murder of three family members, had taken a toll. The only thing that mattered was avenging her parents and brother. She worried that something was going on with the Triads. Kwang Li was visibly upset about the intercepted shipments and strange men were in and out of his office after the regular staff left. By their accent, she knew they were from Mainland China. It gave her a good idea of why they were there, and it frightened her.

Two men were in his office with the door closed. She could hear their muffled angry voices. Suddenly, the door jerked opened and the men walked out. After a few minutes Kwang Li walked to her desk.

He was brisk. "I must borrow your cell phone. My battery is dead, and I need to make a call."

"Why don't you just plug your phone in and use it. You don't need mine."

"My battery charger is at home. I need to use your phone,

now."

She handed it to him, and he returned to his office. She could see him fiddling with her phone and making calls. She whispered a silent prayer that he wouldn't find anything. After about twenty minutes, he returned her cell phone with a curt "Thanks."

She watched him walk to another worker and ask for her phone. He was making the rounds using everyone's phones, but couldn't find any unusual calls. By the time he got to the last person, he threw their phone back at them, stomped into his office and slammed the door.

She sighed with relief. He had found nothing.

May Ling left the office at five and went back to her temporary apartment. She ate a simple meal and then relaxed, feeling drained after the tense day at the office. She was lying on the tattered sofa, tired, and falling asleep. Abruptly, there was a knock on her door. She jumped up and ran to the spyhole and saw Kwang Li's girlfriend, Liza Chin. She slowly opened the door.

"I hope you're not busy, Leona."

"Not at all. Please come in." She smiled slightly.

"Thanks, I need a massage."

Liza waited.

May Ling was silent for a moment but finally stammered, "It's a bit late for a massage, but I'll accommodate you."

"You seem surprised. You weren't expecting anyone, were you?" She smiled sweetly.

"I am surprised. I never expected you to want a massage from me. I wasn't expecting anyone else this evening. My last client left a while ago, and I was cleaning up."

"Oh, I don't want one of those *special* massages, just a regular massage. You do give regular massages, don't you?"

"Of course. Actually I am pleased that you would like to try my massage. I use excellent professional products that all my clients enjoy. This way, please."

She handed Liza a robe and said, "Let me take your clothes."

She waited as Liza undressed and slipped into the robe. May Ling led her to the bathroom, turned on the shower, adjusted the temperature, and said, "You have a nice hot shower, and I'll be right back with a cup of hot tea." She left to get the tea.

Once in the kitchen, she placed the kettle on the fire and put a green tea bag in a small teapot and placed a cup on a tray. Her thoughts were about Liza's strange visit at this time of night.

This is a setup. Kwang Li must have sent her to see if I really do give massages. Thank God I learned from Bette and those tapes.

She poured hot water into the pot then carried the tray into the massage room and placed it on a small table. Liza wore the robe and sat in the only straight-backed chair in the room.

"You enjoy your herbal tea, and I'll get everything ready."

She was aware of Liza watching her every move as she put a clean sheet on the massage table, pulled the movable cabinet with oils and creams next to the massage table, then washed her hands in the sink. As she was drying her hands she turned to Liza.

"OK, Liza. Please remove your robe, and lie face down on the table." She held up the cover sheet so she could not see her naked body.

Liza took off her robe and climbed onto the table. She put her face through the hole at the head of the table, arms by her sides. May Ling dimmed the lights further and said softly, "Just relax."

She rubbed a calming scented oil on her hands, placed them near Liza's nose and said, "Breathe in, breathe out slowly." Liza relaxed.

Next she poured warm oil on her hands and began her first real massage. She had to admit Liza had a great body—broad shoulders, a well-muscled back, firm buttocks, well-shaped thighs, and slender feet.

May Ling started with her feet and then moved up to her

arms and neck, slowly massaging all her muscles. Liza purred like a cat throughout with soft sounds of pleasure as May Ling's hands did their work.

Finally, she finished massaging her neck and head and then asked her to turn over. Liza obliged, lying on her back, hands by her side. May Ling soaked an eye mask with a special solution and placed it over Liza's eyes. She massaged her body for another thirty minutes, and when she finished she removed the eye mask and helped her off the table. Liza took another shower and dressed.

"Would you like a cup of hot tea?"

"No. I have to run."

When May Ling walked her to the door, Liza took her in her arms, hugged her and whispered, "Next time, I want your special." She closed the door behind her as she left.

May Ling stared at the closed door, and her whole body began to shake. She suddenly felt as though she would collapse and quickly moved to the sofa and fell backward onto the cushions.

Her first thought: *I didn't charge her.*

She pulled herself up, walked into the massage room and saw the money on the massage table. Liza had left her one hundred and fifty dollars.

The anti-snuggling canines had, as Chris expected, been extremely effective. They continued to sniff out illegal cargo and helped the border police make arrests. The latest bust was at Westports, the main port near Klang, a port city on the Malacca Straits. Several crates were sitting on a dock waiting to be loaded onto a container ship to China. The dogs sniffed out the animals and the crew and captain of the vessel were arrested. The customs officials involved were arrested and removed from their positions immediately.

On the same day the police arrested a shopkeeper in KL. A large bag of animal parts was found on his counter. Someone had just brought them into the store. An informer called the police, and they immediately went to the shop. They took the man and the bag and then closed down the shop. The shopkeeper would pay a large fine and serve time in jail.

In the northern state of Kelantan on the east coast of Malaysia, the wildlife enforcement team was informed that one family had tiger skins. They went to the small house that sat on the edge of the jungle and knocked.

A woman opened the door a crack, just enough to see who knocked. "What do you want?" She stared at the officers.

"We are here to inspect your house. We have been informed that you have tiger skins."

"Oh, someone gave us the skin as a gift," the woman said, trying to close the door. One officer put his foot in the way and then forced it open. In the small room they saw three large tiger skins on the floor. A cage with several animals sat beside the skins. The officers checked the house and found more animal parts. On the back step, the husband was skinning several snakes. The officers arrested both people and took the contraband.

The next day newspapers and websites had pictures of the animals and their parts from the arrest. Fines were levied and court dates set for their hearings. They all received stiffer fines and sentences than an international animal smuggler.

Suhaimi was reading the papers. "Chris, look at this. The poachers received jail sentences, but a rich smuggler and his wife got off with a slap and short jail time. "

"Looks like there's a payoff going on. Those who can't pay are locked away, and the wealthy smugglers buy their way out of jail. Great system if you have money. Doesn't say much about the judicial system."

"Well, same thing happens in other countries, yours as well."

"Right on. It's always the little guy that gets it."

"By the way, is your boss still pushing you to go back to Seattle? I haven't heard you complain lately."

"Yeah, I get a 'come back' letter every other day," Chris said. "But he is a little more lenient now that he has seen my results and the changes made in the country. So, I guess I'm doing something right."

＊

May Ling and Bette were relaxing in May Ling's apartment— May Ling in her bathrobe, Bette in her sarong dress. They had just finished dinner and cleaned up the kitchen. May Ling hadn't seen Chris for three weeks and missed him with all her heart. She had told Bette little about Chris. She had simply said that he worked in the U.S. Embassy.

"You know, May Ling ... every time you look at Kwang Li, you have such hatred in your eyes. I know there is something going on."

"Is it that obvious?"

"If looks could kill, he would be dead a hundred times over. It's obvious. I've already figured it out. He had something to do with your parents' death, didn't he?"

"Bette, please don't mention it again, OK? I don't want to talk about it."

She hugged May Ling. "I'm sorry. It's just that I care for you and don't want anything to happen to you."

She raised her head to take the soft kiss on her forehead and at that moment, the doorbell rang several times.

"Who in the world can that be?" May Ling peeked through the spyhole. Liza was staring at the door, waiting for it to open.

"Oh, oh! It's Liza!" She turned to Bette and whispered, "Quickly ... go and lie down on the massage table and take off your sarong!"

May Ling poured massage oil over her hands and quickly

rubbed the oil over her body. She pulled the massage trolley over to the massage table and threw two towels in the nearby basket. She called out, "I'm coming," and went to open the door.

Liza walked past her into the center of the room and looked around. "Are you busy? I feel like a massage ... your special massage." She purred like a cat wanting a bowl of milk.

Not waiting for May Ling to answer, she turned and went to the massage room door that was slightly ajar. She peered in and came to an abrupt halt.

She stopped, surprised. "Oh, I see you're busy!"

She was disappointed. "Perhaps I should come back later?" Both women stood at the door looking inside. The lights were dimmed, and they could barely see Bette lying on her stomach on the massage table, covered by the sarong.

Liza opened the door wider and peered into the room again, then turned to May Ling and with a wicked smile asked, "Is that Bette?"

May Ling barely nodded.

"Don't let me interrupt ... in fact, let me finish her massage!" She pushed May Ling out of the way. "You go ahead and go to bed, dear Leona. I'll carry on from here."

She stood and stared, her mouth open in amazement. Liza walked into the room, closing the door in her face.

She went to bed soon after, waiting for Liza to leave. Finally, she heard the soft sound of voices and then the apartment door closing. A few minutes later, Bette came into the bedroom and sat on the bed next to May Ling.

"Well? Come on, Bette, tell me what happened!"

"Better you don't know." She tucked May Ling in. "Good night." She closed the door as she went to her bed on the couch.

21.

AFTER A SWIM AND BREAKFAST by the pool, Chris's cell beeped with a message: *Miss you. Stay safe. MLK.*

He sighed and thought: *She's all right for now, but ...* A sinking feeling came over him.

Minutes later Suhaimi called Chris. "Meet me in ten minutes. We have something to discuss."

Chris met him outside the hotel, and they drove to a park outside the city. They sat in the car near a World War II monument. They were alone in the area.

"What's going on?" Chris asked.

"The Wildlife Department and the anti-smuggling unit raided a house in Sarawak. The Triad member who owns the house is a top feeder in the syndicate. The anti-smuggling unit got wind of an illegal activity at his house. They discovered something very interesting and loaned it to me to show you. I have to return it as soon as you see it. Idris respects the work you are doing and wanted you to see this ledger before the papers got wind of it. Don't mention this to anyone."

"How can you walk out with evidence?" Chris raised his eyebrows.

Suhaimi just smiled. "This is Malaysia, not the U.S."

He opened his briefcase, pulled out a ledger book and handed it to Chris. "The writing is in Cantonese, but I had some of the important items translated." He pulled out another piece of paper with some names written on it.

"This book is an accounting of the Triad's activities. I want you to look at these numbers." Chris scanned several pages and noticed that the numbers were in Cantonese as well.

"I don't read Chinese, but from the number of characters in each row, there must be a lot of something going down."

Suhaimi flipped through several pages and stopped at one full page.

"Here it is. See this line?" He pointed to one line in the middle of the page.

"Yeah."

"It reads: Pangolins. The dates cover fourteen months, OK?"

"Right."

"The total count is twenty-two thousand pangolins smuggled out of Malaysia to China."

Chris was dumbfounded. "Twenty-two thousand? You're joking! There must be very few left in Malaysia. How can that be?" He pulled out his calculator. "That's like fifteen hundred pangolins a month."

"They are now on the endangered list," Suhaimi said. "The ancient spiny anteater that has been around for centuries is now almost extinct."

They both sat in silence looking at the page. "My God! What will it take for the government to stop the trade in wildlife? They had better wake up soon."

"Well, the numbers are overwhelming as well for snakes, lizards, and turtles."

"I feel sick," Chris said. "It's overwhelming. We thought we were gaining on the problem."

Suhaimi interrupted, "We are! That's what's important for you to remember. We have stopped the flow somewhat and can do more to stop it completely before their animals disappear. You have done a great job, and we must keep up the pressure on the syndicate."

"I guess you're right, but it sure doesn't look like it from what you have shown me. We must get that ledger copied before it disappears."

"I'm ahead of you, my man. I did that before I picked you up." Suhaimi dug into his briefcase again, pulled out a thick wad of paper in a plastic binder and handed it to Chris. "This is for you to take back. You can get it translated in the U.S. when you get home. It'll be a nice gift for your boss."

Chris was overwhelmed. "Wow! Thank you for copying it. You saved my job with this one. I might even get a promotion."

Suhaimi dropped Chris off and went to the anti-smuggling unit to return the ledger. He neglected to tell them that he made two copies of the ledger.

Wang Ju answered his cell not knowing what to expect from Zhang Chen. "Yes, what is the news? It better be positive, Wang Ju."

"We have no news from the operation. No word on the patient or the disease. My doctors on the case have found no cancer yet. If there is a tumor, it's well hidden."

Wang Ju breathed easier. They had switched to code for the operation in Malaysia, and no one would know what was in progress except the leaders.

"I thought he would be easy to find. I'm disappointed and very angry. When is the next shipment?" Chen said roughly.

"In progress and will arrive next week. It's a small shipment due to the cancer. Prices will be higher so more profitable with less investment."

"The shipment is priority for a dinner next Friday. Can you

deliver?"

Wang Ju heard the threat. "Yes. It will arrive on time," he said, his voice quivering.

"Keep me informed on the progress."

Wang Ju opened his secret drawer and checked the schedule. The shipment was due to arrive two days before the dinner. He was safe but he worried about the informer and whether or not the shipment would be confiscated. He could do nothing except wait.

❧

May Ling was sitting at her desk printing out the messages for Kwang Li. She carefully read the latest news on the shipments then walked into his office with the folder. He was on the phone, and she listened to his conversation.

"We still don't know what is happening, but are continuing to monitor the progress. I believe we are close to trapping the rat. Your men have been most helpful in this situation. Tomorrow will be important. I'll let you know as soon as I can." He ended the call, looked at May Ling, and smiled pleasantly.

"What do you have for me, Leona?"

"Here are the latest e-mails for you." She handed him several sheets of paper. As he took the papers, he grabbed her wrist and held it tightly. "I am taking you out for dinner tonight. Be ready by eight."

"I can't tonight. I have massage appointments and will be busy."

"Cancel your appointments, my beauty! We'll finish what we started last time." He grinned at her, leaning over his desk.

She pulled her hand free of his and went back to her desk. May Ling sat in front of her computer screen, worried and unable to concentrate. *Perhaps this last shipment was a trap, and I should let it go through. That way no one would suspect me. What about tonight? What's the best plan?*

It was almost lunchtime and Kwang Li would be leaving with the gang. "I am going out for lunch. See you this evening, Leona. Wear something sexy!" He touched her shoulder as he walked past her to the door.

As soon as he was gone, she brushed her shoulder as if removing a speck of dirt, then called Bette. She was at her office and answered the phone.

"Sunset Trading Company. May I help you?"

"Bette, it's Leona! I have to talk to you right away. Meet me at the food court."

Bette worked ten minutes away from May Ling's office, and they often had lunch together.

"OK. See you shortly. Give me ten minutes, and I'll meet you there."

They went to their favorite Chinese stall and filled their plates with the food from the buffet, paid, and sat down at an empty table.

May Ling explained what had happened with Kwang Li. Bette looked worried and grabbed her hands, holding them tightly.

"You can't meet him! You know what he will do to you! Come up with an excuse!"

"I have a plan, but I need your help. Call Liza and talk to her. Casually mention that he is taking me out tonight. She'll be jealous and stop him from meeting me. That's the only thing I can think of."

Bette thought for a moment, drummed her fingers on the table, and finally said, "I think it will work. Liza will stop him from seeing you. It's worth a try and probably the only chance you have. Later this afternoon, I'll call her."

"Thank you, Bette. I am so relieved. Otherwise, he may have other plans for me when he comes over." She shivered as she thought about it.

May Ling was back in the office before Kwang Li returned.

She pretended not to notice him when he walked by her desk. Just before five, her office phone rang. Kwang Li had his door open and could hear her voice. It was Bette. She looked at her computer screen and remained professional.

"Yes, how can I assist you?"

"I called Liza and chit-chatted with her," Bette said. "She asked what I was doing this evening, and I told her that I was looking after clients and that Leona had a date with Kwang Li and couldn't cancel her appointments. She started yelling on the phone, calling you all sorts of cheap names. She said you would never go out with him as long as she was his girlfriend and ended the call."

May Ling remained stoic, pretending to be on a business call. "I understand, and I'll look it up as soon as I can."

Bette continued, "You can probably expect something from her before you leave the office."

"Thank you, and I'll get back to you on the billing." May Ling ended the call and continued working on the document on the screen.

Just before five-thirty, Liza walked into the office. May Ling smiled. "Hi Liza, nice to see you. Can I help you or are you here to see Kwang Li?"

Liza gave her an ugly look and yelled, "Slut!"

She strutted past her into Kwang Li's office and closed the door. May Ling could hear Liza yelling. Finally, it was quiet, and the door opened. Kwang Li walked Liza out of the office, his arm around her.

"I'll wait for you here, darling. Don't be too long. I'm hungry and want a nice romantic dinner with you." Liza watched May Ling. As Liza walked past her, she smiled in triumph.

Kwang Li stopped by her desk. "My plans changed this evening, unexpectedly. It's quite strange how that happened." He gave her a long, knowing look.

Liza grabbed his hand, and they walked out the door.

At that moment, May Ling knew that she could no longer work at the office. Her life was in danger. She had stayed too long.

May Ling had what she needed: enough evidence to destroy Kwang Li. *Let the Triads kill him,* she thought.

May Ling texted Chris regarding the special shipment leaving Malaysia through Hong Kong to Guangzhou. The shipment contained slaughtered animal body parts and was kept in cold storage on the freighter out of the port.

Six days later, a small article appeared in the Hong Kong newspapers reporting that Hong Kong Police had intercepted a lorry carrying a shipment of endangered animal parts and snakeskins. The Hong Kong authorities had received a tip-off from an anonymous source. The explosion of anger and frustration could be heard throughout Guangzhou and Malaysia.

The special dinner was for the Triads Dragon Master and top Chinese government officials. The leaders lost face. They ended up serving an ordinary Chinese dinner, which most of the guests declined to eat. Someone would pay.

22

THE CALL THAT WANG JU HAD dreaded finally came.

"We will arrive in KL this Sunday evening and meet you and Kwang Li at Jimmy's restaurant at eight sharp," Zhang Chen said in a somber, matter-of-fact voice. "Make the reservation and inform Jimmy to close the restaurant to outsiders." The phone went dead.

Wang Ju's hands were trembling as he faxed the information to the KL office.

May Ling read the message, tore the sheet out of the fax, and took it to Kwang Li's office. She placed the message on his desk, returned to her desk, and waited for him to come back. She had a mirror on her desk that, if positioned just right, allowed her to see into his office. She watched as he entered, read the fax, and then began to pace back and forth. Everyone could hear him swearing.

She also had left him a copy of the morning paper. The front page had a large picture of a pangolin being held by a wildlife officer. The headline read: *22,000 pangolins smuggled in 14 months.* The article mentioned the captured syndicate leader and his ledger.

He read the article, and his face turned purple with rage. He slammed his door behind him as he ran out of the office. She watched him storm off, hoping that he would have a heart attack. Kwang Li didn't return and the rest of the day was peaceful for May Ling, with no interruptions.

With no one around watching her, May Ling cleared out her desk and walked out the door without telling anyone that she was not returning.

As soon as she reached home, she double-locked the front door, went to the secret hiding place, retrieved her other mobile phone, and keyed in Chris's number. He answered almost immediately, and she could hear the joy and delight in his voice.

"May Ling ... is everything all right? I am so glad you finally called. When are you coming back to the hotel? Where are you now? I can come and get you!"

"Yes, my darling. I'm OK. I'll be back soon. I have a plan that I must put into action first." She told him of the meeting Saturday evening at Jimmy Lee's restaurant. "The Triads bosses are flying in from China to meet with Kwang Li."

Chris interrupted. "Is it because of the information you gave me on the shipment to Hong Kong?"

"Yes." She told him her plan.

Chris listened, then said, "I think it will work. It's a great idea. Let me put it into action."

"I am looking forward to seeing you, Chris."

That was all he needed to hear.

❧

The dinner at Jimmy Lee's had disintegrated into a shouting match between the Chinese Triads chiefs and Kwang Li. Wang Ju was trying to make himself invisible and moved to the next table, out of the way. The Mainland Chinese ignored the ten-course dinner of Chinese specialties, but the whiskey and cognac flowed like water. Zhang Chen and Kwang Li were both shouting at each other across the table, accusing each of gross incompetence and of being traitors to the syndicate. Jimmy Lee moved to the kitchen, staying out of the way. This was between them, and he didn't want to hear it.

Suddenly, the front door of the restaurant busted open with the sound of splintered wood. Ten police officers in SWAT gear rushed in and pointed their assault rifles at the dinner party. They surrounded the two tables. Another six officers took down the bodyguards and flex-cuffed them. They were hauled away immediately.

"Put your hands on the table, and don't make any moves!" the officer in charge shouted at the men. The officers took the weapons away from them.

"Hands on your heads and stand up."

The men stood up while the officers kept their rifles pointed at the Triads. They moved them to the paddy wagon and took them to the main jail.

Two other officers grabbed Kwang Li, flex-cuffed him, and dragged him out of the restaurant.

Zhang Chen was incredulous. "We will be released before you can take us to the station."

The China Triads and Wang Ju were handcuffed, searched, and their wallets and passports confiscated. The Triads knew they would be out of police custody as soon as Jimmy Lee made a phone call. Jimmy Lee and the lawyer met Kwang Li at the police station. He was released as soon as he was booked and left with Jimmy Lee.

The three gang members and Wang Ju were locked in the police paddy wagon and driven to the main police station in KL. They were fingerprinted, their particulars taken, and placed in a large holding cell to wait for their lawyers to arrive.

One guard stood outside the lockup. The guard was Suhaimi. The Triads chiefs and Wang Ju squatted on the floor, waiting. It didn't take long before Zhang Chen spoke to Suhaimi.

"Where is our friend Kwang Li? He can tell you he invited us to Malaysia for a holiday. We are tourists."

Suhaimi shrugged his shoulders. "He went home already."

"What do you mean he went home?"

"You deaf? He left with his friend, the American."

There was a stunned silence as each person digested this piece of news. They spoke amongst themselves, then Wang Ju slowly asked the question, "What American?"

The rest of the gang members stood behind him listening to the response, then talked together.

"The one from America ... who else. Making trouble for everyone." Suhaimi looked disinterested, as though he was about to walk away.

"What's he doing here?" Wang Ju asked.

"Who?"

"The American, you jerk!" He yelled in frustration. He grabbed the bars and shook them, almost grabbing Suhaimi by the throat, but he quickly stepped just out of his reach.

"How do I know? He always talks about animals."

Just then, the door to the room opened and a uniformed officer walked in and placed their wallets and passports on the table. "OK, everyone. Take your belongings, sign the release forms, and you can go."

The lawyer was waiting outside in his Mercedes. Zhang Chen got into the front seat and the rest into the back. As the car turned into the traffic, he turned to the others in the back and quietly said in a threatening voice, "I think we should have a talk with Kwang Li."

Bette called May Ling early the next morning. "Good thing you left the office when you did."

"What have you heard?"

"This is just gossip, but as of this morning Kwang Li was running for his life. Liza is leaving for Singapore until things settle down here. The new Triads leader replacing Kwang Li is from China and a killer."

May Ling wasted no time calling Chris. "Come and get me now! I'm outside the mall near your hotel." She walked down the street to the mall entrance and waited outside.

Ten minutes later, Suhaimi stopped his car in front of her. Chris bounded out of the car and ran toward her. She rushed into his arms. They hugged each other tightly. He looked into her eyes then kissed her gently.

"I have missed you so much I don't ever want to be apart again, May Ling. You're moving in with me until this is over then we are going to the U.S. together."

He kissed her, holding her tightly. She snuggled into his arms. "I missed you too."

Neither noticed the car that slowly passed by. The driver looked at the American and the Chinese girl hugging each other.

The lineup of traffic stopped, waiting for the light to change, giving him a chance to watch the two lovers. He looked again and thought there was something familiar about the girl in the arms of the American. Suddenly, it struck Jimmy Lee like a thunderbolt. He was stunned. May Ling was wearing a disguise! He recognized her face as she pulled away from the American.

All this time they were looking for a man. How could she have fooled them?

Jimmy Lee sped away, contemplating his course of action.

As he drove, thoughts filled his mind. *Should I tell the gang that it was really the girl in the office that was the informer and working for the American, or should I let it be? After all, I never liked Kwang Li. I am the Deputy Dragon Master and he treats me like a common waiter. He uses my restaurant for free eating for his friends and other gang members. I think I'll let him run for his life. If he escapes and lives, good for him. If not, so what? I want nothing more to do with him.*

He smiled as he parked his car in back of the restaurant, whistling as he entered the kitchen.

As far as May Ling was concerned, he would have to think about her and what she had done. She had been a good friend in the past, and they had been together since they were children. Her family had been good to him. There was a lot to consider.

Chris immediately drove May Ling to the safe house in Damansara, a suburb of KL. She would stay there until the Triads had either left the country or finished what they came to do. She could relax from the terrible strain she had been under. She slept peacefully for a few days.

Chris was already making plans for her in the U.S., thinking about opportunities. Marriage was on his mind, and he knew that she was the one he wanted as a partner. He was content.

She was glad to be out of the gang's office and now had no worries. She was enjoying the stress-free days, debriefing, and trying to forget everything that happened. Kwang Li would not escape the Triads, and she had fulfilled her promise to her parents and her brother. She was free—free to leave with Chris and stay with him in the U.S.

Chris made the rounds of the different ministries, saying his goodbyes. Chris would continue to monitor the project and give them assistance when they required it. He moved into the safe house with May Ling, and each night they consummated their love.

Finally, after one week it appeared that the Triads had returned to China. Chris and May Ling were leaving for the U.S. in three days on a flight to Singapore, then out to Seattle.

The Wildlife Department had a lot of momentum and was

slowly winning the battle with the smugglers. Informers were ratting on the gang members and arrests were being made. The minister would continue the dog training program and the training for the staff until they had sufficient handlers to cover all the borders and ports.

Chris and May Ling had moved back into the Crown Hotel for their last night in town and would leave for the airport from there. She wanted to do some shopping in the morning before they left.

Tonight they would celebrate. Their suitcases were packed, waiting for the final shopping spree purchases to be gathered and stuffed inside.

They dressed for the evening. May Ling wore an understated black dress, long earrings, and stiletto heels. Chris kissed her telling her how much he loved her. She hugged him in return and kissed him tenderly. They walked to the tourist area from the Crown.

"Where do you want to eat, my darling? Any special place you would like to go to?"

"Yes, Chris. Let's go back to the first Chinese restaurant I took you to, Jimmy Lee's restaurant. I want to say goodbye to him."

He wanted to tell her about her friend, but she looked so happy he didn't want to upset her.

Chris gave her a concerned look. "You know the Triads were arrested in his restaurant and you still want to go there? Your friend is a leader in the gang."

"I know, but Jimmy is my oldest friend, and I couldn't leave town without saying goodbye to him. He has been like a brother to me. He doesn't know whom I really work for, how could he?"

"OK, sweetheart. Wherever you say." They walked hand in hand down the road to the restaurant and were greeted by

Jimmy Lee as they entered the crowded place. Jimmy Lee smiled at May Ling and gave her a kiss on each cheek.

"Welcome, May Ling. It has been a while since I have seen you. You look beautiful tonight, as always." He glanced at Chris, nodded a greeting, took them to a table, and pulled out a chair for her.

She smiled and said, "Jimmy, I leave the menu to you. You know what I like."

"Yes, I know. Leave it to me." He left for the kitchen and returned a short while later with a beer for Chris and iced-lemon tea for her. They sat sipping their drinks, waiting for their food.

The waiter brought two appetizers of fish balls and baby octopus, followed by crab soup in small bowls. Next came hot sizzling chicken, spicy pork with green beans, noodles with tofu and rice. They drank hot green tea and at the end of their meal, when the table had been cleared, Jimmy Lee brought two drinks in tall glasses garnished with slices of lemon and pineapple.

"A special drink made for lovers." He smiled as he placed the glasses in front of them and then retreated to the kitchen. They toasted each other and then raised the glasses to their lips. Just at that moment, a passing waiter hit Chris's arm and the drink flew out of his hand and crashed to the floor. Jimmy Lee appeared out of nowhere, shouting and screaming at the waiter in Cantonese. He pushed the waiter out of the way.

"He really went ballistic over a broken glass," Chris said to May Ling.

"Well, maybe Jimmy's having a bad day with his staff."

Some of the drink splashed on May Ling. The waiter swept up the broken glass and wiped the table. He grabbed her glass to take to the kitchen. She stopped him. "It's OK. I'll keep it."

The waiter insisted. "No, miss, there may be broken glass in the drink. I'll fix you another drink, just give me a few moments."

"No, I don't think anything happened to my drink. I'll finish this one."

"Why don't you just leave it and let's go. I think we are both done anyhow. The fuss over the drink really ended the dinner, don't you think? Come on. Let's leave now."

"Yes, let's go, but I think I should take a few sips just to please Jimmy. After all, he said it was a special drink for lovers." She looked at Chris. He smiled and put her hand in his.

Jimmy Lee saw the discussion and walked to the table. He shooed the waiter away. "I think your drink is OK, May Ling." He turned to Chris. "I'll get you another one."

"No, thanks. I don't want anymore to eat or drink." Jimmy Lee looked at him, bowed, and returned to the bar.

May Ling took several sips of her drink, and they walked out of the restaurant saying goodbye to Jimmy Lee. He watched them leave then went to the table, picked up her glass, and returned to the kitchen.

They walked back to the hotel hand in hand and took the elevator to the suite. As Chris opened the door, he kissed her. They went into the bedroom. Both were exhausted and climbed into bed. Chris put his arm around her, and they fell into a deep sleep.

23

MAY LING AWOKE AN HOUR later with stomach cramps. *Why am I having cramps? What did I eat? Was there something at the restaurant that was tainted? Jimmy's food never bothered me before.*

The cramps intensified, turning from discomfort to pain. Chris was sleeping soundly, so she moved his arm slowly off her body so as not to wake him then got out of bed and went to the bathroom, doubled over in pain.

She had a strong urge to vomit and felt bile in her throat. She leaned down over the toilet, heaved, and felt her dinner rising in her throat. She vomited into the toilet and saw blood with the partially digested dinner. She continued to vomit until there was nothing left then fell to the floor, holding onto the toilet bowl. She felt disoriented and became frightened.

She screamed, "Oh my God! Please help me! Chris!"

Chris jumped out of bed and ran to the bathroom.

He saw the blood on the floor and in the toilet. "May Ling! What's happening! I'm calling an ambulance!" He ran to get his phone and called Suhaimi.

"May Ling is vomiting blood! A lot of blood! Call the ambulance for me quickly!"

"Quickly get her down to the lobby and have the hotel drive you to the hospital! There's no time! Just go! I'll meet you there! Go as fast as you can!"

Chris ran into the bedroom, jerked the blanket off the bed and wrapped her in the blanket. She groaned in pain when he moved her. He lifted her into his arms and ran out the door of his suite into the elevator and down to the lobby. When the door opened, he yelled at the staff behind the reception counter.

"Get me to the hospital! Help! I need help!"

A car was brought around immediately, and they got into the backseat. She was unconscious in his arms. Her skin felt clammy and cold. Chris stroked her head as the driver sped toward the hospital that was close by.

The driver went through red lights, not stopping for cars, flashing his lights and honking his horn.

Suhaimi rang Chris and shouted, "The hospital is alerted to her condition! They will be waiting for her! She doesn't have much time! Tell the driver to go to the emergency entrance as fast as he can!"

Chris screamed instructions to the driver. Suhaimi stayed on the phone.

"Is she still vomiting?"

"No, she's unconscious and clammy. I don't know what to do for her!"

"Feel her pulse."

"It feels faint and irregular. We're almost there!"

With tires squealing, the car pulled up to the emergency entrance. The driver jumped out of the car and ran inside to alert the staff.

"OK, get out of the car, and carry her inside! Don't wait for anyone! Time is critical!"

Chris put her limp body gently on a gurney. As soon as she moved, she vomited more blood and lapsed into unconsciousness again. The nurse quickly pushed the gurney into an empty cubicle.

"OK, we're here!" Chris yelled into the cell.

She convulsed on the gurney, her body shook violently. The doctor on duty ran to her and tried to take her vital signs. She stopped convulsing and lay quiet. He checked her blood pressure and shook his head. He shined a light into her eyes and saw no response. Her pupils were fixed and dilated. There was no heartbeat, no pulse, and no movement of her chest—no shallow breathing, nothing.

The doctor looked at Chris and shook his head. "I'm sorry. There is nothing we can do for her. She bled to death internally." He placed his hand on Chris's shoulder, trying to soften the awful shock of her death.

A nurse rushed up and handed Chris a hospital robe to cover himself. He was only wearing boxer briefs. She put the robe over his shoulders. He was in shock. He could not understand what had happened. Suhaimi ran into the cubicle and saw her lying still on the gurney. He looked at Chris and realized that she was dead.

"What happened?"

Chris told him, barely getting the words out. Suhaimi looked at the doctor, and the doctor nodded his head slightly. They both knew what had happened. A nurse pulled the sheet up to cover her face.

Suhaimi put his hands on Chris's shoulders and looked him in the eyes.

"She's been poisoned with santau! You can only get the poison from a bomoh, a Malay man or woman who practices black magic and can cast spells on people. In the States you call them witch doctors. Someone went to a bomoh and bought some santau, a concoction of poisons from plants and animals. Depending on the mixture and the strength, the poison can kill in minutes or over several hours. It's usually placed in a drink given to an unsuspecting person."

"Oh God! We had dinner at Jimmy Lee's restaurant. He prepared a special drink for both of us. I didn't drink mine because the waiter knocked it out of my hand by accident. He tried to change her drink but she said it was fine.

"In fact, Jimmy Lee came over, chased the waiter away, and told May Ling her drink was OK. He's the one who poisoned her!"

He covered his face with his hands and began to cry. Suhaimi held him as he sobbed.

"You can't prove poisoning, Chris. Santau can never be proven. That's the reason it's used. By the way, Jimmy Lee is a Tiger Triads' boss. She didn't tell you?"

"No, she didn't say a word. She said she wanted to have dinner in her favorite restaurant."

Suhaimi said, "He must have been given the order to kill her. I wonder how they discovered it was May Ling? They were all arrested at the restaurant, and no one knew she was involved. Did you give her any details of the arrest?"

"No, I only told her they were captured at his restaurant. It was her plan that we put into action to capture the Triads. She didn't know how deeply he was involved with them. If she had, she would not have gone to the restaurant. She thought he was her friend and just wanted to say goodbye. It's my fault that she died. I should have been more alert."

Chris had tears in his eyes. He finally understood what had happened. He broke down and cried again. Suhaimi held him quietly.

Two orderlies appeared, and the doctor accompanied them as they wheeled the gurney away.

"I'm going to stay with her for a while."

Chris followed the gurney to a small room full of fresh flowers. The lighting was dim, and the room was peaceful, used for family members to be with their deceased relatives.

The orderlies left him in peace as he sat with May Ling. He talked to her about his love for her and the events that led up to her death.

All of a sudden he felt a chill in the room as if the air conditioning was turned up full blast to its coldest setting. He looked around but saw no movement from the air conditioning unit over the closed drapes. He felt something brush his hand, then touch his cheek. He felt May Ling's presence in the room. She was listening to him. He smiled and knew she could hear him. "I love you, May Ling. I love you with all my heart and soul, and I'll miss you deeply. You will be part of me forever, my darling."

He cried as he put his face next to hers and kissed her as the tears flowed down his cheeks onto her face. He felt something brush his cheek again then the chill in the room disappeared.

"Goodbye, my darling."

There was a knock on the door. "Mr. Johnson, may we come in now?"

Chris walked to the door, opened it, nodded to them, and left the hospital. Suhaimi was waiting in the car, and they drove in silence back to the hotel.

❧

It was almost morning, and Chris lay on his bed. He cried into the pillow feeling overwhelmed with the loss of May Ling. He tried to sleep, but sleep wouldn't come.

He heard someone call his name faintly and he listened ... then heard it again. He opened his eyes and saw her standing at the foot of his bed. She smiled at him. There was a faint aura surrounding her.

Chris frowned. "May Ling? Is it really you?"

She had a serene look on her face. "Chris, it wasn't your fault. Don't blame yourself. Jimmy Lee was the one who gave me the poison. He will soon pay for his treachery. Please tell Tan Sri that I am all right."

She smiled sweetly. "I want you to remember me always. I love you." She slowly disappeared.

"Goodbye, May Ling. I love you too." Chris suddenly felt better. She had lifted the pain from his heart, and he immediately fell asleep.

Chris awoke at noon and decided he would pay a visit to Jimmy Lee. He went to his restaurant as soon as it opened. Already customers filled the restaurant for an early lunch. Jimmy was standing beside the door.

Chris walked up the steps to the restaurant. As soon as Jimmy Lee saw him coming, he disappeared inside. Chris followed him in, grabbed him by the back of his shirt collar then dragged him into the kitchen. He pushed him against the wall beside the gas stove and held one hand against his throat, the other on his shoulder.

He said quietly as he stood face to face with him, "What do you know about santau, Jimmy? Used any lately? Did you use it last night? Is that what was in our glasses? Tell me what you know."

Chris held him by the throat. Jimmy Lee gagged out the words, "I don't know what you're talking about. Let me go. I'm clean. I didn't have anything to do with her death."

Chris shouted, his anger building, "What do you mean you're clean?! If you don't know what I'm talking about how can you say you had nothing to do with her death? No one knows that she died last night. Isn't that interesting, Jimmy? I wonder how you found out about it."

Chris reached for the pot of hot water on the stove and picked it up. Jimmy looked at the water and struggled, kicking Chris in the shin, causing him to drop the pot back on the stove.

Chris pushed him back against the wall. "Won't do you any good. You had your fun yesterday, now it's my turn."

24

THE DOCTOR'S REPORT STATED THAT May Ling had expired due to exsanguination from massive internal hemorrhage, shock, and coma resulting from santau poisoning.

Analysis of her blood indicated that the substances placed in her drink caused the destruction of her organs. An autopsy indicated severe irritation in the stomach and small intestine. She hemorrhaged internally.

Suhaimi reported the death to police, who raided Jimmy Lee's restaurant in search of santau. None was found. The funeral was held two days later. Bette told Chris that she was aware May Ling was informing on the Triads even though they had never talked about it.

"She told me that if something happens to her, I am to bury her in the Chinese tradition for revenge."

There were few mourners at the funeral. Her only relatives preferred to say prayers at the family temple. She lay in a simple wooden coffin dressed in a full-length red cheongsam, her face covered with white powder, lips scarlet red, heavy eye makeup on, and her hair parted in the middle and hanging down on both sides of her face, covering her ears.

Both arms were crossed over her chest. Her left hand held a mirror so she could return from the dead and enter the mortal world through her refection in the mirror; her right hand held a double-edged dagger to kill her enemy.

When the monks chanted their last mantras, the coffin lid was put into place but left loose. This gave her easy exit through the mirror and out of the coffin on her return journey of revenge.

The casket was carried to the Kang plot behind their temple as the funeral band played her favorite music. She was laid to rest near the mausoleum where her parents rested. It was a small area with only the Kang family buried in the section.

Large tombstones honored the grandparents and great-grandparents, who were buried looking at the east toward a new day. Behind their site and on each side of their section, other family sites looked toward the east with large tombstones from several generations of family members.

Chris laid a red rose on top of the grave and said another silent prayer for May Ling. He stayed with her for a while then left the cemetery.

That evening, Suhaimi picked Chris up, and they drove to Jimmy Lee's restaurant. Police were stationed at the front and the back, ready to enter. When Chris and Suhaimi entered the restaurant, Jimmy Lee saw them immediately and walked over.

"What are you doing here?" he said to Chris with a sneer. Suhaimi stepped back, his hand on his weapon.

"You weren't at her funeral today, Lee. Scared that something might happen to you?"

"I know nothing about it. I don't know what you're talking about."

"That's too bad, Jimmy, because you killed her, didn't you?"

He reached into his jacket, but Chris pulled out his Glock and pointed it at Jimmy, who stepped back, pivoted, then high-kicked Chris. Chris deflected his foot in the same moment, aimed his weapon, and shot him in the chest. His weapon dropped to the ground. Jimmy looked surprised as he crumpled next to it. The next instant the police stormed the restaurant. People in the restaurant screamed and tried to leave.

Suhaimi yelled, "It's over. Jimmy Lee is dead. Chris shot him in self-defense."

The next day, Chris changed his air ticket to the following Sunday. Each day, he went to the cemetery to her gravesite. Chris would tell her of his love for her. He could feel her closeness and knew she could hear his words and feel his love. Suhaimi also waited near the car giving Chris time alone with May Ling. He was hidden from view and watched the area for any activity.

Chris would spend an hour each day talking to her, telling her what was happening and how much he missed her. It was a cleansing for him and gave him strength to continue living without her presence.

This particular Saturday, his last day in town, he went to her gravesite and knelt, saying a silent prayer. He placed a bouquet of roses on her grave. He was praying when he heard a voice behind him call out, "Turn around, you bastard!"

Chris jumped to his feet, turned, and faced Kwang Li, holding a pistol.

"You and your whore were working together. We've taken care of your whore, and now I'll take care of you."

He aimed his pistol at Chris, ready to fire. Chris immediately hit the ground as he pulled out his weapon. He fired off several shots and saw blood seeping down Kwang Li's forehead from a bullet hole to his head. He had an astonished look on his face as he crumpled to the ground. His eyes were open, staring at the sky, his pistol still in his hand. Suhaimi stepped out from behind a tombstone and walked toward Chris.

Chris was surprised. "Suhaimi! I thought you were in the parking lot."

"Well, this is the seventh day and your last day to visit the grave before leaving for the U.S. I had a tip from an informer that Kwang Li was looking for you. I was hiding behind a tombstone watching for him. You beat me to the draw."

"I never gave him a thought. Another mistake! I was only thinking about May Ling."

"Well, according to Chinese tradition, a person who dies does not know they are dead until the seventh day. They are allowed to return to their home for that one day to see everyone for the last time before they cross over the Yellow River. She was here watching over you. She knew what was going to happen, and she protected you from Kwang Li. She is probably still here, but you can't see her. Turn around and look at her grave."

Chris turned and walked toward it. As he did, he heard faint Chinese music and saw something shimmering just above it. As he continued to stare, a form took shape. It was May Ling in her red cheongsam, floating above the grave, smiling at him. The heavy makeup was gone from her face. She held the dagger in her hand and slowly opened it to let the dagger fall to the ground. She looked at Chris for a moment and held out her hands, palms up in a gesture of love. Behind her, he could see her parents and grandparents waiting for her. She turned and floated toward them and slowly, they all disappeared.

Chris walked to the grave and picked up the dagger. "Goodbye, May Ling. You'll be with me in my heart, always."

Suhaimi called the police, and as they were leaving the cemetery, the police were driving up the road toward the gravesite.

The next day an article appeared in the newspaper:

Triads Leader Found Murdered

Kwang Li Fong was found dead, killed by a shot to his head. It was learned that he was killed at the gravesite of May Ling Kang, who recently died. Fong was involved in the murders of the Deputy Minister of Wildlife and the parents of Miss Kang.

It was also learned that he was head of the animal-smuggling operation in Kuala Lumpur.

As Suhaimi drove by the Petronas Towers, Chris glanced at them for the last time. He knew he would never return to Malaysia and said a silent prayer for May Ling as they passed a Chinese temple. They continued on their way to the airport.

"I have good news, Chris. Two days ago an international animal smuggler was arrested at the KLIA airport. He was changing planes to go to Indonesia and was waiting for his bag at the carousel. When the bag dropped onto the carousel, it tore open and ninety-five snakes crawled out. The police arrested him on the spot and the wildlife control officers captured all the small boas. Anson Wong is on his way to jail for five years and will pay a fine of sixty thousand dollars."

"Hey, that's great! He should stay in jail for longer than five years though. I thought Malaysia had enacted a stiffer penalty this summer."

Suhaimi nodded. "The law was to go into effect in July, but so far it's only on the books. They also removed the assistant director of Wildlife and transferred him to Terengganu on the East Coast. The police think there was coercion between Wong and the director. We've got Wong. We've finally got him."

"What do you mean?" Chris asked. "How?"

"Early this morning we raided the farm that Wong used to store his animals and found two Bengal tigers and a leopard along with a variety of animals and birds. Everything was confiscated, and the animals are in a safe place and will eventually be released into the forests."

Chris smiled. "That's the best news today. Wong should be put away for life now."

Suhaimi hugged Chris and watched him take the escalator down to the immigration booth. The officer stamped his passport and returned it. Chris picked it up and put it in his pocket, then he turned and waved to Suhaimi one last time.

❧

Chris returned to the Seattle office the following day. He settled into his cubicle, turned on the computer and was waiting for it to boot up. His phone rang. "Johnson here."

"Johnson, get down here, now."

"OK, George."

Chris walked briskly down the hall into George's office and settled into the wooden chair facing his desk. He banged his knees as he shuffled the chair to allow for his long legs. George waited patiently, tapping his fingers on the desk.

"Well, Chris, I received all your reports and heard from Tan Sri and the ambassador. Tan Sri said that you did a superb job in Malaysia and thanked us for sending you. He attached a long report on your activities and the results. The ambassador grudgingly said that you added value to the anti-smuggling efforts in Malaysia with the assistance of his staff.

"By the way, the ministry will be picking up the tab for your extended stay. The U.S. government is off the hook and so are you. All in all, we are pleased with your work."

Chris grinned. "It was a good assignment. I did assist with some important changes in their inspection procedures and also in efforts leading to the arrests of corrupt officials."

George smiled. "Well done, Chris. You accomplished more than I expected you would."

"Thanks, George. I appreciate that, coming from you."

"I have put your name in for another assignment, and it's in the planning stage right now. In the meantime there are several folders on your desk that require your attention. So get on those right away."

"OK. I'll take a look when I get back to my desk."

As he left, he closed George's door on the way out, walked down the hall to his cubicle, and then sat in the chair facing his computer. He promptly opened *Soldiers of Anarchy*.

Author's Note

The endangerment of wildlife globally through illegal trafficking has accelerated and has reached vast proportions that place many animal species at risk for extinction. This has aroused increasing concern in the world community that is consistent with the rise of global awareness of environmental issues and the need for environmental law and order.

The WWF (World Wildlife Fund) says the wildlife trade appears to be funding terrorist cells in unstable countries that are threatening national security. The former U.S. Secretary of State Hillary Clinton, in her last months in office, upgraded wildlife trafficking from a conservation issue into a national security threat, ranked second to trafficking in drugs.

There have been varied responses to this threat globally, regionally, and on a country-by-country basis. Meanwhile, the demand for illegal wildlife grows dramatically. The purveyors satisfying this need vary from small-time criminals to powerful organized criminal rings and global syndicates. The black market in illegal wildlife is now third largest in the world, behind trade in illegal drugs and human trafficking. It is estimated to be well over a twenty-billion-dollars-per-year industry.

The People's Republic of China, the United States, Japan, and the European Union are the destination countries with the highest demand for smuggled wildlife. The demand arises from the need for specific organs and body parts deemed to have spiritual or healing properties in the practice of traditional medicine. For others, dining on exotic meat has become a symbol of wealth. It also stems from the desire for luxury fashion items, tourist souvenirs, and exotic pets.

Stricter enforcement mechanisms are on the rise, but actual enforcement still falls far short of stemming the degradation and extinction of wildlife species. A study conducted by the U.N. Environment Programme estimates that up to twenty-five percent of tropical forest wildlife species might become extinct by 2020. This is driven not only by illegal trafficking, but also by pollution and the destruction of natural habitats. A World Bank report indicates that Southeast Asia is a key supplier of global demand for protected wildlife and a global transit point. Within the list of countries with the most endangered mammal species, nine of the top twenty countries are in Southeast Asia.

The choice of Malaysia for the setting of this fact-based novel was incidental to creating the backdrop for the story. It should be acknowledged that despite the pervasiveness of the illegal animal trade, Malaysia has taken steps to stop the blight.

Malaysia's Ministry of Natural Resources has doubled its efforts in the fight by ramping up integration, cooperation, and information networking with other national and international law enforcement agencies to address wildlife conservation. This especially includes enforcement of the Wildlife Conservation Act and the International Trade In Endangered Species.

The Department of the Ministry is also working closely with INTERPOL, CITES secretariats and the Asean Wildlife Law Enforcement Network in combating wildlife smuggling. Further collaborations are taking place with the Royal Malaysian

Customs Department Anti-Smuggling Unit, the Malaysian Armed Forces, the Malaysian Maritime Enforcement Agency, and the Royal Malaysian Police.

These proactive collaborations include monitoring goods entering Malaysia via long coastal seas, border entry points, ports and seaports, including free trade zones for goods in transit.

Malaysia faces a difficult challenge given its geography and determined syndicates. It is nonetheless united in its effort to enforce the laws of the land. It is equally incumbent upon the "demand-driving" nations to do their part to implement and enforce measures against "buyers" and traffickers of illegally traded wildlife.

One key method the public has to prevent the trafficking in wildlife is to use only products that are environmentally friendly. Individuals can play a critical role by abstaining from the use or consumption of illegally traded wildlife and body parts. Using only environmentally friendly products assures that there will be wildlife in the forests for sustainability.

In its enforcement of its Wildlife Conservation Act, Malaysia has closed zoos that demonstrate ill treatment of the animals. After a raid by Wildlife Department officers, one zoo was closed and more than seventy animals, including tigers, lions, elephants, snakes, and crocodiles, were seized. The animals were removed to better quarters and rehabilitation centers.

WEBSITES FOR MORE INFORMATION

Wildlife Trade Monitoring Network
http://www.traffic.org

World Wildlife Fund—The leading organization in wildlife conservation and endangered species
www.worldwildlife.org

Havocscope Black Markets—Online database of black market activities

http://www.havocscope.com/black-market/environmental-crime/wildlife-smuggling/

Malaysian Nature Society (Persatuan Pencinta Alam Malaysia) The Malaysian Nature Society contributes towards the protection of Malaysia's natural heritage.
http://www.mns.my

Planetsave: http://www.Planetsave.com

Australia
www.customs.gov.au/webdata/.../wildlife_smuggling_fact_sheet.pdf

CAWT—Coalition Against Wildlife Trafficking
http://www.cawtglobal.org/

CPSIA information can be obtained at www.ICGtesting.com
Printed in the USA
BVOW07s1133260913

332036BV00004B/9/P